QUITE THE PAIR

BETH C. GREENBERG

A NOVEL

ISOTOPIA
PUBLISHING

ISBN (paperback): 978-1-7359447-6-0
ISBN (hardcover): 978-1-7359447-8-4
ISBN (ebook): 978-1-7359447-7-7

Cover design, illustrations, and Isotopia logo by Betti Gefecht
Interior design by Domini Dragoone
Family tree background image © sabphoto/123RF.com

ISOTOPIA PUBLISHING
www.isotopiapublishing.com
www.bethcgreenberg.com

First Edition

For the talented fanfiction writers
who expanded my mind and my heart—

and the passionate fanfiction readers
who allowed me to practice on them.

BOOKS BY
BETH C. GREENBERG

THE CUPID'S FALL SERIES:
First Quiver
Into the Quiet
Quite the Pair

Isotopia, by Jeff Greenberg
(prepared for publication by Beth Greenberg)

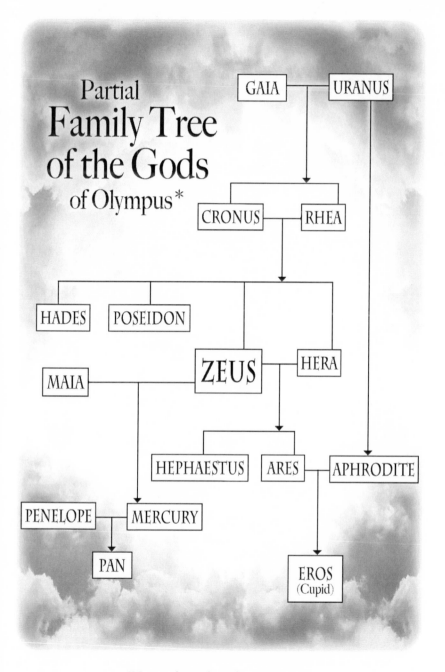

Partial
**Family Tree
of the Gods**
of Olympus*

GAIA — URANUS

CRONUS — RHEA

HADES POSEIDON

ZEUS — HERA

MAIA

HEPHAESTUS ARES — APHRODITE

PENELOPE — MERCURY

PAN

EROS
(Cupid)

*Names chosen by gods in 480 C.E.

A full listing of divine characters can be found
immediately following the story.

Let love steal in disguised as friendship.

—OVID

1

RIDDLES

A fallen Grace, a former satyr, and a heartbroken god walk into a comedy club . . .

Why the hell couldn't Pan stop thinking in riddles?

How many shots of tequila does it take to throw off Cupid's heart radar?

No wonder he was punchy. Of all the places on earth for Cupid to fall in love with Pan, the gods had to pick some rank, beer-soaked corner of a dive bar comedy club with the stench of vomit billowing out every time the bathroom door opened?

"Just checking here," Pan said carefully. "You did just say that your heart is vibrating for *me?*" Turning to Euphrosyne, the goddess of good cheer, Pan repeated his question. "You heard him say he's vibrating for me, right?"

"Yes, that's what I said." Cupid was running low on patience, but Pan couldn't risk a misunderstanding here, not with something this monumental.

"As in . . .?" Pan mimed pulling an arrow taut on its bow and releasing it straight at Cupid's heart.

"Yes, Pan."

Wow.

Yeah, now that Pan was really paying attention, the truth was staring him right in the face. Cupid had worn that same, tragically smitten expression when he'd first stumbled into Mia's yoga studio and again when he'd knocked Ruthie off her feet at Versailles. This time, inexplicably but undeniably, Cupid's boundless, desperate love was dead aimed at Pan.

"I'm ready!" Pan opened his arms wide and launched himself at Cupid before the gods could change their fickle minds. "Quick! Cross us!"

"I can't," came Cupid's muffled reply.

"Quit fucking around and do it, Q."

"Let me go, Pan." The distress in Cupid's voice caused Pan to snap back, allowing Cupid to wriggle free.

Told you it was too good to be true, nagged the weary voice inside Pan's head. "What's wrong?"

Cupid gave Pan those puppy-dog eyes that made him go weak in the knees. "I'm not your Right Love."

"What? You just said you were." Pan looked to Euphrosyne for confirmation; she shrugged.

"I said *I* was beating for *you.*"

Understanding sliced Pan open like a gutted fish. *No echo beat.*

"But I've been a mess for you since you fell, a radio stuck on the same station—all Cupid, all the damn time. How is it even possible I'm not beating for you?"

Cupid shrugged. "It is what they say it is."

What starts with "Aphro-" and rhymes with "spite-y"?

"Maybe you just can't hear it because it's so damn loud in here." Pan's logic was thin, and he knew it, but he was growing increasingly frantic. He had to fix this.

"You know that's not how it—"

"Hey!" Pan shouted at the top of his extremely powerful lungs. "Will you people shut up for a second?"

The boozy undercurrent of laughter and conversation cut off as if a switch had been thrown. *Crap*. It had been many centuries since he'd loosed his panic-inducing battle cry—and with good reason. Attention-getting outbursts were foolish and dangerous. Pan held his breath and prepared for a stampede.

A bright circle of light swung out over the audience and hit Pan in the face. Euphrosyne and Cupid gaped at him along with the rest of the dumbfounded crowd.

"*Allllrighty then!*" came the amplified voice of the comedian on stage. "I've never had a heckler tell the *audience* to shut up before. Everything okay back there, big guy?"

Everything was definitely not okay. Three divines in active peril—including himself—were clearly more than Pan could manage. Squinting into the light, Pan sent a two-fingered salute toward the stage, hoping that would be the end of it. But Mr. Open Mic was getting a rise out of the audience, and he intended to milk it.

"So, it's cool with you if these people laugh at my jokes?"

Pan plastered a big dumb smile on his face and stuck both thumbs in the air.

"Great! Thanks, man. Appreciate it." *Come on, pal. Move on.* "Someone get that guy a decaf. Put it on my tab. Okay, where were we?"

The spotlight rolled away. Heads turned back toward the stage, and Pan turned back toward the two gods in his care, whose alarmed expressions reminded him exactly what was at stake. He could not afford to lose his shit like that again.

"Sorry about that." Pan laced his fingers with Cupid's, a tender gesture meant to channel all their obvious love for each other straight to Pan's heart so the damn thing would perform whatever dance it needed to. "Listen again, Q. Please?"

Cupid met his gaze, allowing a flicker of optimism to pass between the two before pressing his ear to Pan's chest. Pan held his breath so the heart sounds could get through, as if a little oxygen could throw off the God of Love's hearing.

Cupid tensed, and that told Pan everything he needed to know. His brief fantasy of a happily ever after with Cupid dissolved into the stale air. *Damn Aphrodite!* How was it possible a heart that would never beat for Cupid could break so spectacularly for him?

Cupid, bless his cursed heart, made an admirable show of listening harder, even winding one arm around Pan's back to pull him in tighter. *Well, well, well.* It seemed his friend Q had learned a thing or two about lying after all—but only to spare Pan from the awful truth for a few seconds longer.

Enough.

"Q." Pan gently coaxed Cupid's head from his unruly heart.

Cupid swallowed hard as his moist eyes met Pan's. "I'm sorry, Pan."

Pan wrapped him in a bear hug. It was easier to speak the painful words into Cupid's hair. "I was really hoping it would be us after this whole mess was through."

"I hoped so too," Cupid murmured into Pan's shoulder, "but I'm definitely not your guy. Or your girl—or whoever you're supposed to be with."

Pan dropped his arms to his sides. Every inch of Cupid slumped in defeat. Euphrosyne looked away.

Pan probably should have let it go right there—for both their sakes. His heart was clearly not echoing Cupid's beat. But who was to say the gods hadn't rewritten the rules?

"What if it's not just about the hearts this time?"

Cupid shot him a sharp warning glare. "Let it go, Pan."

But he couldn't. Not if there was even a glimmer of hope.

"I want you, Q." Pan's voice quaked with desire.

"That doesn't mean anything," Cupid replied. "You know this isn't about sex."

"Don't insult us both with that crap. We are so much more than a quick fuck."

"I'm just gonna . . . bathroom." Euphrosyne ducked away.

"Pan, *please*," Cupid said, barely registering Euphrosyne's exit. "I'm hanging on by the thinnest of threads here."

Tell me about it.

Pan grabbed Cupid by his shoulders and locked on to his gaze with savage force. "Dammit, Q. You know you're everything to me. You've been my best friend as long as I've been alive. And since your fall . . . the things I want to do to you." Pan gave his head a violent shake, but the images wouldn't let go. "Can I help it if my heart isn't vibrating on your frequency?"

"No, you can't, and neither can I. That's the whole point!"

Of course it was. A frustrated growl rose up inside Pan and reached as far as his throat.

Cupid cupped Pan's cheeks to steady him. "Breathe with me," said the bright-eyed lion tamer to the wild beast.

Pan surrendered to Cupid's measured breaths, nodding when he'd calmed.

"There's someone else who's meant for you, Pan, and it's my duty to find that person."

Pan huffed. "If there's someone out there who makes me hornier than you do, I won't survive the experience."

"You say that now, but when you meet that person, you'll feel differently."

"No, Q. I promise I won't."

"You have to trust me. I've seen it." Cupid's face contorted with anguish. "Twice." *Great.* Now Pan had caused him to relive losing Mia and Ruthie.

"Fuck," Pan whispered for too many reasons to count.

"Look, this isn't a choice we get to make." Cupid's voice quivered with the effort of holding up the mature end of the conversation. Poor guy was close to breaking. "There's a protocol. There are rules. You know this better than anyone."

True, nobody understood the ravages of divine justice better than Pan, but it wasn't so easy to see the hurricane when you were standing inside the eye.

"I don't know *what* I know right now," Pan replied, unable to keep the petulance out of his tone.

"You know what *I* don't know?"

"Thought you knew everything," Pan shot back.

Cupid flinched at the unexpected blow. The hollow of Pan's chest filled with a rare sense of shame. If Pan were a bigger man, he would have apologized.

Cupid pressed on despite the hurt oozing out of him. "What I don't know is how on Gaia's green earth I'm going to help you fall in love with someone else."

2

DIVINE BEHAVIOR

Ares raised his hand before Themis finished the call to vote. "All in favor of approving the minutes from our meeting of 30 September?" While Ares enjoyed the insider access to confidential information and the authority afforded the five-member council to dole out discipline, he had no patience for formalities. Fairness and the will of the majority were so tedious.

Three other hands shot into the air, likely for reasons more noble. Themis nodded and scribbled on her notepad. "Motion passes. First item on the agenda, an update from the Ad Hoc Subcommittee for Disciplinary Action of Cupid. Ares, would you invite Aphrodite to join us?"

Ares schooled his smile as he crossed the room. The "ad hoc subcommittee" of two.

Aphrodite startled at the opened door. She was wringing her hands so hard, Ares feared she might chafe her radiant skin. If only he could kiss her properly, Ares felt certain he could relax the goddess in a matter of seconds. But they hadn't yet crossed that line—not in recent times anyway. He stepped into the hall and let the door close behind him. She'd bathed in lavender, his favorite.

"You look breathtaking today," he said, gently sliding his fingers between hers, rescuing her hands from their torture. "You're anxious."

"I hate this," she answered sharply. "We're his parents. We shouldn't have to ask permission to discipline our own child."

"I know, Goddess." Ares stroked his thumb along her elegant cheekbone as he gazed into her troubled eyes. It certainly wouldn't help to bring up the fact that Ares and Aphrodite were the first ad hoc subcommittee ever appointed, and it was only the high-profile nature of this case that forced Themis's hand. "Don't forget, we're a team. There's nothing we can't do together. Ready?"

Aphrodite gave him a brave nod, and he opened the door.

A gush of warm, protective feelings washed over Ares, taking him quite by surprise. He had to clasp the doorknob with both hands to keep from touching the swath of bare skin between her shoulder blades as she passed in front of him. If all went well, his lips would be there soon.

Apollo hopped out of his seat and remained standing until Aphrodite was seated.

"Thank you for joining us, Aphrodite," Themis said. "The floor is yours."

Aphrodite drew her clasped hands into her lap. She wasn't particularly good at ingratiating herself. The Goddess of Love rarely required consensus.

Ares reached below the table, covered her hands, and squeezed. "Shall I start?" Ares asked her.

"No, but thank you," Aphrodite replied carefully. "As you all know, because of Cupid's transgression with the second Worthy—"

"The kiss," Ares clarified.

"Yes, the kiss that didn't actually happen—" *Oh, how she coddled the boy.*

Surely, Aphrodite could see the danger in underplaying Cupid's misdeeds? It wouldn't do for the Council to decide the two of them had been unreasonably punitive.

"Only because the mortal rebuffed Cupid's advance," Ares added.

Ignoring the interruption, Aphrodite continued. "We have set the third labor into motion. Cupid's heart is set on his next Worthy—"

"Pan." Ares finished for her.

"Pan!" Apollo cut in. "Might I inquire as to what qualifies Pan as a Worthy?"

Apollo's bias was well known; he'd had it in for Pan ever since the satyr had bested him on the flute. If their renowned musical duel had ended with Midas awarding Apollo the victory crown instead, he wouldn't be attempting to cast doubt on Pan's reputation right now, thousands of years later. Even a loser like Apollo might have earned Ares's respect if he could have managed some grace, but a god who couldn't let go of a grudge was just sad.

"The question is out of line!" Ares balled his hands into fists beneath the table. The room stilled, all eyes on Ares. Aphrodite tensed. "Aphrodite answers to no one regarding matters of the heart."

"Brother," Athena answered in her customary, even tone, "due respect to Aphrodite"—the two goddesses exchanged polite nods—"the Council holds ultimate jurisdiction over the execution of the sentence. In this case, since the matter of Worthies is bound up with the disciplinary action, we have a responsibility to ask the question. I'd like to hear from Aphrodite on the matter."

"Of course," Aphrodite answered, leaving Ares to simmer in his own heat. "Let us judge Pan on his good works with our fallen, not on his early life on Mount Olympus. Since Pan's Permanent Descent, every deity sentenced to one of our Tarra colonies on Earth has been successfully rehabilitated and readmitted into our society."

"Hmm," Apollo interjected, setting Ares's teeth on edge. "As I recall, Pan's initial interventions weren't all that successful."

Ares needn't have worried Apollo would persuade anyone; Aphrodite destroyed his argument without lifting a single elegant finger. "It's true, not every fallen has taken the most direct route back to Mount Olympus, and perhaps some portion of the blame can be attributed to Pan's learning curve." She ignored Apollo's snort and pressed on. "I think we can all agree Pan's record is, at least, highly commendable, *and*," she added before he could cut her off again, "let us also remember"—here Aphrodite paused to flash Apollo the sweetest smile that ever delivered the dagger's lethal plunge—"perfection is not a prerequisite for worthiness."

By the gods, the way Aphrodite mastered the Council . . . and an outsider at that! Ares felt the familiar stirring beneath his robes. It seemed he was always on his way to an erection when Aphrodite was nearby.

"In fact," she continued, "a being *without* flaw, were such a creature ever to be conceived"—Aphrodite met each pair of eyes around the table, bringing every member of the Council inside her little joke with Apollo at its butt—"would be impossible to mate. Fortunately, I, personally, have not been subjected to the horror of a perfect husband."

Ares might have laughed a little too hard at that one, earning a subtle but effective glare from Aphrodite.

"The fact remains, Pan has been a valuable asset to us on

Earth, and he's been an especially effective companion for Cupid during this particularly complicated situation, and I, for one—"

"We, for two," Ares added, secretly pressing his thigh to hers. Aphrodite had to feel the heat between them, but she stayed focused on pleading her case.

"*We* believe it is time for Pan to receive his romantic due."

"The satyr is arrogant," Apollo grumbled.

There it was: *hubris*, the root of all the younger generation's ills. Frankly, the grievance left Ares cold. Nothing wrong with confidence if a man had the skills to back it up. But then, what would one expect from a god who fought his duels with a flute?

"How much longer will your petty grievance with Pan last, Apollo?" Ares was not practiced at disguising his vexation in pretty words and smiles.

"This has nothing to do with me, Ares. I simply do not believe Pan has earned this privilege."

A comeback rose to Ares's lips but was silenced by Aphrodite's gentle hand on his knee. He lent her strength; she calmed his rages. They truly were perfect for each other. Their gazes met, gratitude was conveyed in both directions, and the baton was passed again.

"To your point, Apollo," Aphrodite replied, "being chosen a Worthy is most definitely a privilege, but Pan will not cross the Liminal Point without significant effort. He'll need to summon virtues he has not yet been required to find in himself—courage, discipline, and above all, humility."

Ares was flooded with pride. Pride and nearly uncontrollable lust. She really was a force of nature.

"Lest we forget, we are here to discuss *Cupid's* punishment," Themis said, "and it is in everyone's best interest to bring the God of Love home and reunite him with his bow and arrows as swiftly as possible. The cosmos can ill afford the void in new love much longer, especially with the goddess of joy detained as well."

"Thank you, Themis," Aphrodite said. "Yes, Cupid faces his biggest challenge yet, but I'm confident he will rise to the occasion and ascend again to his home."

The others would not have heard the mother's voice crack or understood it was not because she'd been untruthful, but because deep in her bones, she rooted for something other than her son's success—something hot and steamy with the god sitting beside her, who wished very much for the same. Perhaps Ares's lack of conscience had finally rubbed off on her. He could only hope.

"Would that we all had a champion like you as a mother, Aphrodite," Themis said. "If there's no further discussion . . . the Council looks forward to your next update."

3

PAN'S LOGIC

Cupid couldn't find a trace of Pan's usual, easygoing smile as he watched his best friend emerge from Euphrosyne's apartment building. It seemed Pan had settled the wretched Grace for now. Cupid couldn't have said which of their punishments was more impossible—restoring joy or repairing love—but Pan was stuck dealing with both of their miseries, not to mention this newest trial of his own. No wonder his shoulders hunched inward as if Atlas had passed him the heavens.

The security lights shimmered off Pan's copper curls as he strode toward the truck, giving the impression of a wall of fire—ethereal and volatile, stunning and terrifying. Cupid was surely glowing too, his dizzying love for Pan burning white-hot, melting the sticky-sweet mix of shared memories and affections into a rich caramel.

Pan raised his head, locking eyes with Cupid through the windshield. Only someone who knew Pan as well as Cupid did, someone who'd spent countless days kicking up mischief at Pan's side, would have noticed how his mouth twitched downward at the corners for a tick before he fixed it again into a determined line. The rare flicker in Pan's composure sent Cupid into a spin. In just a few more steps, Cupid and Pan would be alone—*together*—inside the confines of the truck, and not even the tight belt across Cupid's chest felt sufficient to hold him in his seat—or tether him to Earth, for that matter.

Pan opened the door and climbed in behind the steering wheel. Cupid stared, breathless and frozen in place, as Pan stretched the belt from shoulder to hip and strapped himself to the seat.

"Sorry I was inside so long," Pan said, his voice gravelly and raw. "I was afraid to leave her alone until she was settled."

"Of course. If you need to stay . . ." Cupid had no idea where he'd found the strength to make such an outlandish offer. The separation from Pan had already left him weak. He wasn't sure he could survive another so soon.

"No, it's okay," Pan said. "She finally fell asleep. I gave her some wheat tea and fixed her a purifying bath—"

Envy spiked in Cupid, sudden and sharp. "You gave her a *bath?*"

Pan's eyes blazed traffic-light green. "Don't tell me you're jealous!"

Cupid wanted to deny it, but the blush had already risen to his neck.

A booming laugh burst from Pan's plump, pink lips. "You're a hot mess, my friend. A very, *very* hot mess."

"Please don't make fun of me right now, Pan."

"Sorry, man. Look, there was nothing even remotely sexual about it. I promise you there was no rub-a-dub-dub in anyone's tub." Cupid was wildly, embarrassingly relieved. "Euphrosyne thought if we could induce a dream, she might see how she's supposed to get home. I ran the bathwater while she drank her tea—that's all. Okay?" Pan set his hand on Cupid's knee. If he'd meant the gesture to soothe, Pan had grossly miscalculated the effect of his touch.

Grasping Pan's wrist with the very tips of his fingers, Cupid lifted Pan's hand off his knee and released it above the gearshift with a warning. "Please don't touch me again."

And now Cupid's every thought consisted of places he wanted Pan to touch him.

"I don't suppose you want to talk about this?" Pan asked.

"Correct," Cupid answered tightly.

"If you change your mind—"

"Pan. *Please.*"

"Okay, okay. No touching, no talking. Got it." Pan tugged on the gearshift and started the truck toward home.

If only they were heading somewhere safer, somewhere they wouldn't be alone and tempted; Pan's house was anything but that place. His scent permeated the walls and the furniture and every speck of air inside. Cupid had resisted the attraction before, mostly because he'd been occupied with Mia and then Ruthie, but how was he expected to refrain now that Pan was his heart's destination? A low moan escaped him, causing Pan to shoot him an anxious glance.

"Are you all right?"

Not even close. But those worry lines on Pan's forehead were troubling, and Cupid couldn't bear to add to Pan's burdens.

"I'll be fine," Cupid said. His throat hitched on the lie. Pan heaved out a sigh.

On they drove into the night, with some music station named for Pandora the only sound penetrating their careful silence. Cupid pretended not to notice Pan's eyes on his profile or the way he would occasionally scrub his fingers across his mouth, as if physically barring the words from spilling out. When the pretending started to feel like lying, Cupid twisted away from Pan as much as the belt would allow, all his feelings for Pan raging inside him like a tornado trapped in a jar.

"Dammit, Q. I'm sorry, but I can't stand this. We need to talk." Pan's anguished tone knotted Cupid's insides. If Pan needed to talk, Cupid would force himself to listen.

He braced himself with a deep, cleansing breath and shifted around in his seat, accidentally knocking his thigh against Pan's knuckles. "Sorry," he mumbled.

"I'll live," Pan said, his mouth quirking into a half smirk as he caught Cupid staring at his arm.

Exactly when had the sight of Pan's bare arm become so damn erotic? *Just this second,* Cupid decided. And once he'd acknowledged the twinge of attraction, Cupid couldn't tear his eyes from the soft whorls of cinnamon-colored hair climbing up Pan's forearm and thinning out at the bulge of his bicep—a wispy, whimsical spray atop chiseled marble—before disappearing under the short sleeve.

"Pan . . ."

"Hmm?"

"You know we can't, right?"

Pan's eyes pinched closed for the briefest blink, two doors slammed shut but refusing to stay closed. "No, actually, I don't."

"Do you happen to remember all that stuff you told me about joyriding? Because I sure do."

"Those were different circumstances," said Pan. "You're in love with me now."

There was no point denying what was disturbingly obvious. "Yes, but you're not—"

"Beating for you? Okay, so what if I'm not?" A vein flared at the side of Pan's neck. "We both know I'm in love with you, Q, have been pretty much since your ass touched down in Tarra. And honestly, it's a huge, goddamn relief not to have to pretend anymore." Cheeks glowing with heat, Pan stole a glimpse at Cupid's reaction. "Wow, okay. I'd kinda hoped my big-ass confession might've made you look slightly less morose."

Cupid scrubbed the heels of his hands over his eyes until they burned. "I'm sorry, Pan. You have no idea how much I wish that were enough."

"I'm not enough for you?"

"You know that's not what I meant."

Pan glared at the windshield, the lines of his face unyielding. "When you think about it, we don't even make sense as friends, really."

Cupid sucked in a sharp breath. "Are you saying you don't want to be my friend now?"

"No!" Pan slammed the meaty flesh of his hand against the steering wheel. "Goddammit! *No!*" Spittle flew from Pan's lips; his breath came in urgent pants.

"Sorry," Cupid whispered, retreating toward his door.

Pan angled his head toward Cupid, his expression softening with despair. "No, *I'm* sorry. Of *course* I want to be your friend. I will never stop being your friend. Got it?" Pan waited for Cupid's nod, then started again, stepping his tone back to a level that didn't make Cupid's skin prickle with fear. "What I meant was, you and I have always been complete opposites, right? Beauty and the beast. The royal prince of Mount Olympus, flitting around with your elegant wings and magical arrows, Aphrodite's favored son—"

A harsh bark escaped Cupid. Pan seemed not to notice.

"Whereas I am the brute, even now. Physical and base. Not fully animal, not fully god, not fully human. Instinct and desire drive me. Have you ever thought about how it is we became such close friends?"

"I didn't have to think about it, Pan. We've always just worked. You saved me from the unbearable loneliness of my existence. You were everything I was not—real, grounded, free. You still are."

"Yes, exactly." At last, Cupid had given Pan an answer that pleased him. "Opposites attract in love, too, or so they say?"

So that's where Pan was heading. His logic had taken a dangerous turn. Dread crept into Cupid's chest. "They definitely *can*," Cupid answered cautiously.

"And there are couples who end up being great for each other even without the echo beat. You told me so." Cupid had no choice but to nod while Pan fit each piece of his argument into place, as if love were some puzzle to solve with words. "Why can't we be that?"

"Because we aren't just any couple," Cupid said, dutifully voicing the answer Pan already knew. "You're a Worthy, and this is my punishment."

"Then why does it feel like they're punishing me too?"

"Probably because love is messy and painful," Cupid answered. Pan huffed. "You're really selling it, Q."

Cupid didn't have to sell anything, but Pan already knew that. "He whom Love touches not walks in darkness."

Pan turned and gawped at Cupid for a full three seconds. "You're quoting Plato to me? Now?"

"I thought you might find it comforting. I do."

"Oh yeah? How is that?"

"If you were in love with me the way I'm in love with you, you would already know."

"What the . . . You're *enjoying* this?"

"Not at the moment," Cupid answered, earning an eye roll from Pan.

"I don't get you sometimes," Pan said, giving his head a rough shake. "I'm really, *really* trying, but . . ." He could only finish his sentence with a pleading look brimming with sincerity.

Poor Pan. It wasn't his fault he didn't get it. The gods had hidden him from Cupid's bow all his life. Explaining Love to Pan was like describing a rainbow to a blind man.

"Before I fell, I lived my whole life without knowing love like this. Without having my breath sucked out of my chest every time our eyes catch or feeling that jolt of pleasure whenever I make you smile. Wishing I could live inside your head so I could give you what you want before you even know what that is. Making sure you never doubt how strong and compassionate you are. Unable to think about anything beyond pleasuring you until your body shakes with bliss, and doing it again and again in every possible combination of—"

"Mercy! *Jeez.*"

"Sorry." Cupid pressed the button that slid his window down, wedged his face into the breeze, sucked in some fresh air, and pushed it out in a *whoosh*.

"Well, pal, if that's you walking in the light right now, maybe the darkness ain't such a bad place to be," Pan said.

Cupid rolled his head slowly to the left along the headrest. "Even with my heart cracked open and my innards leaking all over your truck," Cupid said carefully, "I wouldn't have missed out on this experience for anything, Pan."

The ruddy color drained from Pan's cheeks. Cupid's description had found its mark, sure as any arrow he'd ever shot.

"I love you the same way." Pan's voice crackled with emotion.

"No, Pan. You love me the way I loved you before this punishment set my heart into its impossible spin." Cupid broke his own rule and placed his hand over Pan's on the gear knob. "And as soon as we find your Right Love, you're going to love that person the way I love you now. And then you'll understand how I am so sure that you and I are not fated for each other."

Pan's shoulders sagged. He'd been around long enough to recognize the truth when it kicked him in the teeth. Within seconds, Pan rallied as Cupid had witnessed so many times in their youth. No sooner would Pan have set one hoof outside the headmaster's office than that mischievous grin would appear, and Pan would be right back on his way into trouble again.

"Let's say you're right about everything," Pan said, eyes dancing with fresh optimism. "Who's to say you and I can't have a little fun together while we search for my mate?"

"Oh, Pan. That's a terrible idea."

"You didn't think so when it was Mia you loved."

"And I was wrong. Or have you forgotten the stump you sprouted on your rear end for my transgression?"

"I don't think I'll ever forget that, thanks," Pan said, shifting awkwardly in his seat. "But I'm the Worthy now."

"I trust the gods can find creative ways around that. Do I need to remind you how much we both still have to lose? These glorious human bodies, your fancy Earth job, immortality, phalluses that rise and fall as they were designed to—"

"*Whoa!* Mind your tongue!" Pan lowered his voice to nearly a whisper. "Suggestion is not our friend."

"Neither is joyriding," Cupid reminded him sharply.

"Fine!"

At last, logic seemed to be penetrating Pan's unfounded positivity. "We're in agreement, then," Cupid said. "No rub-a-dub-dub, no kissing, no touching, no joy."

"Well, none for *you*," Pan said with a piercing look.

That stabbing sensation came back; Cupid half expected to see the tip of a knife protruding from his chest. *Here we go again.* Yes, Pan would want to date and kiss and tumble around with someone else, maybe lots of someone elses, and Cupid was duty bound to encourage him.

"Please just do us both a favor and remember what happened to Mia when she picked the wrong guy and ended up beating for that awful Reese."

"You're not going to let that happen to me," Pan said.

"Oh! You're suddenly going to start listening to me?"

Pan's mouth opened, then closed on the lie neither would have believed.

4

DEAD BATTERY

Still mooning over Cupid after a particularly torturous break-fast—they'd sat at opposite ends of the counter, mutely digging up the contents of their respective cereal bowls, both focused on the morning news anchor as if she were the Oracle of Delphi—Pan said a gruff goodbye and lumbered out to the garage. Preoc-cupied by his mood, Pan failed to notice the truck's dome light didn't come on when he opened the door, but the engine got his attention well enough when it rutted three times and went silent. *Dead battery.*

That would be Cupid's door left ajar. Not surprising. The two of them had been walking around in a trance for the last five days and the longest five nights of Pan's existence. While Euphrosyne's sleep remained a dark, still void, Pan's dreams played like a gay porn film festival in high-def, 3D, surround sound. The waking hours were no picnic either. Pan wanted Cupid in the very worst way. Well, that wasn't entirely accurate. He wanted Cupid in every possible way, from hot and hard to sweet and sexy.

Desperate for physical contact, Pan had taken advantage of every flimsy excuse to touch him—reaching across Cupid for the remote, brushing elbows as they passed in the hall, a "careless" hand on a hip as boxes and bowls were pulled from cupboards—always followed by an insincere "Sorry"—insincere on Pan's end anyway. With each touch, Cupid burned brighter for Pan, the sweet aphrodisiac of Cupid's desire a layer of choc-olate frosting Pan could lick off his lips again and again until the taste dissolved into a memory, and then it would be time for his next fix.

It was a fool's strategy. The momentary ecstasies only deep-ened Pan's desire. Even worse, he was an asshole for inflicting the agony on Cupid when his own suffering was a mere pinprick in comparison.

For both their sakes, Pan decided not to pursue the teach-able moment. He'd gathered the strength to leave Cupid once today and had no desire to test his resolve. Instead, Pan grabbed the jump pack from the shelf, propped open the hood, and con-nected the clamps to his dead battery. After triple-checking the connections—because he really didn't trust himself right now and setting the truck on fire wouldn't help—Pan turned the booster pack on, climbed into his truck, and cranked the key.

The engine roared to life, reborn. The pulse of the motor thrummed through Pan's body, rumbling and rocking the truck like a gorilla beating its chest. If only Pan could shock his own heart into producing the magical beat . . .

Yes! Why not? Hell, the love-booster himself, in all his glori-ous flesh, sat right on the other side of that door and just hap-pened to be madly in love with him. A new fantasy popped into Pan's brain: Cupid knelt over Pan's lifeless body, his hands placed like defibrillator paddles on Pan's chest.

Even Pan's sleep-deprived, passion-addled brain recognized

the concept was twisted at best. Maybe he was no better than those divine manipulators of the Council.

Fuck it. If Pan could make this happen for the two of them, the end would justify the means. This wouldn't be Pan's first bout of self-loathing. Cupid would forgive him at some point down the road of eternity. Time was on Pan's side—

And speaking of . . . Pan shot out of the truck and jogged over to switch off the battery pack. *Focus, dammit.* While he was at it, he pushed the button to raise the overhead door before he forgot that, too, and drove his truck right through it.

Pan climbed into the driver's seat again. He would have preferred pacing to driving for sorting out his thoughts, but the newly revived battery needed run time out on the streets, and Euphrosyne was waiting for him across town. Distraction was healthy, plus doing his job would both appease and bore the gods. *Nothing to see here, folks. Find some other mouse to bat around for a while.*

Pan was no shrink, nor was he known for his empathy, but Euphrosyne's mental state was really starting to worry him. They needed some fresh ideas, and Pan didn't expect the Grace to offer much help in her current condition. He sure missed the good old days when he could talk to Cupid about anything and everything: hot nymphs, juicy god-gossip, family bullshit . . .

Ah, family. Maybe that was the glue that had held their friendship together through thick and thin. What a pair of fucked-up mothers those two had! While Pan's mother had taken one look at the abomination of the baby satyr she'd just birthed and run as far as she could, the Goddess of Love took the opposite strategy: spoiling her precious Cupid with every luxury and an utter void of discipline in a misguided attempt to bind him forever to his mother's bosom.

For sure, the lowly Pan had never entered Aphrodite's plan for her sheltered prince, not even as Cupid's friend, let alone his lover. Shunned, maligned, and treated no better than the livestock that ended up on their dinner plates, Pan did not improve his situation with Aphrodite by earning best-friend status with her son; if anything, she'd dealt with him more cruelly for it. Whatever her twisted plan now, she must have been truly desperate to resort to bestowing her highest reward on Pan, though this thick stew of unquenched love and arousal was definitely a grotesque route to the prize. Still, Pan was bound and determined to use his new status to his advantage. He was a Worthy, after all. There had to be some currency in that. At least he hoped so, as the schemes playing out in Pan's head pulled him deeper down the rabbit hole. So much for the distraction of the fallen Grace.

What would it take to shock Pan's heart to Cupid's rhythm? A kiss? A caress? A rough tumble? Something really nasty? Pan licked his lips in delicious anticipation. The possibilities for a horny goat with his own personal jump kit were truly endless. Each filthy idea inspired three more.

It would have to be a sneak attack. Cupid would never agree to this. There were practical, valid, and numerous reasons for Pan to behave himself: his sworn duty to the gods, loyalty to his best friend, and a totally justified dread of repercussions. But if there were ever a risk worth taking, this was surely the one.

5

LAST YOGA

Cupid was weakening, and Pan was about as subtle as a rhinoceros in heat. Hands *everywhere*, his hot gaze following Cupid all around the house, the stench of his desire. There was no break, no off switch, no respite for the mercilessly aroused.

Sex was out of the question. Cupid had no interest in anyone but Pan, who was clearly not an option, nor could Cupid's hand keep pace with his frantic desire. He knew of only one other way to relieve the tension: hot yoga.

Seeing Mia in person again was a risky move, especially in his desperate condition. They'd only spoken by phone since Cupid's heart had moved on. Mia registered surprise when Cupid entered the studio—but most definitely a delighted surprise.

"Q! So good to see you!" She hugged him warmly, temperature of the studio aside.

"You too, Mia. You look well." The familiar twinge of attraction gave Cupid pause—no redirection of his heart could render Mia anything short of perfection—but her charms did not cripple Cupid as they once had.

"Happiness will do that," she answered. Concern clouded her expression; she did not return his compliment. "I have a break after class. Wanna talk?"

"That would be really nice."

Cupid was faintly aware of people vying for the space next to his mat, but he'd come here to take his mind off all that and to exhaust his body. Each time his mind wandered to his worries, Mia guided him back to the pose, the breathing, the tension, and balance. After class, they walked together to the courtyard. She unrolled her yoga mat on the soft grass and offered him half. Their arms brushed when Cupid leaned back onto his palms. He was relieved to find her closeness more of a comfort than a torture.

"Are the boys in the nursery today?"

"Patrick has them. It's his day off." It could have been Cupid at home with those boys. There would have been no Ruthie and Zach to fix, none of this heartbreak over Pan.

"That's sweet. Is Eli still giving him a hard time?"

Mia offered a gentle smile. "Would it make you feel better if I said yes?"

"Not at all," Cupid answered. "Eli was warming up to me, you know."

Mia nudged him with her elbow. "They all love you. Jonah asks about you all the time."

Cupid let the affection wash over him. "I miss you all. Patrick's a lucky man."

Mia exhaled pure contentment. "I never would have guessed I'd fall for a man like him, y'know? He's a grown-up—but not in a boring way. Grounded, steady, sweet. It's effortless to be together, like we've known each other our whole lives. There's zero drama, zero tension. I trust him. He cares about us. He's like this exotic castle in a foreign land, with all these secret passages and hidden gardens. I keep discovering new places to explore."

"I'm happy for you, Mia."

"Thank you, Q," she said with a bright smile. "You know, you should come by the house sometime."

"I *do* miss your banana chocolate chip pancakes."

"We'd be happy to whip you up a batch anytime," she said. "So how's it going with your married lady?"

"Oh. She's not mine."

"You know what I mean."

"Right," Cupid said, recalling how Mia had helped him figure out how to fix Ruthie's marriage. "She and her husband are back together, and they're leaving Tarra."

"Oh. That's good, right?"

"Sure."

"You okay?" Mia's concern nearly broke him.

"I don't think so."

"Oh shit. C'mere." She hugged him to her chest. Soft, gentle, sweet—everything Pan was not. "Can you call her?"

"*Her*? Oh, Ruthie's not the problem anymore. It's Pan."

"The Pan I know? The *guy*, Pan?"

"Is there another?"

Mia laughed. "Not that I'm aware of."

"Yes, that's the one."

"I'm sorry. I didn't realize you and he were . . . *you* were . . ." She shook her head. "Sorry," she repeated.

"Don't be." It felt good to have a friend to talk to about this. Mia didn't know as much as Pan, but she knew enough. "I don't know what to do."

"What's the problem? *Oh.* Is he straight?"

Cupid snorted, a habit he'd picked up from Pan. "No. Definitely not."

"I'm not seeing the problem, unless it's something between you and your god."

The gods were precisely Cupid's problem, but he knew not to share all of that with Mia. "He's not beating for me," Cupid said simply. Mia would understand the rest.

"Wow. You have a busy little ticker, don't you?"

"Yes." Making up for three thousand years of silence.

"I'm sorry, Q. All I can say is when you find the right person, you're going to be so happy you kept looking." Mia squeezed his hand, a kind gesture by a caring friend—but no more than that.

Suddenly, Cupid could no longer bear the light in Mia's eyes, that spark of Right Love that bloomed so bright, it blotted out all others, knowing Pan would soon light up the same way for his truest mate. And how many more unrequited loves would Cupid have to bear after that? Would he be trapped here like Sisyphus and his impossible boulder, to love and lose until his heart had broken for all of Tarra?

Cupid rose abruptly, gripping his queasy stomach.

"Did you remember to drink enough water?" she asked.

"What? Oh, thanks." He took a sip from the forgotten bottle. "I don't think it's a good idea for me to keep coming to your class. I'm sorry."

She offered a compassionate smile. "No, I get it."

"I just don't know what I'm going to do with all this stress." He pushed out a heavy breath.

"Have you tried swimming?"

"Swimming?" He swallowed hard at the bitter memory, the sting of salt water burning the back of his throat. Wings don't fare well in the sea, as Leucothea discovered the hard way. She'd only lasted as Cupid's instructor as long as it took Aphrodite to scream from the shore that she was fired.

"Yes. You know, there's a lap pool at the other end of the gym?"

"I can't swim."

"It's never too late to learn," she said gently. "I have faith in you, Q. You're a real quick study."

That he was, and more importantly, he no longer had those pesky wings to pull him under. Maybe it was time to learn.

"Thanks, Mia. I'll check it out. And thanks for the chat." She started to rise, but Cupid cut off their goodbye before the wall of loneliness crashed down on him.

Unwelcome thoughts followed him to the pool. Through the glass wall, he watched the swimmers cut back and forth in neat, orderly lines as if moving on underwater treadmills. One swimmer caught Cupid's eye, a sleek form bobbing across the surface of the water with the ease of a seabird riding the waves. Enthralled, Cupid entered the pool enclosure. His feet took him to the far lane of the pool, where he stood and watched the swimmer's head rise and dip, rise and dip, as if he were nodding encouragement: *yes, yes, yes.*

The swimmer, surprised to discover a pair of feet at the end of his lane, halted his strokes, grasped the edge of the pool, and pushed his goggles to his forehead. "Can I help you?"

"Maybe," Cupid replied.

The swimmer grinned up at him. "Have you come to offer me a lifeguard job?" He laughed lightly at his own joke.

"Oh, I don't work here."

"Yeah, I got that. So, how can I help?"

Cupid crouched down so they wouldn't have to shout. "A friend just recommended I try swimming to reduce stress."

"And you wanted to see if I looked stressed?"

"I guess I became mesmerized watching you. You make it look effortless."

The man shrugged. "It's certainly easier than running."

"Huh. Well, *I've* never gotten the hang of it." To be fair, Cupid had only tried swimming that once, but it was memorable.

"That's a shame," said the man.

"Do you think you could teach me?"

"You want *me* to teach you how to swim?" The man looked around as if someone might have sent Cupid to play a joke on him.

"You seem very good at it."

"I'm just, uh, I mean, they probably have professionals who do that sort of thing."

"*Oh.* I can pay you."

"That's not what I meant."

"Oh."

The man studied Cupid. "Sure, I'll teach you to swim. My name's Reed." He offered a dripping hand. "Oops, sorry about that," he said, pulling his hand back with an embarrassed chuckle.

Cupid reached for it and shook it heartily. "Very nice to meet you, Reed. My friends call me Q."

"Well, Q, you look like you've just had a pretty intense work-out. Should we try for another day?"

Cupid followed Reed's gaze to the half-soaked shirt stuck to his belly. "Right. How's tomorrow, say nine a.m.?"

"I'll be here."

6

EYES ON THE PRIZE

Pan's sixth ball followed the first five into the fifty-point hole, and the Skee-Ball machine spat out four more tickets. He had to hand it to the town planners; it took some vision—and some brass balls—to design a makeshift pier in a landlocked town. Their bet had paid off. Everything about the Boardwalk was engineered to be romantic, the kind of place you brought a date to hold hands, share a messy gyro, show off your skills at whichever arcade game you were good at . . . and if all went well, steal a kiss on one of the wood benches. Pan had never had much use for the place—or romance, for that matter—but he was counting on the ambience to rub off on Cupid.

Of course, Pan had left out the romantic aspect when he'd coaxed Cupid into an old-fashioned American game night to take his mind off his problems.

Pan sent his last ball up the left side, and it hopped into the one-hundred hole, the highest point value in the game. Any other date would have been impressed with Pan's skill but not a god who'd picked up driving with ten minutes of instruction and the finer points of carpentry from a handful of YouTube videos. Pan waited for the ticket vomit to stop and snapped off the long blue snake.

Pan dropped another token into the slot, sending a fresh batch of wooden balls clacking down the gutter. "Your turn."

Cupid stepped up to the game, and Pan centered him from behind with two firm hands on Cupid's hips. "What do I do?" Cupid asked, turning his head minutely to receive the instructions.

Pan scoffed. "Weren't you watching? I just showed you—seven times."

"Sorry. I guess my mind was somewhere else."

Good. That's right where Pan wanted to keep it. He leaned in, slid his hands to Cupid's shoulders, and squeezed. "Yeah, mine too," Pan said.

Pan felt the shudder shake Cupid's frame.

"Take one of those balls." Pan waited while Cupid reached for the closest ball. "Now roll it hard enough to jump into that little circle at the top." Pan gave Cupid's shoulders one last squeeze before stepping aside.

"Like this?" Cupid released the ball with perfect ease, and they watched it roll straight up the middle, launch into the air, and drop into the fifty hole.

"Yep." Pan chuckled. "Just roll six more exactly like that."

Ever dutiful, Cupid picked up the next ball and repeated his precise motion as if he'd been doing it every day of his life. "Oh, look! Tickets!"

"So, what have you been thinking so hard about?" Pan asked, catching the flicker of Cupid's nervous glance before he answered.

"Trying to imagine how Right Love feels."

Pan didn't even try to hide his delight. "And what have you come up with?"

Cupid released the next ball, his face screwed up with concentration. "It, uh, feels like a castle." The ball flew slightly to the right and skittered into the ten-point trough. *Hmm.* A rare miss for Mr. Coordinated.

"A castle?" said Pan. "I think I need a little help connecting the dots."

"Feeling like the other person is your home but also having new rooms to discover." Satisfied with his answer, Cupid sent the next ball straight down the middle.

"That makes sense," Pan said.

"And trusting each other. And caring about each other." Cupid seemed to be ticking off items from some invisible list. "Oh, and not being bored."

Pan brightened. "So you're saying we're perfect for each other."

"I wasn't . . . not exactly . . ." Cupid sent another ball flying into the ten-point trough. Poor guy, all this talk about love was really throwing off his Skee-Ball game.

"I know, I know," Pan replied. "The echo beat thing." Cupid gave him a sad nod, and Pan clapped his hand on his friend's shoulder. "Good news, Q. I have a solution."

"You do?" The mix of hope and skepticism in Cupid's voice almost made Pan reconsider his cruel strategy.

"Yes. You're going to jump-start my beat."

Cupid pulled away, a cross expression replacing everything that came before. "We've already discussed this."

"I have a new idea"—Pan slid in front of Cupid and yanked their hips together—"how you can get my heart beating the right way . . ."

"Pan—"

"And before you object, this is something we've already done, and nothing bad happened." Pan cupped Cupid's cheek, drawing him near. "Remember? At the station? When you kissed me?"

"You kissed *me*!"

"Right. I keep forgetting." Pan parted his lips, and Cupid's gaze followed. "Nothing bad happened, Q," Pan whispered. "We can do that again."

Cupid's eyelids fluttered, but he fought his desire. "But that didn't make you beat for me!"

"*Becauuuuse* you weren't beating for me then. This is our chance—don't you see?" Pan snaked his hand behind Cupid's neck and held him close. "One harmless kiss could change everything."

"Come on, Pan. Since when is anything harmless where the gods are involved? Even if they miraculously allowed us another kiss, how could we ever trust ourselves to stop there?"

"We stopped last time," Pan said.

"Patrick nearly had to pry us apart!"

"Okay, fine. Then get us a chaperone."

Locked in Pan's grasp, Cupid growled in exasperation. "Like who?"

"Anyone." Pan gave him a carefree smile. "Just grab one of these random tourists passing by and tell them to hose us down at the first sign of smoke."

A giggle escaped Cupid, and Pan joined in with a snort, the first genuine laughter either had enjoyed since leaving the comedy club.

"See?" said Pan. "We've got ourselves a solid plan."

Cupid's laughter died first. "No, Pan. You know the reason I'm still here suffering is because I tried to kiss Ruthie. I just can't risk it. Not this time, not with you." The heart-twisting sigh almost broke Pan's resolve. *Crap*, he hated putting his friend through all this.

Eyes on the prize.

"Man, I really hope the Council is watching. You should earn your wings for that alone. You're a better man than I am, Q. That's for damn sure."

Cupid's guard slipped for a split second. That was all Pan needed.

Tightening his grasp, Pan trapped him in an openmouthed kiss. Cupid gasped. Pan sucked Cupid's breath into his lungs. His head swam with pleasure, but it wasn't enough. Pan needed that jump.

He pressed his tongue between Cupid's pretty lips. *Zap!* Tongue met tongue, two live wires colliding. Cupid let out a surprised squeak. Pan's heart thudded faster and stronger.

It was working!

Pan yanked Cupid's hips to his own. Their breaths came shallow and quick. Cupid's heart thumped out its mating call against Pan's chest, and Pan willed his own to match it. If he didn't know better, he might have prayed.

A firm hand on Pan's chest shoved him backward. Their bodies broke away from each other, two mouths gulping for air.

"Stop it, Pan! What are we doing?" Fear and confusion tore at Cupid, but soon enough, that would all be replaced by eternal bliss—Pan was sure of it now.

"Quick! Listen!"

"Listen to what?"

"My heart. It's all over the place. I think we did it!"

"What are you talking about?"

"Please, Q. Just listen." Pan opened his arms to clear the space around his wildly beating heart.

Cupid's expression twisted into a pained grimace. "That's your big idea? You thought one little kiss was going to change your beat?"

"Goddammit! Just tell me if it worked."

"No, Pan. It didn't work. Your heartbeat is the same as before, a little faster maybe. Don't you think I've tried that already?"

Fuck. Of course he had, with Mia. And maybe if Pan had fully set himself in Cupid's shoes, he would have realized that.

Cupid leaned in closer, his voice a strangled whisper. "We talked about this. We had an agreement. How could you risk everything like that?"

"I'm sorry, Q. I really thought—"

Cupid snapped away from him, his eyebrows two furious slashes. "*What* did you think, Pan? Huh? You thought this would work out well *for you*." Cupid jabbed his finger again and again into Pan's chest. "You, you, you!"

"Okay, okay. I see your point." Pan grasped Cupid by the shoulders, tried to tamp down the wild flailing that seemed to be getting him even more agitated.

"Get your hands off me!" Cupid shouted.

Passion throbbed in the air around them. Here was the energy Pan had been after, enough to power a city block. But it was all for naught. Not even Zeus's thunderbolt could have changed Pan's heart rhythm while Aphrodite held it in her clutches.

There would be no happily ever after to justify Pan's underhandedness. He had failed them both. And he would have to live with the burden of his choice every time Cupid looked at him as he was right now: as if looking at a stranger.

"Q—"

"You *promised* me—no kissing! Do you remember that? Do you?"

Pan hung his head. "Yes."

"Patrick never would have done something so selfish to Mia."

Heat rose from Pan's neck and radiated to the tips of his ears.

"You know the saddest part?" Cupid waited for Pan to lift his gaze. "Even though I'm furious with you right now, I can't deny I liked that kiss, and now I won't be able to get it out of my head."

A twinge of pleasure at Cupid's admission brought Pan a fresh stab of guilt. *What kind of a friend am I?* One not worthy of

Cupid's friendship, let alone Right Love. Pan wondered again why Aphrodite would squander her highest gift on his sorry ass.

"Take me home, Pan. I need to pack my stuff. I think it's for the best that I move out."

"What? No. Come on. I promise I won't try anything like that again. Please, Q."

"I'm sorry, Pan. I don't trust either of us right now."

7

SWIMMING LESSON

Reed felt those eyes on him again. His nerve endings tingled with anticipation and buoyed him a good two inches higher in the water.

Reed checked his form, squeezed his glutes, and stroked his right arm in a perfect arc, hyperconscious of every muscle in his body but not in a bad way. *Christ. Was he . . . preening?*

Cutting neatly through the water with cupped fingers, Reed pulled hard. One more stroke would get him to the wall before Q noticed how one leg flutter-kicked for both.

"Good morning!" called the voice from the deck.

Q, he'd said. Reed had chewed on that one all night. Quinn? Quaid? Quincy? Something exotic, for sure, much like the man himself. Not that it mattered, obviously. The important thing was being useful again. A man's ego could only handle so many disability checks.

Reed gripped the coping and made sure to tuck his legs underneath him as he pushed the goggles off his face. There he was, the mysterious Q, crouched at the pool's edge, youthful and eager and fit. His toned physique conjured efficiency and grace, making Reed wonder if he might be a ballet dancer. The young man was beautiful, breathtaking even; there were no two ways about it.

The word "unfair" popped into Reed's mind, but not as it ever had before. Not as a mangled man's bitterness toward the able-bodied or a middle-aged professor's envy of a coed stud's effortless charm. No, this emotion was entirely foreign to Reed—a brand-new and extremely confusing *stirring* of the sort that had only previously been inspired by the female form.

Curious. But Reed would have to push it aside for now. Water and distraction didn't mix well.

"Good morning to you," Reed answered, glancing conspicuously at the clock mounted high on the wall, "and right on time."

Having arrived at the gym at 8:15, Reed had left himself plenty of time to disrobe, enter the pool, and swim four warm-up lengths so he'd be in perfect form by nine without diminishing his stamina. If Q had arrived late, none of it would matter; Reed couldn't abide disrespectful behavior, a holdout from his teaching days.

"Of course," said Q. "But if I've interrupted your workout, I'm happy to wait." On time *and* considerate.

"No, it's fine. I was just finishing up."

Q bestowed another perfect smile on him, then slid the towel off his shoulders and tossed it onto the bleachers. He strode to the edge of the pool and curled his toes perilously around the edge of the coping as if about to dive in.

"Whoa! Whoa!" Reed thrust his hands out. "Back up! Wait a second!"

Q's toes retreated. "Sorry."

Reed's racing heart slowed to something resembling normal. What kind of fool was he, agreeing to teach this person to swim?

The PT who had supervised Reed's aquatic therapy had classes and training and experience, not to mention liability insurance. Reed was no Kane. If pressed, he could probably recall some CPR basics from his last recertification at the university, but Reed had never needed to revive anyone, thank God. And how could he know if his upper body strength could compensate for all he'd lost? There was a life at risk here. This was insanity or sheer vanity or—or something else Reed wasn't ready to name.

"Look," Reed said, "I've never taught anyone to swim before."

"I know. You mentioned that yesterday."

"You should know that other than screaming for help at the top of my lungs, I probably can't save you if something happens." Pride kept Reed from elaborating.

"Got it," Q said simply, entirely nonchalant. *Ah, youth in all its reckless glory.*

"You need to wait for instruction before you go trying anything yourself, okay?"

"Of course."

"We'll be working in four feet of water. At any point, you can always stand up." Reed released the wall and let his feet touch the bottom. "See?"

Q grinned. "Okay."

This kid's cavalier attitude was starting to worry Reed. The last thing he needed was some arrogant fool drowning on him. "Look, I know you think this is silly, but a person can drown quite successfully in just two inches of water. Honestly, I don't need that on my conscience, so if you're not going to take this seriously—"

"I am," Q said, dropping to one knee. "Reed"—Q's voice went sober on his name—"I hear what you're saying, and I appreciate your concern. I will be extremely careful and listen to everything you tell me. I promise nothing bad is going to happen to me, but I want you to know I do not hold you responsible for my safety. I just want to learn what you know, okay?"

Everything about this was a bad idea, but there was something about this kid that pulled Reed in. He didn't just believe in Q; he believed in himself again.

"In that case, I can promise you'll get your money's worth—if you don't drown." Reed allowed himself a smirk, which Q returned. "Shall we get started?"

"Yes!"

"Here." Reed patted the deck at the end of his lane. "Sit down and slide in, feet first."

"Got it," Q said with a solemn nod, barely giving Reed a chance to snap his hand away before the bright-red trunks met the tiles.

Reed stood close, his whole body on high alert as Q pushed off the side and slipped into the pool like quicksilver, seeming not to register the change in temperature or the enormity of his courage.

Back when Reed was in rehab, they'd occasionally get an adult who'd never learned to swim, for whatever reason, forced into aquatic therapy by injury or malady. It was rare to see a first-time swimmer enter the water without any trepidation. With Q, the only sign of anxiety was a series of exaggerated shoulder rolls though the water stopped just above his waist. A nervous tic? Reed would have to keep an eye on that.

"Congratulations! You're in the water!"

"So I am," Q said, his mouth breaking into a grin exactly at Reed's eye level.

Q stood a good two inches above Reed, about the same height Reed had been when both legs had straightened properly. Q's strong, sculpted shoulders anchored a taut chest, but it was the two peaks of soft, pink flesh Reed had to work hard not to stare at.

Q dipped his hands below the surface and watched the blurry lines of his own fingers trailing through the water. Q's eyes widened with childlike joy. That Reed found himself sharing Q's sense of wonder took him completely by surprise.

"What now?" Q asked.

What now, indeed. Teaching was easy . . . and safe. Reed followed the lesson plan he'd made last night—force of habit. His curriculum for Q entailed a combination of remembered swim lessons from early childhood and techniques Kane had taught him after he'd been injured. He showed Q how to float on his back, how to hold his breath and bob his head below the surface, and—with less embarrassment than Reed would have thought— how to blow bubbles.

The moment of truth came sooner than Reed expected and hit him harder than he cared to admit. If only he could have taught Q to tread water without actually demonstrating it himself. But of course, there was no better option than Reed gliding first into deeper water so he could show Q the movement of his arms and legs.

With Q observing Reed as if his survival depended on it and imitating Reed's form as if playing back video footage, of course he would snap his right leg the same way Reed did. Even with the hitch, though, Q's technique was sound enough to keep him from drowning—which was, after all, its purpose. Reed could have left it alone, and he might have done just that if anything else about Q had been even slightly off, but it felt like a crime against humanity to inflict his own imperfection on such an impeccable specimen.

"Here's where I tell you to do as I say and not as I do," Reed said to his puzzled student. "If you can imagine my right leg as a mirror image of the left, that would be the ideal." Q took in the information, made the adjustment, and perfected his own motion.

They repeated the process with each new skill: Reed's demo and self-critique followed by Q's near-perfect first attempt. Reed's light touch, tweaking Q's crawl stroke or adjusting the angle of his neck, was all he required to achieve precision.

Reed had been subjected to enough HR seminars at the university to be alert to the concept of "inappropriate touching," not that the boundary had ever challenged him before this moment. Reed was being careful with his hands—probably overly cautious, if anything—but only because his feelings toward this man were so confusing. These days, Reed wasn't anyone's employee but his own. Still, the last thing he wanted was to make Q uncomfortable.

For his part, Q seemed eager for any and all of Reed's feedback. "How was that?" Q asked, pushing dark, wet curls off his forehead.

Perfect. Everything is perfect.

"That was very good."

"What's next?" he asked, the ever-present, expectant grin lighting his expression. The simple truth was that Q had not only already learned everything Reed knew; he had, in fact, eclipsed his skill at every turn.

If only Reed could teach Q the butterfly. What a joy it would be to watch this graceful creature arc through the water like a dolphin! But Reed was no fool. He lacked the physical ability to demonstrate anything close to a proper stroke, and he lacked the words to bring alive what he'd never experienced.

He would have loved to have kept Q to himself a bit longer, but Reed knew enough to quit while he was ahead. He glanced at the clock, shocked to note that two hours had passed. He could not remember the last time he'd felt so energized.

"Well, let's see. You've gone from basic water safety to mastering crawl, breast, and backstroke. I'd say that's a good day's work."

"Ah, okay," Q replied. "I guess we have been at it a while." It might have been wishful thinking, but Reed heard a note of disappointment.

Q turned to the wall, set his palms on the deck, and pushed his spectacular body out of the water. He seemed to hang there forever, suspended ramrod straight against the side of the pool while the water rolled down his nicely muscled back, over the curves of the clingy red material stuck to his butt cheeks and even—brazenly—between them. He swung his feet onto the deck and stood, tipped his head back, and squeezed the water from his hair.

There was no arrogance about him. Reed understood that now. It wasn't Q's fault he was perfect. He wasn't trying to flaunt it. Reed couldn't stop leering—there was no other word for it—as Q grabbed his towel from the bleachers and bent to dry his calves.

"I can't thank you enough for spending all that time with me," Q called out to Reed, then smiled when he saw he already held Reed's rapt attention.

Reed's reply juddered out of him like one of those movie aliens laying a giant egg. "It was my pleasure." And *that* was exactly why Reed needed to stick to a lesson plan.

Now that his confession was out there, the best Reed could do was try for diversion. "So, what's the verdict, Q? Do you feel relaxed?" Because Reed was anything but.

"Yes, actually. And starved! Is swimming supposed to make you hungry?"

Reed chuckled. "I'm not surprised. You worked hard today."

"I'd really like to buy you lunch."

Reed hadn't counted on that. "Oh, no, no, no. That's not necessary," he said, waving his hands like a drowning man.

Q walked over to the edge, scrubbing at his hair with the

towel. *Good God.* Since when did the sight of a man's armpits cause Reed's groin to tingle? What was happening to him?

"You're not going to swim some more, are you?" Q asked him.

And now, Reed was truly trapped. "Uh . . . no. I'm good." If only Q would walk away and leave him to his fish-out-of-water routine in privacy.

Q crouched at the edge, one knee pointed toward each of Reed's ears. "So, you're planning to *stand* in the pool for a while longer?"

The man had a point. Reed was acting ridiculous. This whole morning was ridiculous: showing off for this kid, attempting to hide his injured leg under the water, and if he were honest, fantasizing about what was staring him down behind those red trunks.

For crying out loud! Reed was a man of letters—a scholar of classical literature!—not some silly schoolgirl with a silly crush . . . on a *man,* no less! And the age difference! The idea that this young man would give a second thought to Reed's body suddenly struck him as so ludicrous, it cured him of his temporary insanity.

"No. It's definitely time to get out." He felt Q's eyes on him again as he breaststroked to the opposite end of the pool. Reed forced his focus elsewhere—the clock worked well—as he flipped down the seat of the handicap-assist chair and pressed the button to start the lift.

Out of the corner of his eye, Reed saw Q jogging toward him. It had been a long time since Reed had felt disabled, *less than.* Maybe it was just a different flavor of foolishness, but since his injury, swimming had always made Reed feel exactly the opposite—in control, competent, *powerful,* even.

The chair slowed to an undramatic halt, and there was Q, all youth and ease and beauty.

"I'm sorry, I had no idea—" *And now you do.*

Reed tried but couldn't avoid meeting Q's eye. Yep, there was *that look* he'd hoped never to see again, let alone from this young man who had thirsted with such intensity to soak up everything Reed had to offer. And by god if Reed hadn't wrung out the very best of himself. No wonder he felt like a spent rag.

"Here, let me help you—" The magnificent, graceful Q turned awkward and clumsy, tripping over his words and hands to help the invalid out of his chair. Reed supposed it should have made him feel minutely better that Q was human after all, that the distance between them was maybe a tiny bit smaller. But all he felt was crushed to have diminished the young man who'd achieved godlike status in his eyes.

And that was the straw that broke Reed's back.

"Thanks, I've got this," Reed said, meeting Q's gaze one last time with all the kindness he had left to give.

Quick study that he'd shown himself to be, Q nodded mutely and stepped away from the chair.

The sequence Kane had drummed into Reed came back to him in well-practiced clips. *"Take your time"* was the hardest to heed. Reed would have sprinted to the locker room if he could have. As he painstakingly traversed the expanse of concrete—*"right, left, breathe"*—Reed saw Q scrubbing a hand over his chest.

Yeah, kid, my heart's broken, too.

8

UNWORTHY

Pan shoved the milk carton back in the refrigerator and slammed the door. Who cared how much noise he made? There was no sleeping god in the next room to worry about waking—not since Cupid had left last night.

The Cheerios sloshed over the rim as Pan lifted the bowl off the counter. Shielded only where his briefs happened to cover his bare skin, Pan was slightly more careful with the hot coffee.

Just days earlier, he and Q were the easy pals they'd been growing up, conquering the problems of the cosmos together. Now, Cupid couldn't stand the sight of him. Pan's ill-conceived plan had seemed worth the risk at the time, but he would do anything to take it all back, even settle for being strictly *platonic*, as his old buddies on Mount O might say.

Nothing on TV was going to distract Pan from the fact that he'd broken his promise to Q. And worse, every new idea that popped into his mind was dumber than the one before: injecting himself with some substance that would alter his heartbeat to match up with Q's (as if love were some chemistry experiment); flaunting another man-woman-gender-ambiguous being (as if jealousy had any power to influence Cupid's hearing); fucking everything in sight (as if Pan could rid himself of the physical need for Q).

Or . . . what if . . .

Well now! He shot up from the couch, lifted the cereal bowl to his lips, and drained the milky dregs. The idea had been niggling at his brain since this thing started, but now it came into sharp focus. If Pan couldn't fashion Cupid into his Right Love, he would just fashion himself right out of being a Worthy. Surely, Aphrodite had made a mistake. How hard could it be to help her see the error of her ways? Once Pan was released from the "privilege" of Worthy-hood, he and Cupid would be free to explore this thing between them without the gods pulling the heartstrings from above, and everyone would see that they truly belonged to each other.

Sure, the Council would rev Q's heart again and again and again until they'd exacted their revenge, and Cupid would fall for each new Worthy just like before. But this time, it wouldn't hurt quite so much because Cupid would *know* that he and Pan belonged to each other even if his heart tried to convince him otherwise. It would all be okay because he would find that Worthy's Right Love, and two more people would be happy forever, and Q's heart would be freed to return to Pan.

And if Cupid would go ahead and make one little slipup each time—nothing major or dangerous—maybe he wouldn't have to ascend, *ever*, and he could just stay here with Pan. Permanently descended. Unofficially.

With fresh determination, Pan grabbed a black marker and slapped a blank piece of paper onto the kitchen counter. He thought about titling his page, "Reasons Pan is NOT a Worthy," but in his experience, the gods preferred to believe they'd drawn their own conclusions.

He started by writing a fat "1" in the upper left corner. "Number one," he said in a tone intriguing enough to draw attention, "Syrinx." Ah, the beautiful wood nymph who'd fled to the river to escape Pan's advances. The eerie sound of his mouth pipes was an enduring reminder of his wrongdoing. If he hadn't thought it too obvious, he would have gone and played them now.

"Number two, Pitys. Now a pine tree," he added, just in case. "Number three . . . through twelve, goats."

Pan paused to admire his growing list. He was going to need more paper.

"Number thirteen, that time I—"

"What are you doing?"

Pan startled at the intrusion. Nothing like ruffling a few divine feathers to get a house call from dear ol' Dad. "Hello, Pop. What brings you down to earth this fine morning?"

"I asked you a question, son." Mercury stepped warily toward him, eyed the paper, and studied Pan's face—no doubt, looking for signs of madness. Pan wouldn't have been the first deity to break under pressure.

"I'm taking a moral inventory."

"Don't tell me you've enrolled in one of those New Age self-improvement programs the mortals love so much."

Pan scoffed. He had never been one for reflection unless something horrible was staring him down, something as bad as losing his best friend forever—again. "I'm helping Aphrodite with a project."

"Helping?" Mercury was fluid, one of the hardest gods for Pan to read, but even the fleet-footed messenger had a tell: a tight clench of his jaw. "Last I checked, Aphrodite was doing just fine."

Pan set down his pen. "I'm afraid she's made a miscalculation where my character is concerned. I wanted to make sure

I cleared that up before we get another Worthy tangled up in this business."

"The gods don't miscalculate." The warning in his voice was clear. Mercury loved his son, but he was a company man through and through.

"Come on now, Dad. You don't think it's a bit of a coincidence I'm suddenly a Worthy after all these years? Just when Cupid happens to fall?"

Mercury answered in measured tones. "I don't believe the timing is a coincidence, but that doesn't mean you don't deserve it."

"Spoken like a father," Pan said.

Mercury glided to a spot directly across the counter from Pan, making it impossible to avoid his steady gaze. "Perhaps I'm not entirely objective, *but*"—Mercury paused at Pan's huff—"you must admit I've never condoned your bad behavior, of which there has been, ahem, *plenty*." Mercury leveled him with a glower, and Pan began to wish he had pulled on a pair of shorts before his company arrived. He didn't enjoy feeling so exposed.

"However," Mercury continued, "since your descent, your work as god-catcher—"

"Concierge."

"Your work as 'concierge'"—Mercury never could pronounce the hoity-toity French title without cracking a smirk—"is highly regarded. Not perfect," Mercury said quickly before Pan jumped in to remind him of his early fiascoes, "but impressive."

Pan's gaze fell to the paper he'd curled under at the edges. He knew he wasn't the same beast who'd pursued those nymphs to their untimely deaths, and he'd mostly let himself off the hook for their fates, but there'd been others. He wasn't proud of his first few centuries in human form. He'd sown his wild oats and then some.

Ah, but times change, and even an old goat grows wiser, gentler, and—dare he believe?—more sensitive. The sixties threw Pan for a bit of a spin, what with all the free love and psychedelic drugs everyone was passing around, but he'd been a pretty good boy since Woodstock.

"Pan."

"Hmm?"

Mercury smiled kindly at his son. "Has it occurred to you that you earned the honor of Worthy precisely *because* of how you've behaved since Cupid fell?"

Well, that was a new one on Pan. He'd felt anything but virtuous where Cupid was concerned. "No."

"Everyone knows how you've desired him, and yet, you've managed to set your personal feelings aside."

"You mean I've managed to keep my dick in my pants," Pan said gruffly.

"I suppose you could put it that way," Mercury answered, "but I wasn't simply referring to the physical." Mercury's reasoning was wreaking havoc with Pan's strategy to prove himself unworthy, but there was a part of Pan that had secretly started rooting for Mercury to convince him otherwise—a self-destructive part, apparently. "You've put Cupid's needs first, ahead of your own. That night you shared a bed at the Miller home, you proved yourself to be the truest kind of friend."

"You saw that?"

"No. *I* try to respect your privacy. Hephaestus told me about it. He believed I would be proud of you."

Uncomfortable with the touchy-feely moment that had snuck up on him, Pan dropped his gaze.

Mercury clasped his hands together on the counter. "Hephaestus was correct."

Despite his best intentions to deflect Mercury's compliments, a lump had formed in Pan's throat. "You give me too much credit. I was a crap friend yesterday. Did you know Q moved out?"

Mercury nodded. *Of course he knew.* "Probably for the best."

"I cannot imagine how," Pan said. "This whole situation is just so fucked up." Mercury's upper lip twitched at the obscenity.

"Be that as it may, this is the situation you're in. Fighting your fate is not going to help you *or* Cupid. Aphrodite is not famous for changing her mind."

"She is when it suits her."

"Son!" Mercury's rebuke was sharp but laced with concern. Gentler, almost playfully, Mercury added, "You know, Right Love is not the worst thing that could happen to you. At least, that is what I've heard."

By unspoken agreement, they never discussed Mercury's whirlwind romance out loud, but both father and son understood that the memory of Mercury's beloved water nymph Larunda had just been invoked. Theirs was no Right Love pairing but a theft of the soul Mercury had been ordered to deliver to the gates of the Underworld. Along the way, Mercury and Larunda fell in love, had sex, and *poof,* two half sisters for Pan. Pan still wasn't sure how his father had disobeyed Zeus and come out of it with his balls intact.

"Frankly, I don't see it happening. I've been living in this Tarra for twelve years, longer than I usually stay anywhere. I've met pretty much everyone here I have any chance hitting it off with."

"Forgive me for pointing out the obvious, but you didn't have the God of Erotic Love at your disposal until now. Why don't you give him a chance to do his job?"

"Do his job?" Pan snorted. "I've seen this play out. Trust me, he has no idea what he's doing."

"He's made two pairings already, has he not?"

"One was literally an accident, and the other was a couple who were already married! That's hardly rocket science."

"Who says love is rocket science?"

Frustration swept through Pan. He strode to the refrigerator, opened the door, stared inside without seeing, then slammed the door shut. A terrifying thought occurred to him, one that hadn't struck him while he was still focused on winning Cupid.

"You do realize, aside from the fallens and me, the only beings down here are mortals."

Mercury shrugged. *Aggravating.*

"Okay," Pan ranted on, "for argument's sake, let's say I buy into all this. I throw myself into this search, Cupid finds my person, we fall madly in love, and we're perfect for each other. And then I screw up somehow—because you know I will—and Aphrodite decides to revoke my status?"

"I wish I could say, son, but I'm a messenger, not an oracle. The only thing I can tell you is that Aphrodite holds love in the highest esteem—which is why your good friend is down here in the first place, as you'll recall." Mercury was making sense again, and Pan was having the hardest time trying to decide if that was good news or bad.

"I get that, but it's just so hard for me to believe this whole thing isn't a test of some sort."

"Oh, I believe it is the *greatest* test . . . but not yours." Mercury gave his son a gentle smile. "This will be Cupid's biggest challenge yet. And isn't this the pattern of your fallens, each failure ratcheting up the difficulty level of the next feat? It seems to me if Cupid can succeed in pairing you, he'll be released from his torture here on earth, which is what you both want. Right?"

"He'll ascend," Pan said, staring past his father into the empty great room.

"One assumes."

"Sure. Yes. Of course that's what I want for him."

Mercury gave him a sober nod. "I must go now."

"Thanks for popping in."

"Right. Here is your message from the gods . . ." Mercury stuffed a tightly folded piece of paper in Pan's hand, and he was gone.

"Goodbye, Father. Thanks for the heart-to-heart."

Pan chuckled to himself as he unfolded the paper to find it blank on both sides.

9

OBJECTIONS

No surprise, Cupid's heart signal had brought him to Pan's front stoop, where he'd battled a full sixteen minutes against the inevitably of ringing the bell. The front door of Pan's house swung open, and just like that, the hollow space in Cupid's chest filled to bursting.

"Hi. Sorry I didn't call first." Only as the apology fell from Cupid's lips did he realize the thought hadn't even crossed his mind. Really, no thought had crossed his mind since the awful motor started—beyond how to make it stop.

"Well hello, stranger." Grasping the top of the doorframe, Pan arched forward into a luxurious stretch. His T-shirt rode up, revealing a mouthwatering sliver of skin. "What's it been, three days?"

"And three nights." A pretty awful three nights at that, but at least they were both still on the same astral plane—for now.

Pan scanned the mess of a god standing on his stoop and let out a grunt. "Change your mind about moving out?"

"No."

"You know, you don't have to ring the doorbell. Your garage door opener still works. You can come over anytime you want."

"I don't even want to be here now."

Pan huffed. "Gee, you sure know how to make a guy feel good."

"You know what I mean. May I come in, please?"

Pan dropped his hands and stepped out of Cupid's way. "You wanna beer or something?"

"I guess." The taste of beer would never grow on Cupid, but Pan always seemed a little more relaxed with a bottle in his hand and a few drinks in his belly. That could be helpful.

He followed Pan into the kitchen, about twice the size of the cooking area in his new apartment, not that he used anything but the refrigerator and microwave. Pan popped the caps off two bottles and handed one to Cupid.

"*Na pane kato ta farmakia.*" With a brief bottle-to-bottle salute, Pan gave him a wink and knocked back his drink. *May the poison go down indeed.*

Cupid took a polite sip of the sour swill. One corner of the label had curled away from the brown glass bottle. Cupid nudged his fingernail under the edge. "So . . . I've been working on your situation."

"Oh, *my* situation?"

"Yes. I have a few ideas I thought we could explore."

Surely, Pan must have been expecting this. And yet, his eyebrows banged together, forming a sharp V. "Is that right?"

A pearl of sweat rolled down the back of Cupid's neck. "Yes. I know the dating apps can be a bit brutal, but—"

"You can stop right there, pal. I'm a demigod. I don't need some dating app."

"I thought it might be a good place to start."

Pan's bottle met the counter with a scary *ping*. "Well, I happen to think it's an awful place to start."

"Do you have a better idea?"

"Yes," Pan said, leveling Cupid with a menacing glare. "Leave it alone."

"I'm sorry, but I don't see how that is helpful."

"Seriously, Q, what's your rush?"

That dizzying tilt snuck up on Cupid again. Dread seeped into his bones.

"Only the gods playing tug-of-war with our hearts," Cupid answered. "Or is your heart no longer afflicted?"

Pan's desire for him hadn't decreased, Cupid had divined that much as soon as his friend's scent had slapped him in the face, but there was an apathetic air about him now, chillingly reminiscent of his old self. This was not the same open-minded Pan who had brainstormed with him about Mia and Ruthie.

Pan wrapped his lips around the bottle, drained the remaining liquid, and headed to the refrigerator for another. "Just so we're on the same page," Pan said, spinning around with his new beer aloft, "once you find this person for me, that's the end for me, right? No more fooling around?"

"That's the general idea."

"Huh." Pan took a long, thoughtful guzzle, then leaned across the counter. "I have to be honest with you, man. I'm not sure I'm ready to give up bachelorhood."

"Three thousand years of running around wasn't long enough for you?" Cupid's irritated tone wore like the screech of metal on metal to his own ears, but Pan seemed not to notice.

"You really can't count my first thirteen hundred years as a satyr. That was more frustration than fulfillment."

"Pardon me. Only two thousand years of fornicating with anyone you want."

"It's been a good run," Pan said with a casual wink.

"Wow." Anger smoldered inside Cupid until it became too

hot to contain. "Of all people! You know the futility of fighting this. You know the reward. Why are you making this so hard for both of us?"

"I really love sex. I'd just hate for a meaningful relationship to get in the way of all that."

"That's what this is about? Sex?"

Pan shrugged, nursed his drink, and fixed his mouth into an impassive smirk. Cupid stared back at the face he'd once known better than his own, albeit a slightly more civilized version of the wild, pointy-eared satyr.

How hard Pan was working now to maintain his cool façade. The realization filtered into Cupid's consciousness like a childhood melody tucked away in his brain. There was no outward sign Cupid could pinpoint but rather, something moving through his friend—an undercurrent of emotion rushing up against a mighty dam, straining to blast its way out.

Oh, this force that made powerful men and gods hide from themselves. Cupid knew it well: fear. Pan would be furious with him for pressing, but there was far too much at stake to skirt the issue.

"Have I failed to mention that the physical expression of Right Love is the pinnacle of erotic experiences?"

A spark flared behind Pan's green eyes. One eyebrow twitched.

Cupid lifted the beer to his lips, forced himself to drink and to wait.

Pan cleared his throat. "So . . . just the once, or . . .?"

"From what I understand," Cupid replied, "there's no limit."

"Huh." Pan gazed off, no doubt running his mind over a list of erotic experiences he'd probably never imagined topping. "But still," he said after a while, then shook his head rather sadly. "This isn't really about sex, is it, Pan?"

Pan tried to protest, contorted his face into disbelief, irritation, even boredom, but Cupid was not fooled.

"What's going on? Talk to me."

When Pan met his gaze again, the fear was right there on the surface. "I don't really think I'm cut out for love. Everyone I've ever wanted has needed saving—*from me*. Look what happened to Pitys and Syrinx."

"Lust is not the same as Love, Pan. Have you never loved anyone?"

"Not counting you?"

Cupid frowned. "Not counting me."

Pan blew out a heavy sigh. "I don't know, Q. I don't think I was capable of love as a satyr, and now . . .? Is it even possible for me to love a mortal?"

"I did," Cupid answered. "Twice."

Pan regarded his friend warily. "I'm not sure it counts if there's divine intervention."

"Is love possible without it? Let's face it, there are forces that transcend the realm and capacity of mortal beings: life, death, love."

"Point taken," Pan replied.

"We could both list examples of Olympians coupling with mortals. Zeus and Poseidon and"—Cupid hesitated—"okay, yes, Mother, too. Who's to say whether those unions were love?"

Pan's mouth turned up at the corners. "At the risk of pointing out the obvious, most of those unions inspired violent responses on the Mount."

"Yes, true."

The two fell into their own thoughts. Pan put down another two beers; Cupid managed half of the first. He needed his mind sharp to refute whatever new objection Pan might throw at him. Cupid held his tongue while Pan plumbed the depths of his own mind, chasing the tail of one question to the next and the next, until he landed on the one to ask out loud.

"Okay. Let's say we do this. Say you find my person, and we fall madly in love." Cupid's emotions reeled like stones tossed into a tornado. "Wouldn't the gods have to bring us both to Olympus?"

"Why would they revoke your Permanent Descent? You're not being punished."

"If that's true," Pan said, "that means the person I love will die."

There it was at long last, the darkest corner of Pan's heart laid bare. During his lengthy span of time on Earth, Pan had surely lost people he cared about; moving every ten years would not have shielded him from attachment.

"Yes," Cupid answered with a somber nod.

"What will I do *then?*" The last, shuddered word caught in Pan's throat. Cupid swallowed over the lump in his own.

To see tears pool in Pan's eyes over the death of a person he had likely not yet met afflicted Cupid with a wave of pain no more bearable for being thirdhand. The kitchen counter between them kept Cupid from pulling Pan into a treacherous full-body embrace, but he stretched across the stone slab for Pan's shoulders and held Pan's bleary gaze like a man grasping the edge of a cliff by his fingernails.

Cupid steeled himself to speak, but his voice came out in a strangled croak. "When my mother told me you'd been killed—"

A moan escaped Pan. "Q, *please* . . ." A tear started down Pan's cheek and disappeared into his bushy beard. "I can't do this now . . ."

"I remember this strange thought taking hold of me," Cupid continued. "I wanted to die."

"I'm sorry," Pan whispered. His head began to move side to side, then picked up speed.

"Hush," Cupid said, cradling Pan's head between his hands until it stopped shaking.

Pan blinked his reddened eyes, spilling fresh tears onto Cupid's fingers. Cupid swiped Pan's cheeks with his thumbs, but new tears fell faster than he could wipe them away. As his own tears had soaked Aphrodite's robes all those centuries ago.

"Until that moment, I'd never even considered death. But if you'd gone to the Underworld, that's where I wanted to be, too."

Pan's eyelids fell shut. He clenched his lips, but the flood of emotion found release in his shoulders as they trembled and shook. Cupid coaxed Pan's head to his shoulder. The big man went limp, his warm, wet sobs absorbed into Cupid's embrace.

"It's okay, Pan." Cupid pulled his fingers gently through Pan's thick red curls. "I survived. Apollo survived Hyacinth's death. Mother survived Adonis. Look what Ruthie survived. Grief and loss change you, for sure, but you will survive, too. If you're very lucky, you might even love again." Cupid pressed his lips to Pan's head and held him while he quieted.

It wasn't until Pan pulled away that Cupid realized his own eyes and nose were dripping, too. Pan took one look at Cupid, declared him a "fucking mess," and sent the two into a fit of uncontrollable laughter.

"All right, *fine*," Pan said. "Let's get this party started."

10

MATCHMAKING

"Can I get you another beer?" asked Cupid.

Pan suspected a whole case wouldn't be enough to get him through this matchmaking session, but he quite liked the idea of Cupid waiting on him hand and foot. "Sure, and grab one for yourself, huh?" As if he hadn't noticed Cupid never finished the first.

"Here you go," Cupid said, handing one bottle to Pan and setting the other, presumably for himself, on the coffee table. "Are you comfortable?"

"Actually, could you just slip that pillow under my feet? Ahh, nice. Mind giving me a little foot rub while you're there . . ." Pan waggled his toes for effect, earning a cross look from Cupid that died as quickly as it flared. Dude really did deserve a damn medal for self-control.

Cupid perched his ass on the edge of the armchair and leaned toward Pan. Smoothly sliding his phone from his back pocket, Cupid tapped in his password without looking. "As I said before, we don't have to go with the dating apps. I'm open to suggestions."

"I tend to play better in person. It's hard to convey 'demigod' through the screen."

"Oh, I totally agree," Cupid said. "You're a man of great passion, clearly, which is why we'll want to set up the meet-and-greet as soon as possible."

"Listen to you with the 'meet-and-greet'!" Pan had a momentary twinge of nostalgia for the good ol' days before Cupid knew his way around apps and power tools and dealing with mortals, when Cupid still relied on Pan for everything earth-related. He marveled briefly at the turning of the tables that placed his future in Cupid's hands.

"So the apps will just be a starting point, to help us narrow the field a bit."

"Hey, you're the expert." Nobody knew that better than Pan, but that didn't keep the skepticism out of his voice.

Cupid either didn't notice, or he was too focused to let Pan slow him down. "All right. I set up a profile for you on OkCupid."

A dozen glaring objections popped into Pan's head, but curiosity overshadowed them all. "Don't you need my phone for that?"

"Oh, I used my number."

"Of course you did," Pan said. *Kid's got game.* "And what, pray tell, do you have so far?"

"A first name and"—*click!*—"a profile picture." Cupid examined his screen and grimaced at the photo he'd just taken. "Hmm. Maybe we should try that again."

"Gimme that!" Pan snapped his fingers, and Cupid surrendered his phone. Yeah, that one wasn't going anywhere but the tiny digital trash can. "It helps if you warn a person first." Pan squared his shoulders, smoothed out his facial hair, snapped a selfie, and handed the phone back to Cupid. "Here."

Cupid's grin stretched wide as he checked out the new picture. "Yes, that's much better."

"Why do I feel like I just got played?" *Taught by the best.* The thought warmed Pan. Or maybe that was the beer sliding down his gullet.

"What should I say for age?" Cupid asked.

"A well-preserved thirty-three hundred seventy-five?"

"Thirty-three, it is." Cupid tapped the screen while he talked, imperturbable.

"And holding," Pan replied with a chuckle. He'd been thinking about these details too—quite a lot lately.

At what point in the relationship would it be appropriate for Pan to disclose to his supposed life-mate that he was a god? It seemed an overly intense revelation for date one or two, but then, these big truths had their own built-in points of no return. You wait till date three to drop a bomb like immortality, and the other person can't help but wonder what else you've been hiding—a wife, a hacked-up corpse, a tiny penis?

But how could Pan ever hope to share his real identity, hooves and all, with any sane person? And how could Right Love bloom and thrive if it were rooted in lies?

"Gender, male," Cupid mumbled, more or less to himself.

"Sorry, was that a *question?*"

Cupid peered up from his phone. "Should it be?"

"Are you asking me to whip it out?"

"I wasn't," Cupid said, but his eyes went straight to Pan's lap, where the evidence was piling up, so to speak. "Moving on?" The question had a frustrated edge to it that wasn't there a second ago.

"You're the boss," Pan huffed.

Cupid's gaze tipped downward to the safety of his phone. "Next—what are you looking for in a match?"

Now there was an interesting dilemma. Lately, it was "dick all day," but nymphs had once been Pan's bread and butter, and mortal females offered an impressive range of exotic delicacies he wouldn't have wanted to miss out on. What with the moderns' ever-growing array of non-binary options, Pan honestly had no clue how his Right Love might gender identify.

When in doubt, deflect. "Isn't that *your* department?"

"Fair enough." Cupid tapped in his selection.

"Wait, what'd you put?"

"I just checked everything."

"Good thinking." A smorgasbord of options. Maybe this wasn't such a terrible idea after all. "What's next?"

If Cupid noted the hint of eagerness in Pan's tone, he let it slide. "This next part asks how your best friend would describe you."

"Lemme guess"—Pan chuckled—"stubborn and horny."

Cupid cracked his first smile. "They'll figure that out soon enough. I was thinking along the lines of fun-loving and adventurous, enjoys traveling and working out."

"Great, that'll really differentiate me from the pack."

Pan's sarcasm failed to dampen his friend's enthusiasm. "Should we mention your job?"

Pan snorted. "Absolutely. Intercepts degenerate deities and facilitates their cockamamie schemes . . . *this*, for example."

"Concierge," Cupid said as he typed. "Okay, now they list a bunch of multiple-choice questions so they can calculate your best matches. Ready?"

"Fire away." If this little exercise accomplished nothing else, at least Pan was reminded how fortunate he was not to need all these machinations just to get laid.

"Carefree or intense?"

"Too easy," said Pan. "Next?"

"Could you date someone who is messy?"

"C'mon, Q. Don't they have anything more challenging than that?"

"What's more interesting to you right now—sex or love?"

Pan laughed out loud at that one. "Seriously?"

"Oh!" This time, it was Cupid who glanced up from his phone and broke out in a giant grin. "How important is God to you?"

Just like that, Pan and Q were the terrible twosome again—except they were no longer the young rabble-rousers who could thumb their noses at authority without repercussions. Poking the beast with a snarky comment might have felt satisfying in the moment, but for Cupid's sake, Pan behaved himself. "I think we better skip that one."

"Agreed," said Cupid. "Ah, here's a good one. About how long do you want your next relationship to last?" Cupid answered his own question without waiting for Pan's response. "The rest of my life."

Pan swallowed his objection. *Fill in your little boxes, Q.* Ultimately, Pan was still in control of who he hooked up with.

"Okay, that's it for the questions." Cupid stood and extended the phone toward Pan. "You ready to start swiping?"

"Really? Are you sure you trust me to do that?"

"I'm sure I don't," Cupid said with an amiable grin. "That's why I'll be sitting right next to you." The cushion hopped when Cupid plopped down practically on top of Pan. "Want me to hold your beer?"

"Nope. This is one of many tasks I can manage with one hand," Pan said, tossing Cupid a wink as the first potential match, a tasty, blonde morsel, appeared on his screen.

Whatever. Pan could barely remember that once-familiar sting of rejection, but it was hard to argue with a curated collection of attractive choices set literally into the palm of his hand.

"Good start! This one is just my type."

A swipe right brought a hot, green-eyed brunette holding a cat. "Also my type, though *cats . . .* eh, whatever," Pan said, licking his lips as he swiped right again: a gym-stud with thighs bigger than Pan's waist. "Hello, sir." *Swipe right.* "Gotta say, Q, this app's kinda growing on me."

Big-chested woman: *Swipe right.* Big-chested man: *Swipe right.* "Hmm, maybe I do have a type," Pan cackled. "Ooh, stripper. Athlete. Yum. Chef? Good idea . . . hey, a handyman. Maybe he knows my buddy Rayne at Home Warehouse." Pan waggled his eyebrows; Cupid smiled benevolently. "Beard? Yassss. Silver fox? Hmm. Eh, why not? Oh, wait, no, not this one." Bald guy with a beer gut busting out of a short-sleeved button-down: *swipe left.* "Fail," Pan said with a chuckle. "Okay, okay, we're back on the swipe-right train."

Cupid watched over Pan's shoulder, not speaking a word as Pan collected three dozen possibilities before coming up for air. "That should get things rolling," Pan said playfully. "Here's your phone back."

"Keep it. Your matches are going to start coming in. You should see them first."

"Right, right, my matches. Just think, Q—my 'echo swipe' could already be inside here waiting for me." Pan jiggled the phone by his ear like a kid shaking a present on Christmas morning.

Cupid's sober response sucked all the air out of the room. "Yes, that would be the hope."

Pan met his best friend's unflinching gaze. In a rare moment of perfect clarity, Pan grasped the inevitable: Cupid was going to succeed. Even more shocking—Pan wanted him to.

The jolt of insight shook him to his core. Pan's casual swipe-fest had suddenly taken on the gravity of three people's futures:

Pan, Cupid, and some unsuspecting mortal about to be drawn into this divine drama.

"Okay, I'll hold on to your phone for now," Pan said, "but just till we get three good matches—"

"Six." Cupid's tone left no room for bargaining.

"Fine, but that means you have to stay. You're not leaving here without your phone." It was the closest Pan had come all night to taking care of Cupid, a role he was far more comfortable inhabiting.

Cupid nodded and picked up the same beer he'd been nursing all night. "Anything good on Netflix?"

11

A TASTE OF BAKLAVA

Aphrodite tipped her forehead to the gaia wall in Ares's War Room. The cool glass against her skin was a stark reminder that her son was worlds away, not the few meters below her that Pan's great room appeared through the Earth window.

"Cupid's behaving honorably," Aphrodite said.

Ares harrumphed. "For now," came his flat response.

"You think he'll weaken." It wasn't a question, and she didn't turn for his answer, unsure whether she'd emerge from his steely gaze unscathed—or at all. Bad enough they were alone in the War Room. Ares had a way of filling the spacious chamber that made Aphrodite marvel at how the walls could contain him.

He materialized behind her, as swift and noiseless as Mercury, his robe swishing to a halt against her bare calves. "Look at the two of them together, both of them barely holding on."

Barely holding on. He might have been describing Aphrodite. *This*, being alone with Ares again, was all she'd been able to think about since their appearance before the Council. It thrilled her to guess what new, bold intimacies the God of War might inflict on her today. Begging was beneath him; seduction was not.

"You see how they pine for each other," Ares said, his words wafting over that spot on her neck that always drove her crazy. Ever the strategist, Ares wouldn't have forgotten that detail. "It's even worse than before. I don't know about Pan, but Cupid doesn't stand a chance."

Aphrodite felt the jab; she was still a mother. "I think you're wrong."

"And you hope I'm not," Ares retorted.

It was a dare: *Tell me you don't want him to fail. Tell me you don't want to finish what we've started.*

When she didn't answer, Ares stepped closer, meeting the curve of her bottom. She felt his mouth curl into a smile against her cheek. He loved winning.

"Goddess." His warm whisper entered the shell of her ear and filled her with heat. "I accept your surrender."

Ares spun her to face him, and she became fully his, even as his audacity was still sinking in. *Yes*, the god was arrogant and stubborn—and those were his better qualities—but there was a need behind his eyes, too, and Aphrodite knew it was all for her. She didn't ask him to name it. If she'd wanted soft and fluffy, she would've stayed home with her husband.

Still, Aphrodite was a goddess of considerable station, and she had her pride to protect. She met Ares's grin with one of her own. "And I accept yours."

His eyes sparkled with boyish glee. "A stalemate, then," he said. "I can live with that."

His hand cupped her cheek as tenderly as she could ever remember, and he pressed his lips to hers. Her breath left her in a giddy *whoosh*. She'd forgotten how his kisses made her head spin, but he seemed determined to make sure she wouldn't forget again. He tipped her backward, catching and trapping her with his powerful arms when she lost her balance. His tongue slipped between her lips, and she opened for him.

They kissed until there was no more *his* and *hers* but a singular blur of lips and tongue and heat. He lowered her deliberately but gently, cradling her head as her back met the stone floor. Shrugging off his outer garment, Ares stretched out alongside her, his face hovering just above hers, eyes swimming with desire. Only the thin layer of his linen tunic muffled the full effect of his manhood pressed against her thigh.

"I love that *this* is where I'll have you," he said, smiling almost cruelly as he took in their stark surroundings, the seat of his power.

Aphrodite shivered. She wanted him to conquer her, to peel away her royal robes and take her against the hard, bare floor, to claim the deepest recesses of her body. She needed all of that, even his brutality, now that she'd won his surrender.

As if he could see right into her fantasies, Ares climbed astride her and threw off his tunic. He paused to allow Aphrodite a moment to admire the hard lines of his chest and the glorious tumescence she had inspired. Virility was a gift Ares had never squandered. Aphrodite feasted her eyes on the banquet above and around her. Ares drank in the potent nectar of her hunger and seemed to desire her all the more for it. Gazing into the mirror of the other, they created an infinity of reflected desire.

"By my calculation," Ares said, "we've had six weeks of foreplay."

No other lover would have gotten away with such a brash maneuver, but the God of War was exempt from normal rules of engagement. Besides, foreplay would have required patience neither of them possessed. Her silence told him everything he needed to know.

With a growl that curled Aphrodite's toes, Ares plucked apart the clasp at her bosom and spread the silk to both sides. Glorious in his conquest, he bent and grasped her nipple between his teeth. Her thighs fell open as if he'd unlocked a secret door. The sting was followed by a tantalizing brush of tongue, leaving Aphrodite to squirm beneath him and wonder which torture was worse. She had only one coherent thought: *More.*

She groaned; he laughed, then bent to her other breast.

He bit down harder this time. Her hips jerked up and smacked into his groin. Ares grunted and pressed her to the floor. It seemed he'd won, but Aphrodite found a way to snake her hand between their bellies and curl her fingers around his heavy phallus.

He sucked in a sharp breath and stopped laughing. Aphrodite had the upper hand now.

He retaliated, of course, going straight to her pleasure spot with his lethal fingers. Aphrodite wasn't fool enough to think Ares was out of practice simply because she'd made herself unavailable for the last three thousand years. Still, every woman was her own puzzle to solve, and it pleased Aphrodite that Ares remembered exactly how to drive her to her bliss.

He worked her into a froth, describing in graphic detail exactly what he was going to do to her and extracting the final submission—making her beg. The orgasm that tore through her surprised her with its blinding intensity.

When the stars cleared from her vision, all she could see was Ares's triumphant leer.

"I quite like you this way," he said, sweeping the pad of his thumb across her breast. "I'm not sure I'll let you go, after all."

As if to confirm that she very much enjoyed being his captive, an aftershock rippled through her body. She tried to wriggle free, but he held her immobile and pressed a kiss to her lips. Power was always his greatest aphrodisiac.

She blinked up at him, woozy with awe and desire. "What will you do with me?"

"To the victor go the spoils," he said, crawling between her legs. "Don't worry, Goddess. You'll be begging me soon enough for your next orgasm."

He wasted no time, spearing her with his mighty sword. Inside her at long last. The world outside the one-way windows sped by all around them; neither cared. All that mattered were the two lovers inflicting pleasure upon each other. Ares made good on his boast. She did beg again, but this time, he, too, was lost in ecstasy.

Afterward, they lay sweaty and sticky in each other's arms, staring at the map of the cosmos painted on the ceiling. Ares put voice to it first, though the exact thought had passed through Aphrodite's mind. "We're going to do this again," he said, turning to bestow his winning smile on her. Typical of Ares, it was a statement, not a question.

A flush rose from her neck. Stumbling into unfaithfulness out of passion somehow seemed less deceitful than planning for it. "You'll have to up your foreplay game next time," she said.

His laughter shook them both. "Challenge accepted."

Curling his arm to draw her toward him, he kissed her, this time with a tenderness that stirred her. When he pulled away, she thought she read wonder in his eyes.

"I fear I won't be able to get enough of you now," he said. For all his posturing, Ares would have been surprised to learn it was his vulnerability that gave him the most power over her.

"It's a terrible thing to know what you've been missing," Aphrodite said. Only Adonis had ever pleased her as thoroughly as Ares did, and far more sweetly, but her beautiful prince was long gone from this world.

"Indeed," Ares agreed. "All these years, I'd decided I must have embellished the details."

"It was easier that way," Aphrodite said.

A brilliant, dreadful idea popped into Aphrodite's head. Just the act of saying it out loud would seal her infidelity. There would be no coming back from this.

"Goddess?" Ares cupped her cheek and forced her gaze to his. "You're not having regrets?"

"No, no. It's not that," she answered too quickly, piquing his curiosity.

He tensed, raised his upper body off the floor, and leaned on a bent arm. "I think you'd best tell me what's on your mind." Demanding, controlling, unyielding—he was not going to let this go, and Ares was the one god Aphrodite couldn't lie to.

"Promise you won't think me terrible?"

Ares's mouth curled into a wicked grin. "I like it already."

"It strikes me . . . *now* . . . that it's a whole lot easier to resist, say, *baklava* if you've never tasted it."

"All right . . .?" Ares sat up straighter, setting his mind to the puzzle.

"So, if I want to make you *desire* baklava, my best strategy is to find a way to get you to taste it. Wouldn't you agree?"

"Yes, I suppose." Ares's forehead creased with the effort of deciphering her code. "So long as it's tasty."

"Oh, it's tasty," she replied. "And after that, you're bound to want *more* baklava, and that's no good because—"

"Because if I keep eating baklava," Ares said, his smile breaking with understanding, "I'm not going to give a fig about stuffed grape leaves ever again."

Aphrodite nodded cautiously.

As she'd both hoped and feared, Ares picked up the thread and spared her the burden. "We offer a taste to Cupid and Pan, a special dispensation for one . . .?"

Hmm. One *what,* exactly? The knotty question hung between them.

"Maybe one *day?*" Aphrodite suggested.

"Yes, a time limit would be effective," Ares said, his evil grin widening. "We'd have to offer immunity, of course."

"Of course," she agreed.

"But after that . . ."

He didn't finish the sentence. He didn't have to.

12

INTERMEDIATE SWIM

Cupid had no reason to expect Reed to be at the pool at nine the next morning. He didn't know the man's schedule. It wasn't as if they'd made an appointment for today. Still, when Cupid emerged from the locker room all suited up and keen to swim some laps with Reed, he couldn't help feeling forlorn and so very lonely when Reed wasn't there.

Respectfully obeying the protocol Reed had taught him, Cupid entered at the end of an open lane, feet first. He centered his new goggles over his eyes, pulled the straps snug at his temples, and dipped his head underwater to check the suction.

Cupid's first length of crawl stroke was not his best. How could he concentrate on his rhythmic breathing when Pan had six dates set up over the next three days? To make matters worse, Pan insisted on a *whole* date with each one. "None of that catch-and-release crapola you pulled on Mia." Apparently, Pan fully planned to bed each one, and the only thing that might make him reconsider sleeping with number six was if number five happened to be his Right Love. And Pan had made it abundantly clear how Cupid would be dealt with if he tried to interfere. "Thumbs up if you hear two echo beats, thumbs down if you don't. Either way, you signal, then you scram unless you want those thumbs to end up where the sun don't shine."

Can you believe this guy? Cupid railed silently, pulling vigorously at the water with his cupped fingers, flutter-kicking extra hard with pointed toes.

He couldn't tell Reed the details, obviously, but Cupid had hoped to blow off some steam with his swim partner. At least being with Reed would have pulled Cupid out of his own head, but now, on top of all his Pan troubles, Cupid had a new worry—that his awkward behavior had made Reed uncomfortable enough to avoid him.

Cupid switched to breaststroke and set his thoughts on how he could apologize to Reed. Would the membership desk give him Reed's phone number? Was it creepy of Cupid to ask? What if Cupid left his number for Reed or maybe a written note—

"Impressive."

The word reached Cupid's ears through the muddled acoustics of water, but he recognized Reed's voice immediately. Cupid swam the rest of the length with his head fully above water and a smile spanning his face.

There stood Reed, wrapped from waist to knees in his towel, leaning slightly on his cane as he dissolved into laughter. "Well, not so much that doggy-paddle to the wall, but the rest of the lap looked to be fine form."

"I have a great teacher," Cupid said, basking in the compliments almost as much as in Reed's mere presence. He was inordinately happy the man had shown up.

"Apparently."

Cupid hooked his folded arms over the edge of the pool and craned his neck to look at Reed looming large above him. The towel and cane lent the appearance of a shepherd tending his flock. Cupid pushed the goggles off his face, but his perception didn't change.

"Look, Reed, I want to apologize for how I acted last time."

"No need," Reed said. "I've been told I can act a little prickly about my . . . situation. Especially around new people."

"My stepfather walks with a limp, so I'm used to it. It's just that I hadn't noticed when you were in the water. You're so graceful."

"Yeah, not so much on land. If only I were a fish." Reed chuckled. "Speaking of which, I should probably stop procrastinating."

Cupid watched with a cautious eye as Reed hobbled over to the bleachers, unwrapped his towel, and kicked off his sandals. Setting his cane on top of the bench, Reed turned and limped toward the pool about half as quickly and twice as labored. Upon reaching the edge, Reed hitched his right leg out of the way and descended abruptly toward the ground. Cupid lurched forward to catch him, sloshing a wave onto the deck.

Reed froze in his grasp. "I'm fine. You can let go," he said tightly.

Cupid released his grip and retreated into the water. "I'm sorry. Again."

"I realize it's not the most elegant entrance"—Reed lifted his body using his arms—"but I always end up in the water eventually." Reed shot him a quick wink and slipped into the pool and underwater.

He emerged in front of Cupid, his brown hair slicked back, goggles slung around his neck, his eyes glimmering with regained confidence. "Now . . . let's see that crawl stroke."

A queasy unrest had settled into Cupid's belly. Reed may have been ready to move on, but Cupid wasn't. "Would you mind answering a question for me?"

"Sure, no problem. What is it?"

"How do I do *this*"—Cupid gestured back and forth between them—"so I don't offend you again?"

"Ah," Reed said. "It's pretty easy, actually. Just treat me like anyone else unless I ask for your help."

"Okay." Sounded simple enough, but Cupid wasn't entirely sure he could stifle his reflexes if Reed were to stumble again. "I'll try."

"Fair enough," Reed answered, "and thank you for asking, by the way. Most people would just pretend not to see the elephant in the room."

Relief surged through Cupid. Reed was here, and they were good.

Cupid propped his foot against the wall and prepared to push off. "Are you going to follow me?"

"Not yet. First, I want to make sure you're not about to reinforce any bad habits."

"Oh, *okay*," Cupid teased, raising an eyebrow before pulling on his goggles. "As long as you're not procrastinating."

Reed huffed. "Thanks for your concern. I'll be over here, warming up and stretching so I can keep up with you."

Cupid set off across the water, focused on the rhythm of the *pull, kick, breathe*. Now that Reed was here, it felt critical to do it right.

Approaching the far wall, Cupid remembered the flip-turn he'd come across on YouTube. He tucked his legs into his chest, somersaulted, turned, and pushed off the tiles as hard as he could. He slowed as he reached Reed, who was observing him from the end of the lane.

"I didn't teach you that turn," said Reed, eyeing Cupid with awe.

"I found it on the internet."

"Did they explain about blowing air out of your nose when you flip?"

Cupid shrugged. "No, I just did it."

"Huh." Reed bit back his little smile but not before Cupid tucked away his surprising jolt of pride. "Ready to work up an appetite?"

"Always."

"Why don't you lead the first twenty laps, alternating breast and crawl, and then we'll see where we are, okay?"

They could have spread out; there was a lane open right next to them. Cupid had no interest in suggesting it, nor did Reed seem motivated to put space between them.

Cupid pushed off and started swimming at a moderate clip. Hyperaware of maintaining a consistent gap between his kick and Reed's head, Cupid settled into Reed's rhythm. Each time they passed each other coming and going at the wall, Cupid would make a silly face to get Reed to smile. His heart felt lighter than it had in days, and it wasn't just the water carrying his weight.

After the twenty laps, Cupid pulled to a stop. Reed tapped the wall beside Cupid, then dunked under the water again and came up, pushing his hair and goggles off his face.

"You were holding back on my account," Reed said.

Reed was right, and Cupid understood that denial would have insulted him. "It was a comfortable pace. Gave me a chance to really focus on my form."

"Your form is perfect," Reed said. Cupid couldn't be sure the tinge of pink in Reed's cheeks wasn't simply caused by exertion, but it seemed Reed might have been blushing. "I guess you don't need me anymore."

"No, I *do*," Cupid said.

The truth came easily to Cupid's lips. He needed Reed now more than ever, with Ruthie leaving and Mia settled in with

Patrick and Pan about to strike out and meet all kinds of new people, and Cupid's home so very far away.

Reed cocked his head, skeptical but not displeased. Cupid took the opening.

"I'm, uh, having some trouble with my rhythmic breathing on my right side. I was hoping you might take a look?"

Reed was nobody's fool, and Cupid was still a terrible liar. "Okay, let's see it," said Reed.

An agreement had been struck.

It wasn't easy for Cupid to flub the rhythm that came to him so naturally, but he set his thoughts on all those exasperating hours spent on Mount O with Chiron, desperately trying to learn how to run hurdles: the wings flapping whenever he leaped and screwing up his timing; his stubby legs unable to properly calibrate his stride and never quite adequate to lift him over the hurdles.

He swallowed a mouthful of pool water and came up coughing. It tasted worse than beer.

Reed was at his side in a heartbeat, arm wrapped around Cupid's shoulders. "Easy now. Just breathe."

"See? Need you." Cupid rasped, proud of himself for spinning truth from his lie. *Cough.*

"Mm-hmm," Reed said, barely containing his grin. "Are you okay?"

Cupid nodded.

"Good." Reed gave Cupid's shoulder a squeeze before letting go.

A warm, more-than-a-friend tingle lingered where Reed's hand had been. Despite the heavy concentration of chemicals in the air, Cupid definitely detected a waft of musk coming from Reed. *Yes, that works, too.*

"Thank you," Cupid said, staying close to Reed, drawing out the delicious intimacy.

"I didn't really do anything."

"No, I mean thank you for all of it, for teaching me."

This time, Reed pulled Cupid's gratitude inside and gave it a home. "You're very welcome."

"Can I make you dinner?" Cupid remembered that first meal at Mia's, the newness of it all, the nice alone time, not having to share her with a restaurant full of people.

"Oh. That's not necessary." Reed's gaze, shining with confidence just moments ago, darted away from Cupid. "We should start swimming again before our muscles cool down. Cramping is no fun. Trust me."

Reed was procrastinating again, this time using swimming as the excuse to avoid Cupid. He was a complicated man.

"You know, Reed, you're going to have to let me do *something* to thank you for helping me learn to swim."

"You just thanked me." Reed lined up against the wall and sank to his shoulders in the water, but there was a hesitation to his movements that made Cupid persist. *One last try*, he told himself.

Cupid squatted in front of Reed and glided so close, their knees brushed underwater. "*Please, Reed?*"

The glassy eyes blinked once, twice. Reed sighed. Another deal had been reached. "Sure."

Remembering Mia's thoughtful invitation, Cupid asked, "Do you have any food allergies?"

13

SUCH A DEAL

Cupid was not a fan of Pan's choice of rendezvous point, and he was even less a fan of any woman who would agree to meet him at this seedy hotel for a first date. Thinking back on how anxious he'd been for Mia's safety, Cupid had to wonder why this girl didn't have a friend to talk her out of making such a reckless decision. He had half a mind to do it himself. It eased his conscience to know that Pan would never harm a mortal. More importantly, Cupid had made a promise to Pan that he fully intended to keep.

He checked the dashboard clock: twelve minutes until three o'clock. "Take your time showing up," Pan had told Cupid, torturing him further by adding, "but don't expect us to wait for you in the bar once the mood strikes." Oh no, Cupid had no intention of taking his time.

He'd arrived thirty minutes early, just in case, and he planned to wait right here in his car until both Pan and the girl had arrived and made their way inside. He'd approach the pair only as close as absolutely necessary to make his determination, give Pan the agreed-upon signal, and get far, far away from this place as quickly as possible. From the looks of the exterior, the walls were thin, and Pan was not a quiet lover. Cupid's nose wrinkled at memories of Pan's loud and pungent sex with that dancer Jagger.

A knock on the passenger window startled him. Expecting Pan, Cupid was even more surprised by the face from home. Lacking context and his signature winged sandals and petasus, Mercury was almost unrecognizable. His Earth form had a filmy quality that made the god appear to be both here and on Olympus at the same time, even clothed as he was in blue jeans and a black leather jacket.

"Greetings from the gods. It's urgent that I speak with you."

Terror ripped through Cupid. There was only one reason Mercury would have come to him: Cupid's ascension!

That day Cupid had left Mia's in a fog of heartache and pain, when he was sure he was about to shoot up into the sky alone and without warning, Pan had explained the mechanics of ascension. Mercury would come down from the Mount to retrieve Cupid in a spot where his sudden disappearance wouldn't be witnessed by mortals. Cupid had called up that information after crossing Ruthie and Zach, but again, he had failed to ascend.

Cupid's gaze darted around the deserted parking lot. Not a mortal in sight. Was this it?

Why now? He scrubbed at his heart with a tight fist. He hadn't finished with Pan. There had been no painful release of the tight grip of his punishment. Surely, the girl of questionable morals meeting Pan here would not turn out to be his Worthy. And surely, Pan's crass "C U at 3" text did not constitute crossing their Liminal Point.

Was Cupid to be dragged home a failure, then?

The passenger door opened, and Mercury slipped inside. The car pulsed with the god's eerie glow. Cupid gawped, unable to speak.

"I have an urgent message from your mother."

Mother? She's finally realized her terrible mistake! They're retracting the punishment! But what will happen to Pan?

Cupid couldn't organize his racing thoughts, but he knew he couldn't leave like this. "*Please.* I'm not ready to go."

Confusion then tenderness broke across Mercury's expression. "I'm not here to take you."

"You're not?"

Mercury smiled warmly. "You don't want to leave."

"I–" Cupid searched his heart of hearts. "No, I don't. Not yet."

Mercury placed his hand on Cupid's shoulder. "You've always been a good friend to my son."

A lump formed in Cupid's throat. "I love him, Uncle."

"I know, Cupid. He loves you too."

Cupid's head filled with questions. Until Pan's so-called death, Cupid had always shared a close relationship with Mercury. On the family tree, Cupid hung from the branch of Mercury's half brother Ares, but because of his friendship with Pan, the "uncle" title had always carried more weight than mere biology. Whatever questions felt too big for Hephaestus or too embarrassing to ask his mother, Cupid had brought to Mercury. After Pan's disappearance, Mercury changed, became distant. Hurt and more alone than ever, Cupid had turned to his mother for an explanation. She'd blamed it on grief, explaining why being around his son's best friend would be too painful for Mercury.

It took Cupid a few seconds of staring into the face he'd once trusted so completely for the betrayal to filter through. Tears stung Cupid's eyes. Yes, he'd gained back his best friend, but he'd lost much, too.

Cupid shrugged out of Mercury's reach. "What is the message?" Cupid asked, shaken by the detachment in his own voice.

Mercury held his gaze long enough to watch the boulder settle across the entrance to Cupid's heart. He reached into the back pocket of his jeans and pulled out a folded piece of paper. "Before I read this, I need you to know how sorry I am about the deception. It nearly broke me to see you in so much pain."

Cupid looked away, blinking his angry tears in the opposite direction. He wouldn't send Mercury home to report that he was still the crybaby of Mount O. "Is that all?" Cupid asked evenly.

Mercury sighed. "No." He waited for Cupid to turn back or ask him to continue; Cupid did neither. "I beseech you to set aside your feelings and remember this is not Pan's punishment but your own."

How dare he! Cupid's station might have been temporarily lowered by his punishment, but was he not still the prince of the palace of Aphrodite, a god deserving of Mercury's respect?

Cupid drew a deep breath and released it slowly. Yoga had proven to be a useful practice. Emotion would detract from his authority. As composed as he was likely to get, Cupid faced Mercury.

"You overstep your station, *messenger.*"

"I am aware," Mercury whispered, lowering his sorrow-filled eyes.

Humility was a trait few of the pantheon possessed. Mercury's display sucked the air out of Cupid's sails. How many terrible deeds had the gods required of Mercury, and yet Cupid had never seen him rail or make demands. Only now, sitting next to Mercury in the tight confines of his car, did Cupid begin to appreciate the burden carried by Mercury for Pan's disappearance, the unbearable weight of silence.

"You are wrong if you believe I would put my needs above Pan's now or ever."

Mercury lifted his gaze to meet Cupid's. "My apologies," he said solemnly. "I should not have underestimated you."

"Apology accepted." Fresh tears rolled down Cupid's cheeks. This time, he did not turn away. "How could I fault a father's blindness over his son's welfare?"

The stark truth was understood without being said aloud: Cupid had no such parent.

"I pray you would not," Mercury replied. "Now . . . can we go back to calling me 'Uncle' again?" Mercury's request was meant to soften the blow. It worked.

"Perhaps you should read the message now."

Mercury's nod halted abruptly when something caught his attention over Cupid's shoulder. Cupid swiveled around as the door beside him was yanked open.

"It's show time! What the—" Pan poked his head inside the car. "*Father?* Two visits in one week?" *Curious.* This was the first Cupid had heard about the other visit.

"Hello, son."

"You'll be pleased to know I'm about to have a date with my first potential Worthy."

Mercury glanced over at the hotel entrance, then back at his son. "Far be it from me to stand in the way of your . . . romantic afternoon."

"Really? You're judging me now?"

"No, Pan," Mercury answered, shaking his head. "Not I."

With an eye roll that could've been heard in the next state, Pan jerked his chin toward Cupid. "Hey, you ready?"

"Your father was about to deliver a message from my mother."

Mercury flashed the paper, finally catching Pan's attention. "This concerns you too, Pan."

Pan scoffed. "Get on with it, then. Brandi's gonna be here any second."

Cupid didn't relish stepping into the path of Pan and Mercury's storm, but he also didn't want to risk Pan's chances with this Brandi on the off-off chance she was the one. "Pan, don't you think maybe you should get in the car or something?"

"Good point." Pan slammed Cupid's door, opened the back door, and slid to the middle of the seat. "Okay, let's have it." Pan tucked his hands between his knees.

Mercury ignored his son's temper tantrum and read from his document:

BY SPECIAL DECREE OF THE
AD HOC SUBCOMMITTEE FOR
DISCIPLINARY ACTION OF CUPID,

Judgment is hereby suspended until the stroke of midnight tonight [local Earth time] in the case of Cupid v. Hera, such that any activities [i.e., carnal behaviors] engaged in by the transgressor [Cupid] with any being, mortal or divine [including but not limited to Pan], will be exempted from official judicial consequences, now and for all time.

WITNESS OUR HAND AND SEAL,
Ares
Aphrodite

"I can vouch for the authenticity of the signatures," Mercury said morosely. He turned the page around so Cupid could see the official seals of the God of War (a blood-smeared sword) and the Goddess of Love (a kiss of her balm-stained lips).

Pan burst into raucous laughter.

"What's so funny?" Cupid asked, looking to Mercury, who seemed equally puzzled.

"Your parents want us to fuck. Apologies for the rough language, Father," Pan said before Mercury had a chance to complain.

Cupid took the document and reread it to himself. He had to admit, the language left little to misinterpretation. They'd even specifically mentioned Pan.

"But why?" Cupid asked.

"C'mon, Q. You know this one."

"It's a test of some sort?"

"There ya go!" Pan answered with a wink, then started fiddling with his phone.

"But it states right here there will be no consequences."

"No 'official judicial consequences,'" Mercury said, then turned to Pan. "What are you doing?"

"Rescheduling Brandi and Garrett for tomorrow," Pan replied. "I don't plan to waste precious time." He slid his phone back into his pocket, rubbed his hands together, and licked his chops at Cupid as if sitting down to a feast. "As good fortune would have it, there's a hotel just a few steps away. Father, always a joy. Q, shall we?"

Should they?

"I don't know, Pan," Cupid answered. This unexpected gift from the gods didn't sit well. Cupid couldn't see the strings, but neither had the Trojans. Leave it to the God of War to apply military tactics to Cupid's heart.

"Remember, this is merely an *offer*," said Mercury, seemingly heartened by Cupid's hesitation. "You don't have to—"

"Whoa! *Hey!*" Pan threw his hands up. "When did you get promoted to *commentator* of the gods?"

Mercury's downcast expression only served to tighten the grip of dread's cold fingers around Cupid's heart. His earlier plea on behalf of his son made more sense now.

"It's time I take my leave." Mercury reached for the door latch.

"Father, do me a favor, please. If the gods decide to send you down with any revisions before midnight strikes, do your very best to get lost on the way."

"Goodbye, Uncle," Cupid said, drawing a warm smile from Mercury.

"Good luck, boys," he said, then vanished on swift feet.

"Now, where were we?" Pan asked. "Oh yes, about to go inside."

"Pan, why do *you* think they're doing this?"

Pan huffed. "Who knows? Maybe Brandi was my person, and they want you to work harder—"

"There is no way Brandi is your person," Cupid answered hotly. He had resigned himself to humoring Pan and letting him have his fun—as long as there were no one-way beats—but he was not about to believe the decree had anything to do with Brandi. "C'mon, Pan. Help me think this through."

"Okay, okay. Let's play this out. Here we are, the two hottest gods in the cosmos, set loose to indulge in a no-holds-barred sex marathon, limited only by our imaginations and the number of times we can get it up, both of which are damn near infinite. Would you agree we're both about to have the most mind-blowing sex of our lives?" Pan paused while Cupid nodded woodenly, belying the storm of arousal brewing inside him. "I guess the big question is what happens after that?"

Trying to project his thoughts past all the wild fantasies of what he and Pan were about to do to each other felt very much like picking his way through the Minotaur's maze blindfolded and standing on his head. "I suppose we'll be right back where we started—here, at the top of your list."

"With one giant difference," Pan said. "We'll both have this impossibly high bar to carry with us forever."

"Yes."

"Well, my friend, not to beat a dead gift horse, but this is *your* judgment we're living out, which leads me to believe your postcoital existence is going to be a whole lot more unpleasant than mine."

"I'm sure you're right about that." The longer Cupid had coupled with Mia, the more attached he'd become, the harder to let her go, and the more agonizing to see her with someone else.

"I have to confess, Q, I'm not feeling particularly objective about this."

"I understand. Your feelings are important, too, and I need to hear them before we make any decisions."

"You're about to find out exactly how selfish I am," Pan said, blinking away a flicker of pain, or was it shame?

"I know you, Pan. Just be honest with me. *Please*."

"Okay, here goes. I want you, Q, as much as I've ever wanted any being—god, human, or anything in between—and not just for the physical pleasure, but the chance to reach that level of intimacy you can only have with a lover. I felt a hint of it when we kissed, but there's so much more there. We've barely scratched the surface."

"I want that too, Pan." So badly it was hard for Cupid to risk Pan talking him out of this.

"I can't tell you how we're going to deal when midnight comes around. I assume at some point in the not-too-distant future, you'll find my Right Love for me, and I'll be granted a reprieve from my feelings for you."

A *reprieve*. The pain of losing Cupid would fade into the shadows of Pan's past. Not so for Cupid unless Aphrodite inflamed his heart for another Worthy.

"I should be talking you out of this." Pan paused as if he might change course, then shrugged. "Well, I'm sorry. I'm not going to do that."

"I don't want you to," Cupid said. The dizzying certainty hit him with a force that could have propelled him all the way across the parking lot. This was happening.

"Just to be clear, that's a yes, right? Because I am barely holding my shit together. This is no time for a misunderstanding."

"Yes," Cupid said. "That's a yes."

14

CARNAL BEHAVIOR

Pan wriggled his shoulders between the front seats, grabbed a fistful of Cupid's shirt, and lunged. There was an audible gasp just before their mouths crashed together.

Pan tipped his face to the well and drank the sweet nectar from Cupid's lips. Did he taste like ambrosia to all the others? Was Cupid's gift the ability to become exactly what every lover desired? Deep questions for another time—a time when Pan's head wasn't crowded with the voices—*slow down, take your time, mine, mine, MINE.*

It was happening again, just like that first kiss Pan had stolen at the station. Instead of quenching Pan's thirst, Cupid's kiss consumed him. The more of Cupid he took, the more Pan needed. They kissed and kissed until Pan was delirious with desire.

The air inside the tiny car thickened with grunts and groans and the exquisite agony of *want.* Pan's torso wedged between the seats, writhing to get closer to Cupid. Pan needed to get them both upstairs—and fast.

He pulled Cupid's lower lip between his teeth and bit down hard. Cupid jerked away, panting, wild-eyed, and confused.

"Ow! Why did you do that?" Cupid glared at him as he swept his tongue across the wound. "I'm bleeding!"

"It was the only way I could stop." Yeah, that had sounded less crazy inside Pan's head. "Don't worry. You'll heal up faster than you can say, 'Kiss me, you fool!'"

Without waiting for a response, Pan shimmied out of the back seat and coaxed Cupid out of the car. "Ticktock."

"Are you sure you want to do this . . . in *there*?"

Granted, the Tarra Arms wasn't the Four Seasons—*hell*, it wasn't even two seasons—but the venue was less about romance and more about containing the wreckage. Also, not for nothing, they were already here.

"Yes," Pan said simply. When his short answer failed to move Cupid, Pan elaborated. "When I get done with you, the place is gonna look like a crime scene. I'd really rather not have to burn down my house tomorrow."

"Fair enough," Cupid said, the corners of his frown edging up toward a smile.

"Good. I need to make a quick pit stop." Pan wrapped his fingers around Cupid's and gave him a persuasive tug toward his truck. Pan had recently added lube to the stash of condoms in his glove compartment, and he was never more grateful for his foresight.

"Do I even want to know what that's for?" Cupid asked, watching Pan shove a tube into his pocket.

"You're cute, but your questions are slowing us down."

At the reception desk, Pan splurged for a "deluxe king," all the more square footage to defile. The desk clerk grinned at them both as she handed over the room key. "Enjoy your stay!"

They stood side by side in the elevator, seemingly focused

on the doors ahead. Cupid had done an admirable job following orders to "blend in" by choosing a generic black T-shirt and skinny jeans, nothing out of the ordinary except for the sinful way the denim hugged his thighs and ass. If not for the cameras, Pan might have taken Cupid right there against the wall, but he'd learned the hard way that hotel security did not look kindly upon such acts.

Pan reached over and swept his thumb across Cupid's lip. "See? No blood. Good as new." He made a show of bringing the thumb to his tongue and taking a long, slow lick.

Cupid watched like a mouse eyeing a tiger about to pounce. The sexual tension inside the chamber could have Willy Wonka'd the elevator right through the roof.

The doors opened, and they spilled down the hallway like an overturned barrel of apples. Pan slapped the key card at the lock four times before the light turned green. He threw his shoulder against the door, stumbled inside the room, dragging Cupid along with him, and kicked the door shut behind them. He didn't plan on seeing that hallway again before midnight.

The furnishings barely registered as Pan unbuttoned his shirt and tossed it away.

"Your turn," he said, crowding Cupid against the door so he barely had room to reach over his shoulder.

The shirt passing over Cupid's hair released the smell of chlorine into the air along with that body wash from the gym. *Hell yeah*, those pecs and biceps had been recently worked. *But when had Cupid started swimming?*

Pan's mouth went dry as Cupid's treasure trail was revealed from the jeans up to Cupid's belly button. A growl rumbled out of Pan. *Want.*

Obviously, they'd seen each other bare-chested, but this was no friendly toweling-off in the locker room or two roommates scarfing down Cheerios at the kitchen counter. This was a lover's body—hello, *the quintessential* lover's body—revved for sex. Cupid was a bull ready to charge, or *be* charged, and Pan was quite sure he looked the same.

Cupid swallowed hard, bouncing his Adam's apple up and down inside his throat. Pan opened his mouth to say something clever. Nothing came out. *Fuck it.*

He hooked his fingers through Cupid's belt loops and tugged their hips together. The friction made his head swim. *More.* He leaned in, grinding denim against denim until Pan thought he might explode.

Later, Pan would take his time, draw Cupid out and tease him for a full hour on the edge of release. Later, he'd treat Cupid to his full repertoire of moves. Later, there would be time for feelings and sweet, whispered words. Pan lacked the discipline and the inclination for any of that now.

He pried open the button on Cupid's jeans and worked his hand inside Cupid's fancy silk boxer briefs. At Pan's first stroke, Cupid tipped his head back with a groan, a tempting flash of pink tongue peeking out between his kiss-swollen lips.

Cupid reached for him, pawing at the belt buckle in his way. Pan was gonna blow the second Cupid touched him—sooner, if he didn't *hurry the fuck up.*

"I'm trying!" Cupid said. Whoops, had Pan said that out loud? "Damn these human restraints!"

Finally, miraculously, the belt opened, the button popped, the zipper slid, and Pan leaped into Cupid's palm. *Fuck yeah.* Pan's world shrank to the white-hot bullseye gathering between his legs. When his orgasm hit, Pan grasped Cupid by the shoulder and held on so hard, he left five red fingerprints on Cupid's skin.

Cupid let loose a string of curse words Pan hadn't heard

since their childhood as his face contorted into the O-face Pan had imagined so many times since his friend's fall. Oh, but the real thing was better *by far*—that split second of surrender, the suspended breath of anticipation, the bright spark of pleasure, the blessed relief of release.

Cupid's ecstasy was nothing short of glorious.

Number two would be even more so, and number three after that. Pan would see to it.

Cupid wrapped his arms around Pan and held him close. Their stomachs squelched together, ginger fur meeting soft, dark curls. Pan set his palm to Cupid's heart and absorbed its rhythm into his bones.

Fingers stroked Pan's hair, Cupid's tender caresses a stark reminder of the powerful storm of emotions that must have been raging inside him.

"Hey," Pan said quietly, waiting for Cupid's soft hum before continuing. "Sorry. That's not exactly how I'd planned to start things off."

"It's all right," Cupid murmured in a dreamy, faraway voice. "We have hours ahead of us."

"It won't be enough," Pan said too quickly, already hating himself for tainting their bliss, when what he'd meant to do was promise Cupid every possible pleasure.

"How could it ever be enough?" The heavy words vibrated in Cupid's chest. Gathering a handful of Pan's hair into his fist, Cupid leaned in with a gentle kiss, stealing Pan's breath when he pulled away with a soft sweep of his tongue.

Pan blinked up at him, muddled and mellowed, to find Cupid grinning.

"What's that for?" Pan was already reflecting Cupid's smile back at him, musing whether this was how their lovemaking would go—the two so attuned, they would mirror each other all night. If only his stupid heart could echo Cupid's beat, their joining would be complete and perfect and eternal.

"I kissed *you* that time," Cupid said. "For the official, judicial record."

"Noted . . . and extremely hot."

A sudden blush rose to Cupid's cheeks. "Pan, I—" He shook his head shyly.

"I've got you, Q. C'mon, it's *me*."

"That's what scares me."

"Hey, I know that wasn't the most romantic start, but you can trust me to be"—he couldn't promise to be gentle—"careful with you."

"It's not that." Cupid rubbed his hand across his chest, back and forth over his heart. *Oh.* "I can't mess this up."

"Okay look, this isn't difficult. I want you. You want me. I'm the horniest creature in the cosmos, and you're the God of Erotic Love. We can't break each other, and we're not going to run out of stamina. So really, the only way you can 'mess this up' is by leaving. You're not going to leave, are you?"

"No, of course not," Cupid said. Pan thought he saw Cupid's shoulders relax just a little.

"Then we're golden. And guess what else: no love glove required!"

"Well, *that's* good news."

Pan paused to plant a kiss on Cupid's adorably surprised expression.

"Do you trust me?" Pan asked.

Cupid lifted his gaze to meet Pan's. "I always have."

"Then let's do ourselves and each other a favor for the next eight hours. No more worrying what comes after this. No wondering if we'll be good enough. No holding back. Let's just enjoy this miracle while it lasts. Okay?"

"Okay."

"Good!" Pan closed his mouth over Cupid's and stole a steamy kiss. "Now, take your pants off and get your ass on that bed! I'm already hard again, and . . . *looky there!* So are you."

Cupid proved Pan right once again; it took him no time to adjust to the contours of a male lover. The bed held up admirably to the two gods slamming each other around. The love seat, not so much. Sprawled on top of each other amidst a pile of splintered wood, they laughed their asses off until the next wave of arousal grew too intense to ignore.

A few hours later, when their bellies demanded food, they paused long enough to call in a room service order. Huddled against the headboard, they scarfed down burgers and fries while watching Daddy porn on the giant screen. Their ice cream sundaes melted on the side table.

Close to midnight, having fucked each other silly and sore, they lay contentedly in the bathtub, hands twined together.

"Are you watching the time?" Cupid whispered.

"I set an alarm on my phone."

"Okay, good."

"Yeah, we need to make sure we're dressed and out of here by the stroke of midnight." Neither knew the penalty for overstaying their welcome, but Pan suspected Aphrodite would do worse than turning his truck into a pumpkin. He had a feeling genitals would be involved.

Cupid's mouth fell into a frown Pan couldn't kiss away. Time to say the things that needed saying.

"You know I'm not much for the mushy stuff," Pan said, rolling his eyes at Cupid's snort, "but today was by far the best day I have ever spent on this earth or on Mount Olympus."

Cupid answered with a tender kiss that tore at Pan's heart.

"Q, I want you to know now and always, I will never love anyone the way I love you."

"I'm afraid I feel the same. That doesn't bode well for either of us."

"No, I suppose not," Pan replied with a sigh. "So, tomorrow . . ."

Cupid tried on a brave smile, but it wouldn't quite stick to his face. "Right. Maybe you could take your dates somewhere else?"

"*Jesus!* What kind of monster do you take me for? Did you honestly think I'd make you come back here and watch me go upstairs with someone else?"

"Sorry," Cupid said with a shrug.

"*Fuck.* I'm sorry too. This sucks." Pan squeezed his eyes shut, but the problems didn't get smaller. "It kills me to know that I'm the one who's going to destroy you."

"It's not your fault, Pan."

"That's not even the worst part." So much for the relaxing bath. Pan's agitation was creating a whirlpool, sloshing water over the edge of the tub. "I can't even be there to pick up the pieces this time. Not to sound like a dick here, but how are you going to get through this without me?"

"I've been making other friends."

Pan huffed. "Euphrosyne? I think she's more depressed than you are! Besides, you can't count on other fallens. Either one of you could be called up at any moment."

"There's a guy at the gym who's teaching me how to swim." That explained the chlorine.

"You signed up for swim lessons?"

"I couldn't keep going to Mia's class. It was just too painful."

"No, I get that."

"I heard swimming was supposed to be relaxing, so I decided to give it a try. I saw this guy doing laps and asked him to teach me. You know I could never get the hang of swimming when I had wings."

Pan snorted. "Try it with hooves." He lifted his feet out of the froth at the other end of the tub and wiggled his toes, a luxury he'd never tire of. "So, you and this swim teacher are getting to be friends?"

"Yes. He's coming over for dinner tomorrow."

"Dinner?" Well, this had taken an interesting turn, a very date-like turn. *Keep it light, Pan.* "You cook now?"

"Not exactly. Euphrosyne said she'd help me."

"Oh, she did, did she?"

Cupid's eyebrows pinched toward the middle. "You don't have a problem with this, do you?"

"What? Me? No!" Pan slipped his arm around Cupid's shoulders and sighed dramatically. "It's just this stupid midnight deadline getting to me, I guess."

"You know," Cupid said, "if you're stressed, you could give swimming a try."

"Thanks, but I'll stick to punching my bags at the muscle gym. You stick to your"—*don't say guy*—"friend at the pool."

"Hmm." For a long moment, Cupid seemed lost in deep, dangerous thought territory. "But what if your Right Love is at *your* gym? If I don't go with you, you'll never know."

"That's a chance I'm willing to take." Considering Pan had used his gym as his own personal hookup app for the last two weeks, the last thing he wanted was Cupid sniffing around among the wreckage.

Pan's phone ended their talk with a "*Cuckoo! Cuckoo!*" He dried off his hand on the closest towel and silenced the alarm.

"Time to get our wrinkly asses out of this tub. But first," said Pan, raising his phone high above the bubble bath, "one last selfie for the road."

15

SMITHING

Hephaestus returned his wife's gaiascope to its mahogany stand, taking great care to compensate for his fury-induced tremor. The looking glass only revealed what was happening on Earth—in Room 508 of the Tarra Arms to be specific—but he'd seen enough to deduce exactly what was happening right under his nose.

He swept the soft cotton cloth across the inscription carved into the bronze with his own two hands such a very long time ago: *For My Divine Prize.*

Prize, shmize. As if the bride's heart were included in the dowry when Zeus ordered their marriage.

How easily Aphrodite had slipped inside the folds of Ares's robes at the slightest opportunity. This time, Hephaestus feared her well and truly lost to the God of War. As much as he would have loved to piss on those long-smoldering embers and extinguish their flame once and for all, he'd never beat Ares by spite or might. He'd never beat Ares at all. But that didn't mean he had to stand idly by while they made a cuckolded fool of him *again*, destroying Cupid's and Pan's lives in the process.

Ever since Cupid's near-kiss with Ruthie, Hephaestus had feared it would come to this. Heart as heavy as his footsteps, Hephaestus clomped down the stairwell to his workshop. There was smithing to be done.

After the Cerberus incident, Hera had thundered through Hephaestus's workshop as if Lyssa had set a mad rage upon her. Once every last arrow had been thrown to the floor from its ordered shelf, Hera commanded Hephaestus to destroy them all. He'd briefly considered disobeying her and tucking away one of Cupid's arrows for just such an emergency, but he did not wish to become his mother's next target. Fortunately, her tirade had fizzled before demanding Cupid's bow. Hephaestus could no more craft Cupid a new bow in his absence than Daedalus could fashion his son Icarus a new set of wings.

Here, at his mighty forge, the God of Fire had always felt more at home than anywhere else in the palace—or for that matter, all of Olympus. Hephaestus snapped his fingers to ignite a stack of shavings from his woodshop, added dried cedar chips for kindling, and topped off the pile with yesterday's coke, all while forcing just the right breath from the bellows. He shoveled clumps of coal into the belly of the fire as patiently as a father spoon-feeding his child, and . . . *ahhh, there she is!* As many times as Hephaestus had stoked the fire, the sight of the gorgeous yellow-white flame roaring to life never failed to stir his ancient soul.

Rivulets of sweat trickled down Hephaestus's cheeks. He pumped the bellows, then eased off, leaving the coals to settle into a low burn, throwing clouds of thick, black smoke up the chimney.

Destroy, Hera had demanded. With metal and wood requiring completely different processes, Hephaestus had first separated all of Cupid's gold arrowheads from their shafts. Onto the coals went all the lovingly whittled hazelwood shafts with their perfectly balanced gray-goose fletching. Next, the precious lengths of deer-sinew cord were fed to the fire, never mind Hephaestus's wheeling and dealing with the goddess of the hunt for the backstrap of a freshly killed buck, all for the strip of silver skin where the finest sinew could be found. Never mind that after separating the sinew from the filmy membrane, Hephaestus had to pound each individual strand between two rocks and chew the long, gristly fibers to dissolve nature's glues with his saliva. Only then could he braid the strands together to form the special cord.

Yes, creating new shafts would require some effort, but Olympus would provide the raw materials. Deer, hazelwood trees, and goose feathers were plentiful. The special gold for Cupid's arrowheads, on the other hand, now *that* was irreplaceable.

If pressed about his failure to execute Hera's orders, Hephaestus would've fallen back on good, old-fashioned chemistry. Short of a nuclear reaction, gold could never be entirely destroyed. Not even the highest gods of the Mount wanted anything to do with harnessing nuclear power, possibly the one force in the cosmos stronger and more volatile than the gods themselves.

Thus, when Hephaestus melted down the golden arrowheads, he'd technically complied with Hera's demands. And when he'd poured the liquid gold into his ingot molds, it could be argued he still hadn't violated the spirit of the mandate. But now? Sixty-seven days into Cupid's punishment, the moment had come for Hephaestus to cross that line. His only hope was that the boys would make use of the arrow before Hera—or worse, Aphrodite—got wind of his scheme.

Hands steady and sure in his element, Hephaestus placed the crucible containing a single ingot over the hot coals. He dared not risk crafting more than one arrowhead, and that one would have to be perfect.

The gold brick heated to a gleaming yellow-white. Hephaestus leaned in to feel the glow on his face, to gaze into the borrowed chunk of sun, primitive and pure and mesmerizing. The ingot glowed brighter and redder and blurred at the edges with the effort of holding its shape. Gold was a gloriously stubborn element, but even the most tenacious must eventually surrender. Hephaestus held his breath for the dramatic moment the solid form collapsed into a brilliant yellow pool.

But even the fluid fought equilibrium. Hephaestus watched, awed as always by the rich liquid climbing the walls of the crucible. Eventually, a ball began to form at its center. Hephaestus readied Cupid's mold and poured the molten gold exactly to the top.

And now, the wait.

While the gold was hardening, Hephaestus shored up his justifications for interfering with Cupid's punishment. Pan and Cupid made perfect sense together. Best friends from childhood, the unlikely pair were always joined at the hip. Now, they were joined at the heart. To keep them apart would have been unnecessarily cruel. Pan didn't deserve to be a pawn in this lovers' scheme cooked up by Ares and Aphrodite. *For that matter, neither do I*, Hephaestus observed with an inward huff.

He tipped the mold and released the arrowhead into his weathered palm, barely registering the searing heat, then quenched the metal in the trough of cool water at his side. The fire's work was complete. The rest was up to craft.

Shifting with a practiced ease to his worktable, Hephaestus braced the arrowhead in a vise. The forge was his first love, but as the God of Craftsmen, Hephaestus was a gifted artist in his own right. His superior metalwork had earned him the respect and awe of his fellow gods. Why else would he have been trusted to craft Zeus's aegis breastplate, Mercury's winged helmet and sandals, and the armor Achilles wore into battle?

With divine patience, Hephaestus filed the tip to a sharp point, then smoothed the entire surface with fine sandpaper until the metal felt like silk under his rough fingertips. He bent to inspect his work. *Flawless.*

Hephaestus chose his softest chamois and buffed the finish until he could see his own reflection. A metalsmith of lesser genius might have argued the polish was more about style than flight, and that was mostly true. But the purest of Love could not be inspired with sloppy engineering.

Hephaestus wrapped the precious arrowhead in a deerskin cloth, secured it in his carry-pouch, and set out for the forest to gather the rest of his supplies.

16

A WELL-MANNERED MAN

Reed sliced through his porterhouse like a cellist bowing his strings. Polite-sized chunks of food were set onto his tongue, then chewed thoughtfully behind closed lips. His wine disappeared gradually in savored sips. The napkin tucked onto his lap was pulled out at regular intervals and used to wipe his mouth whether it needed wiping or not. Cupid had never seen a man eat so delicately.

Pan's meat-cutting technique was more of a two-armed sawing motion, and he tended to down his drinks in guzzled gulps. Crumbs were swiped away with the back of a hairy hand, not a napkin in sight. As for Hephaestus, if he used utensils at all, it was only after Aphrodite had bullied him into it with one of her blistering looks. Cupid sorely lacked genteel male role models in his life.

"You eat the way you swim." Cupid's observation caused Reed to grin at him from across the small dining table.

"*Heh*. Swallowing mouthfuls of liquid?"

"Elegant. Smooth." Cupid switched his fork to his left hand, picked up his knife with the right, and made a clean cut through his steak. "Like you're dancing."

"Dancing," Reed repeated with a dark chuckle. "With this bum leg."

Cupid felt his cheeks heat with embarrassment. He'd meant it as a compliment, but Reed had a way of twisting things. "All I meant was I'm not used to being with a man who has actual table manners. My last, *uh* . . . the last guy's idea of fine dining was eating off the lid of the pizza box."

"I suppose pizza boxes can have their charms," Reed answered with a kind smile.

"I suppose so." Indeed, the memory of sharing a pizza with Pan that night at Ruthie's filled Cupid with a surge of warmth for their repaired friendship, followed swiftly—and quite unfortunately—by a fevered memory of sharing french fries last night in bed.

"Did you want to talk about him?" Reed asked carefully.

"Who?"

Reed tilted his head. "That 'last guy'?"

Pan, whose kiss Cupid could still taste, whose touch still lingered on Cupid's skin, whose bulk Cupid could still feel moving above him, around him, inside him.

"Not really. Do you?"

"Not particularly," Reed answered, "but if it would make you more comfortable, I could drop some food on the floor." Reed's serious expression broke into a playful grin.

"No, thank you."

"Honestly, that's a relief. I'm not actually sure I could drop food on the floor on purpose."

The two chuckled together. "You're basically the anti-Pan," said Cupid.

From Reed's thin build and quiet, contained manner to the shirt tucked neatly into his trousers, the leather shoes with their fancy tassels, and the owlish, black-rimmed glasses framing his face, Reed could not have been more different from Pan if he were actively trying.

"Pan? Is that his actual name?" So they'd ended up talking about Pan after all.

"Uh, yes," Cupid answered, his brain scrambling to remember Pan's cover. "It's short for Panthino."

"Hmm, Greek?"

"Originally. Though he's been here for two thou—a very long time."

Reed drew the base of his wine goblet in small circles along the table, swishing the wine up and down the sides. "I see."

After a few thoughtful moments, Reed took a sip of wine. He blotted his mouth with the napkin, leaving a deep burgundy stain on his lips. Cupid had a sudden urge to lean in and kiss it away.

"What about you?" Cupid asked. "What do you do when you're not swimming?"

A shy smile tugged at Reed's lips. "I spend a lot of time reading."

"What kind of reading?"

"Classical literature—the poetry and drama of ancient Greece and Rome. Homer, Virgil, Euripides, Sophocles, Plato, Aristotle . . . have I lost you yet?"

"No, not at all. I've read all those too."

"You *have?*" Reed seemed unsure whether Cupid could be believed.

"Yes, in fact, I have a Plato quote on my back." He'd never been happier for his mysterious tattoo.

Reed's eyebrows lifted over the rims of his glasses. "Plato, really? Huh. I saw some kind of tattoo, but I didn't want to be nosy."

"Here, look." Cupid turned his back to Reed and pulled his shirt up to his shoulders.

Reed leaned in closer. His warm breath hit Cupid's skin, sending a shiver up his spine. *"He whom Love touches not walks in darkness.* Hmm, how'd you come to choose that passage?"

"It was chosen for me," Cupid answered as his shirt slid down his back again.

Reed smiled. "I think I understand."

He couldn't have understood, but there was something about Reed that made Cupid wish he could tell him everything.

Spearing his last piece of asparagus, Reed said, "It's rare nowadays for young people to study the classics, but everything makes more sense when you have the foundation."

For once, all those years toiling at the family histories didn't feel like a waste of time.

Releasing a contented sigh, Reed rested his knife and fork together across his dinner plate. "Well, Q, you are quite the chef. This meal was delicious."

"I might have had a little help from a friend."

Earlier that afternoon, as he'd watched Euphrosyne grill the steaks on an open fire, he'd soaked up the details, wishing he had paid more attention to Pan's meal preparations when they'd lived together. Cupid had never imagined his Earth stay lasting this long or not having Pan around to take care of him.

"You know what Socrates had to say about friends," Reed said.

"Remind me," Cupid said, and Reed smiled at him the same way he'd smiled when Cupid had pretended to need help with his rhythmic breathing.

"Be slow to fall into friendship, but when you are in, continue firm and constant."

"Firm and constant. Right."

"Right," Reed repeated, twisting the stem of his nearly empty goblet between his fingers.

"I haven't really kept up with my reading." Cupid wasn't ready for Reed to find out what kind of student he'd been.

"The good thing about books is they're always there for you when you're ready for them."

Cupid raised the wine bottle. "May I?" When Reed did not object, Cupid filled his glass with the remainder of the wine. It hadn't occurred to Cupid until just then how long it had been since he'd been able to just sit and relax with someone without that cursed motor in his heart acting up and pushing him to do something he didn't even know if he wanted to do.

"You know, the other day when you approached me about teaching you to swim, it made me realize how much I've missed teaching."

"You taught swimming?"

"No. Literature."

"Aha!" Cupid said, drawing a smile from Reed. "You don't teach anymore?"

"No. I've been on disability for"—*sigh*—"many years now."

Cupid glanced at Reed's leg. "Mind if I ask what happened?"

"The short answer is I stuck my nose in where someone thought it didn't belong, and a very bad man used me for target practice."

"Just for being nosy?" Cupid would have been murdered a thousand times over by now.

Reed huffed. "I guess you want the long answer."

"Only if you're comfortable sharing it."

Reed studied Cupid's expression for a moment, then straightened up in his chair, exhaled slowly, and seemed to brace his whole being.

"Reed, you really don't have to talk about it."

"It's okay. I'd like to." Cupid nodded, and Reed disappeared into his memory. "I was out jogging at the edge of campus before my evening class when I heard a commotion coming from behind a car—a woman's voice, then a man's. I called out to ask if they were okay. The man yelled at me to get lost. I knew something bad was definitely happening."

Cupid swallowed hard but didn't interrupt.

"The next sound I heard was this horrible, scared whimper coming from the girl, as if she realized her very last hope was about to disappear. Pure instinct took over. Before I even had a chance to think about it, I was jogging their way."

The story flowed out of Reed as if he were in a trance, watching the scene unfold before his eyes. "When I was close enough to make out the bodies, I saw that the man was dragging this woman into a car by her hair . . . *by her hair!*" Anger and pain pooled in Reed's eyes. "His other hand was inside the pocket of his jacket, pointing what looked like a gun at me. He yelled at me to mind my own business. This was between him and his old lady."

How many times had Cupid seen Zeus behave like this? *Io. Europa. Echo.* It never ended well for anyone but Zeus.

"Her eyes caught mine for a second, and I tell you, Q . . . something inside me just snapped. I have sisters. You know?"

No, Cupid didn't know anything about sisters, but he held his breath because Reed was about to get hurt.

"I charged him. He pulled the gun and shot me in the hip."

"Wow! That's horrible."

"Horrible for me, yes, but when I hit the ground, Caroline—that was her name—found her voice and started screaming at the top of her lungs. I was fading fast, but I could see feet running toward us, a crowd forming. I heard a thud, and the screaming stopped. Caroline landed next to me on the ground, her face all bashed in and bloody. The bastard took off in his car. I blacked out after that."

Cupid shuddered. Violence of any sort sickened him.

"When I woke up in the hospital, Caroline was there in my room, all bandaged and bruised but alive," Reed said, looking up at Cupid with the awe and relief that must have been written on his face in that moment. "Together, we got that monster locked up. She told me she couldn't bring herself to do it on her own. They gave him ten years for first-degree assault with domestic violence as a kicker."

"And you lost the use of your leg."

"I lost some mobility, yes," Reed answered. "Tell me, Q, do you believe in fate?"

"The Fates?"

A flicker of recognition crossed Reed's face. "The concept that our lives are predetermined?"

"I believe that Clotho spins the thread of each mortal's life, Lachesis allots the length, and Atropos snips that thread at the end."

"*Well* now," Reed said, smiling, "you do know your Greeks."

Oh, Reed. You have no idea. "Yes."

"And what about our actions during that length of life? Do we have free will in those?" It was so clear why Reed missed teaching. He came alive with his questions.

Cupid thought for a moment about all the bad life choices he'd made before his fall and the better ones he'd made lately. "I guess there wouldn't be much point trying to be good if we didn't have a choice."

"And no hope for reforming those who do bad things." Reed was probably thinking about his attacker, but Cupid took the words to heart.

"But people can and *do* change," Cupid said.

With a delighted smile, Reed raised his goblet as if to toast Cupid's comment. "There are certainly many great thinkers who would agree with you on that."

Cupid held Reed's gaze as they tipped back their wineglasses together. Basking in the glow of a teacher's approval had been a rare occurrence for Cupid at the academy, but since landing on Earth, Cupid had become quite the model student: yoga, driving, carpentry, swimming, lovemaking . . . he'd mastered each in turn. Still, there was something surprisingly gratifying about impressing Reed with his intellect.

"And what do you believe?" Cupid asked.

Reed leaned forward, sliding his glass to the middle of the table. "I believe we have the power to create our own destiny. That's why this bum leg is not the worst thing to happen to me even though it cost me my job."

"You lost your job?"

"'Early retirement,' they called it," Reed replied.

"But why? Why would a damaged leg end a teacher's career—if you don't mind my asking?"

"Actually, your honesty is a breath of fresh air."

After his earlier missteps, Cupid was pleased to hear that Reed welcomed his questions.

"After the trauma, I startled easily. I found myself wary around people—especially men—in a way that wasn't healthy. I tried to work, but I was unable to find my confidence again with my students, especially in large groups."

"But you didn't hesitate to help me when I approached you at the gym."

"It took me many years of therapy and a lot of hard work to get where I am today. The university was patient with me up to a point, but eventually, they were forced to move on and fill my position."

It broke Cupid's heart to imagine the pain Reed must have felt stepping away from his whole life, everything he'd learned, his obvious love for teaching. "What about now? Couldn't you go back to teaching?"

A small huff left Reed's lips as he shook his head. "It's a whole new world out there. I'm a dinosaur in the teaching world. You can't step off the track for fifteen years and expect to hop back on where you left off. Everything has changed. Life marches on."

"But your subject matter is . . ."

"Ancient?" Reed supplied the missing word with a smirk.

Cupid shrugged. "I was going to say 'unchanged.'"

"No, it's really not," Reed answered in his gentle teacher-voice. "But besides all that, the modern delivery methods are beyond my grasp. Smartboards and virtual lecture halls . . ."

"You could learn that part," Cupid said. "I could teach you!" He'd have to first learn them himself, but Cupid was confident he could master whatever was needed and pass his skills along to Reed. The man was brilliant. And Cupid owed him.

"You're very kind," Reed said, "and believe me, I appreciate the gesture . . . and your faith in me. Funny thing, the university is not banging down my door to come back."

"I'm sure if they knew you were interested—"

"It's too late for me, Q. I've accepted that."

But Cupid could not. "That sounds like a terrible price to pay."

Reed shrugged. "It could have been worse."

"Yes, of course. You might have died."

"Sure, but that's not what I meant."

"No?" Cupid shifted to the edge of his seat, bolt upright and attentive.

"It was my decision to insert myself into that situation. I could have kept right on jogging and pretended not to hear the cries for help. I might have even convinced myself later that I couldn't have made a difference." A pinch of anguish crossed Reed's expression as he must have imagined how that would have turned out for Caroline. "But what would my two good legs be worth if they carried me in the wrong direction, hmm?"

Cupid tried to imagine how Reed could have lived with such a terrible weight on his conscience. Would the guilt have faded after a few years' time, or would every step Reed took from then on with two healthy legs have reminded him of his choice?

Would Cupid have wanted *that* Reed as his friend—or whatever they were becoming?

"Besides," Reed continued, lighter now, "my wounds are relatively minor. My leg doesn't always behave the way I'd like it to, but I can walk! I can drive. I can swim. I can share a nice meal with a new friend." Reed raised his wineglass toward Cupid, then took another sip while Cupid digested his story. "I can breathe now—well, most of the time." A shy smile flickered, then disappeared.

"What do you mean?"

Reed leaned back in his seat, sliding his hands to his lap. "I never gave much thought to my, uh, preferences, I guess? Is that what you people would call it?"

"What people?"

"LGBT . . . Q . . . X? Did I get that right? I can't keep up with the proper lingo anymore."

Now he had Cupid truly baffled. "Lingo?"

"I guess what I'm trying to say is I feel extremely ignorant about all this, and I'm trying really hard not to offend you."

"Why would I be offended?"

There was a lot of fidgeting on Reed's side of the table. "Look, I know how it feels to be on the receiving end of morbid curiosity. I would never do that to you."

"Okay?"

"I think I'm attracted to you." Reed's cheeks colored a deep red.

Finally, *finally*, Cupid caught up with the conversation.

"I'm attracted to you too."

"You don't understand," Reed said. "I'm not gay. I've never even *thought* about a man this way."

"Oh," Cupid answered simply, while a part of him ached to tell poor, bewildered Reed everything.

"Is it okay for me to ask if you're, uh, just into men, or what?"

"It's fine to ask, and I've only been with one man."

"This Pan, the pizza lid fellow?"

"Yes." The image of Pan walking around with a pizza box on his head brought a smile to Cupid's face—until it didn't.

At noon, Cupid had met Pan in the parking lot of the Tulip Tree Inn to listen for the echo beat, only to discover his heart-pull toward Pan was now bound up with a violent, full-body craving so vivid in Cupid's mind and senses, he could hardly bear the torture of sticking close enough to hear Pan's heart.

Of course, Cupid had no choice but to listen. As expected, there was no echo beat to be found, but that didn't stop Pan from taking Brandi upstairs. At three o'clock, Cupid returned as planned for an excruciating round two with Garrett. Different person, same result. For all Cupid knew, the two of them were still together in that dingy hotel.

"Women too?" Reed asked.

"A few, yes." Cupid could still count the women on one hand, but how many more might he know here on Earth before he returned home? *If* he returned home.

"So you're bisexual?"

Cupid shrugged. Humans and their labels. Things were much more fluid where he came from. "I don't really know what all that means. I just like who I like."

Reed nodded, a small smile settling on his face. "That seems like a good way to be."

"It's not as if I have any choice in the matter." Though it did feel nice that his heart seemed to be making a choice this time without any compulsion from the gods.

"No, clearly. A young, fit guy like you . . . why would you ever *choose* someone like me?"

Dread crawled up the back of Cupid's neck. "Someone like what?"

"Broken," Reed said, gesturing toward his injured leg. "Lame. If I were a horse, they would've shot me." The melancholy in his voice was palpable.

Cupid tucked his napkin under the edge of his plate, then rose and moved into the chair beside Reed. "I don't understand why mort—people seem to only see the parts of themselves they don't like."

With Cupid so close, Reed spoke softly. "I guess it's easier to take than enduring someone else pointing out our faults."

"Someone would see this as a fault?" Cupid lowered his hand toward Reed's leg, then thinking better of it, clasped his hands together on the table. "I see your wound as a mark of courage."

Reed's gaze slid away from Cupid's, his mouth straining with the effort of leaving Cupid's words unchallenged.

"But it's not just your leg, Reed." Cupid's gentle voice coaxed Reed to turn back. "I could tell there was something different about you from the first time I watched you swim. Yes, you made the choice to intervene in that altercation, however quickly or instinctively that happened, but I don't think you could have acted any differently, given who you are."

Cupid's words circled around the two of them like twine, cinching them closer together.

"I definitely changed that day," Reed said. "I never realized I had a sense of innocence about the world until I lost it."

"I know all about losing faith in the world you think you know," Cupid said. *In my own mother.*

"You're a surprise."

Deep in his own thoughts, Cupid had failed to notice that Reed was looking at him as if he'd just had his first taste of frozen yogurt with all the toppings. "A good surprise, I hope."

"On every level," Reed assured him. "You have a certain wisdom about you, an old soul. I guess I expected you to be shallow. That wasn't fair. I apologize."

"You don't have to apologize."

"I do. Truth is, I've spent the last fifteen years getting angry for people prejudging me. I'm starting to understand I've been doing the same thing without realizing it."

Cupid shrugged. Reed didn't know judging until he'd seen the Divine Council in action.

"All that might be true," Cupid said, "but you're here with me now."

Reed smiled. "Yes, I am, aren't I?"

The air buzzed with anticipation. There was no question Reed wanted him, but Cupid wasn't about to take what had not been offered.

Cupid inched closer. "Would it be okay if I kiss you?"

Only Reed's eyelids moved while he mulled over the question. *Blink, blink, blink.* Desire. Curiosity. Fear.

Cupid smiled. "I've been told I'm a good kisser."

Chuckling, Reed replied, "Oh, I'm quite sure you are." Reed shook his head and let out a long sigh. There would be no kissing tonight.

Cupid swallowed his disappointment. The last thing he wanted to do was jeopardize this fragile, new friendship.

"Look, Q, I like you—a lot," Reed added with an adorable huff, "and I'm definitely feeling something . . . something new and confusing. But this is all happening so quickly, I think I just need to give this a little room to breathe."

"I understand," Cupid said, pulling back. They were sitting way too close for conversation.

"I hope I didn't spoil the evening."

"Not at all. It's been nice getting to know you."

"Likewise," Reed said. Reaching across the space between them, Reed placed his hand on Cupid's. "I'm hoping a man who's studied the classics might have the patience to give me a little time?"

"Of course," Cupid answered, knowing full well that time was not his to promise.

17

UNHAPPY DELIVERY

Each of the next three mornings, Reed and Cupid swam together. *Give me a little time*, Reed had said. While Cupid respected Reed's request for time, he also wanted to send a clear message: he was ready for Reed.

Cupid tried his best not to push, but did he smile and flirt? Did he graze Reed's shoulder as they passed in their swim lane? Did he towel off at the end of their swim using only the tiniest corner of the towel so as not to impede Reed's not-so-sly ogling? Yes, Cupid did those things, and he did them without apology. He'd learned from the best. *Sigh.*

The very next day following the motel marathon, the evil genius of Ares and Aphrodite's scheme had revealed itself. That afternoon, Cupid had met Pan in the appointed parking lot at noon and again at three o'clock, listened for the echo beats, and attempted to survive when Pan took each not-Worthy human upstairs. Three days and six failed matches later, Cupid finally allowed Pan to convince him to suspend the search.

Agreements between friends were well and good, but the gods above had their say the next morning. Cupid had just loaded four bags of groceries into his car when his heart-GPS powered up. Bad enough he was about to be forced into close contact with Pan, but now his cookie dough ice cream was bound to melt before he could get it home to his freezer.

Ignoring the pull of his heart was not a good idea, as Cupid had learned the hard way, so he started up the car and drove where the gods led him. He'd driven several blocks toward Pan's house when inspiration struck. Cupid could obey the gods and have his ice cream too.

He speed-dialed Pan, who picked up after four rings, breathless. "Is this urgent?"

"Yes," Cupid replied.

"Make it quick!" Deep-voiced moans could be heard in the background.

"Can you meet me at my apartment in ten minutes?"

"I'll be there in twelve." Pan clicked off, leaving Cupid dazed and aroused.

Happily, his plan worked. Once Pan's truck started moving in the direction of Cupid's apartment, Cupid's heart motor pulled him there too.

Twelve minutes gave Cupid just enough time to reach home and unload his groceries. It wasn't until the reek of sex followed Pan through Cupid's door that he realized the precarious situation he'd put them both in by inviting Pan into his cramped living quarters. The heart-motor had slowed to a manageable hum, but the activity level in Cupid's groin more than made up for it.

"Sorry about that," Pan said, seeing Cupid's nose curl as he passed through the opened door. "You didn't give me time to shower. Why am I here?"

"My heart," Cupid answered simply.

"So much for giving each other space."

"Maybe I shouldn't have asked you to come here, but I had groceries in my car. Then when I called, and you were with—" Who *was* Pan with? Did Cupid recognize that voice?

"It's fine, Q. Breathe." Pan reached for Cupid's shoulder but pulled back when Cupid flinched.

"Would you like something to drink? Flavored seltzer?"

"Wow. Fancy," Pan said, slipping into one of the chairs at the small dining table. "Sure. Whatever you've got is fine."

Cupid unscrewed the cap on the raspberry-lime seltzer, sending bubbles over the top. "I guess I was in a bit of a hurry to get home," he said as he ran to the sink.

"Well, here we are," Pan said. "Now what?"

Cupid poured Pan's drink, set it on the table, and retreated to the other side of the room—not that the distance helped much. "I guess this means we need to get back to work on your list."

"Think you can handle it?" Pan asked, glugging down half his drink.

"Do I have a choice?"

After much brainstorming and compromise, they agreed Pan would meet his next potential Worthy at the park. Outdoors might be bearable for Cupid. Match or no match, Pan and his date would take a hike. No hooking up.

"If nothing else, you'll get some exercise," Cupid said.

"Oh, I've been getting plenty of exercise," Pan replied with a smugness Cupid did not appreciate.

Their conversation was cut short by the sudden, startling presence of Mercury. Where Cupid's fall to Earth had been a lengthy, clumsy tumble, Mercury's speed and stealth translated into appearances out of thin air. "Greetings from the gods."

"Back again so soon, Father?" Pan said. "Wait, don't tell me— the Council has issued us an extension on the carnal behavior decree? Q, quick! Grab your toothbrush! There were a couple pieces of furniture we didn't break."

Mercury groaned. "Sometimes I really hate my job."

"Tell me about it," said Pan.

"Is that my bow strapped to your back?" Cupid peered around behind Mercury though he could practically see right through his ethereal Earthly figure. "It is! And my quiver!"

"Yes," Mercury agreed, shrugging Cupid's bow off his shoulder and handing it to him with a frown. "Hephaestus sent me."

"Looks like we're going old school," Pan said with a grin.

Cupid turned the bow over in his hands. The hazelwood handle tried to find the familiar groove in his palm, but of course, these Earth-hands had never held Cupid's bow.

Pan rose from the table and strode over to Mercury. "Wait, *Hephaestus* sent you?"

"Correct."

"Wow. Stepdaddy's got some brass balls on him," said Pan.

Leaning in, Mercury drew Pan and Cupid closer. "It's a mess up there, and without Euphrosyne"—Mercury side-eyed Pan for not getting that case resolved—"Olympus is that much darker. Ares and Aphrodite are rumored to be—" Mercury shook his head sharply; he knew better than to fall for the false security of plaster walls. "Hephaestus is a wreck. I think he believes Aphrodite will be grateful to him for returning Cupid home."

Pan snorted. Before he could say out loud what all three were thinking, Mercury handed Cupid his cowhide quiver. A single, gold-tipped arrow protruded from the lip. "The shaft was sanded just this morning. You can still smell the sawdust."

A sense of deep foreboding overtook Cupid. The last "gift" from the gods had only put distance between Cupid and Pan and delayed his mission. Cupid couldn't imagine how the arrow would help.

"Uncle, what am I meant to do?"

Mercury shrugged. "Hephaestus said you would know."

Thoughts raced through Cupid's head almost too quickly to register. With just the single arrow, Cupid held the power to change one heart's course. In order to create a match for Pan, Cupid could either pierce someone Pan was already beating for, or he could find someone already beating for Pan and send the arrow into Pan's heart.

"Cupid," Mercury said, as if reading his thoughts, "duty required me to deliver this to you. That does not mean I endorse the idea of your shooting my son's Earth form in the heart with a potentially lethal weapon."

"I understand," Cupid replied.

Mercury let out a long, weary sigh. "I must return home now." He turned sad eyes on Pan. "Be well, son." Mercury gathered Pan into a tight embrace as sudden and unexpected as his arrival, and then he was gone.

18

THE ARROW

Still rattled from the finality of his father's farewell, Pan collapsed onto the sofa and attempted to organize his thoughts. Eighteen minutes ago, he was happily riding one of his favorite booty calls to oblivion, blissfully unaware he'd be standing here now, pondering his own mortality. "Something tells me raspberry-lime seltzer is not strong enough for this conversation."

Keeping a healthy distance, Cupid shook the golden arrow at Pan like a forefinger. "Was this your idea?"

"*Heh.* I'm flattered you think I have that much power. You don't seem to have noticed the messaging only flows in one direction. I do, however, think it's the best solution I've heard yet."

"Shooting an arrow through your heart?"

"Yes. Look," Pan continued, ignoring everything about Cupid that was screaming *no*, "you're already beating for me. Shoot me right now, and *boom!* We're done here! We echo for each other. That's how it works, right?"

"Assuming it's not a trick . . . *and* assuming you'd live through it." Cupid dropped his arms to his side, bow in one hand, arrow in the other. "We have no way of knowing what they did to this arrow, Pan. What if . . ."

"You heard my father. Hephaestus wants to bring you home. He loves you. He wants you to be happy, and I'd like to believe he's fond of me too."

"You know he is," Cupid said.

"Right. He took an awful risk to give us this chance. I think we should take it."

Cupid's reply was thick with emotion. "Even your father doesn't know if you could die down here. A direct blow to your heart could kill you."

Pan fixed a smile on his face in the hopes it might ease his friend's wretchedness. "Come on. You shoot mortals all the time. Ever killed anyone?"

"No, but I've only shot my arrows from a mountaintop high above the clouds. Not standing right next to a person on Earth."

"Q." Pan leaned forward, elbows on his knees, and waited for Cupid to meet his gaze before continuing as gently as he knew how. "You've been killing me since you got here. You might as well just get it over with already."

"That's not fair, Pan." And which part of this effed-up scenario *was* fair?

"What about your tattoo? You said it yourself—you wouldn't have wanted to live without the experience of love. That's me. Living in darkness. You have the power to change that."

"Yes, by finding your Right Love. Only the Goddess of Love can choose your true Right Love."

"I'd settle for you." Pan had hoped his remark to come off as lighthearted, but Cupid wasn't having it.

"There's more to it than that, Pan. We'd be skirting Mother's designs—and Father's as well. You know they won't tolerate being outmaneuvered."

Of course Pan knew this. His entire job description was dealing with the fallout whenever a Major was crossed. Reason was not on Pan's side, but that didn't stop him from trying. "Hey, you and I weren't the ones who forged the arrow or sent my father to deliver it. Let's not forget that."

"I don't think the Council will deal in subtleties when they're deciding how to punish us. How'd you like to be a goat again?"

Pan clasped his hands between his knees and shot Cupid a smug grin. "Depends. Would you still love me?"

"With the heat of a million suns." There was not one ounce of sarcasm in his friend's tone.

"Okay, then. There's your answer." Pan had shifted into serious bullshitting mode now, and judging by the scowl on Cupid's face, he knew it too.

"What's our best-case scenario? I shoot you. You live. You beat for me."

"Exactly! Sounds glorious, no?" For a moment, Pan allowed himself the fantasy before Cupid snatched it away again with his damn logic.

"Oh yeah? And then what? The gods are done with me, and I ascend? Your descent is permanent. You're not coming with me, Pan. Have you thought this through? Eternity is a long damn time to be separated from your true love. Is that what you want?"

"Of course not." If Cupid hadn't forced him into a corner, Pan would not have then told his biggest whopper yet. "You know, they might decide to let you stay too."

Cupid seemed unable to decide between hurt and anger. In the end, he made yet another attempt to shut Pan down with incontrovertible logic. "Have you forgotten the goddess who used her considerable influence to make sure everyone would have me believe you'd died, just so I would never learn such a thing as Permanent Descent existed? What could ever possess you to think Mother would let me go now?"

Pan didn't, really. This time, he kept his yap shut and offered up only a contrite nod.

"Right," Cupid said, acknowledging if not exactly accepting Pan's unspoken apology. "So I'll go back to my days as a sexless, flying man in a teenager's body, only now I'll know what I'm missing. And what about you, Pan?"

"Hmm?" Pan was still processing the idea of this new version of Cupid tragically trapped inside his old, winged body like some horrifying remake of *The Fly.*

"Do you plan to be celibate down here?" Cupid asked.

"Hell no." Celibacy did not suit Pan. Not in his past, not now, and most definitely, not for eternity. "There are work-arounds, Q. We could negotiate—" But Pan had already been called out for crying wolf, and Cupid was done giving Pan's desperate theories an audience.

"And what if my punishment *doesn't* end there? Say the gods set my heart on a new Worthy *while we're together in love.* Where will that leave you?"

"Polyamory is always an option."

Cupid's expression twisted with pity. "Spoken like a soul that's never been in love."

"Enough!" Pan leaped up from the couch. "Too much thinking. Just point the damn thing and shoot me."

"Don't you see?" Cupid scoffed. "That is *exactly* what got me sent down here in the first place."

"There's a difference between that stupid prank you pulled on Hera and mating a truly matched couple."

"Maybe," Cupid said, "or *maybe* this setup is the ultimate test to see if I've learned my lesson. If that's the case, shooting you would bring a whole new level of torments my way."

"Yes, well"—Pan huffed—"I suppose there are hazards involved for both of us." Having made his point, Pan unbuttoned his shirt and thrust out his chest, offering the target without ambiguity.

"What'd you do that for?" Cupid demanded.

"You need me to draw you a damn bullseye? We only have one arrow. No margin for error. Right"— Pan grabbed Cupid by the wrist and drew his palm to his chest—"*there.*"

"For the love of Zeus! I could find your heartbeat blindfolded with nine fingers tied behind my back."

"As amusing as that might be, let's try it with both eyes and all ten fingers, hmm?"

Cupid yanked free of Pan's grip. "Stop trying to turn everything into a joke, Pan. This isn't funny."

"Oh, come on. It's a little bit funny. Who'd have thought this would be us, back in our glory days days when we were the horny satyr and the flying love-god baby?"

"That's not helping," Cupid said, visibly working to psych himself up for the job.

"We should kiss."

"*Now?*"

"Why the hell not? If I'm about to die, I'd like you to be the last taste on my lips."

"And if you're not about to die, we will both be in a heap of trouble."

Pan burst out laughing. "Dude, make up my mind. Am I dying or not?"

Cupid searched Pan's face as if it held all the answers. "I guess we'll never know," Cupid said, turning away with a huff.

Pan lunged forward, catching Cupid by the arm and spinning him back around. "Do it," Pan said, matching Cupid's serious tone for the first time.

"What if I kill you? *Really.*"

"It's worth it. No matter what happens, I love you, Q. I always have."

Cupid stared him down. Ever so slowly, Cupid lifted his bow and nocked the arrow onto the string. Pan worked to slow his breathing; the last thing Cupid needed right now was a moving target.

Cupid took aim, stretched the bowstring taut . . . sighed heavily, and lowered his arms.

"I'm sorry, Pan. I just can't."

"Well, I can!" With a move too swift for Cupid to track, Pan stripped the arrow from Cupid's hand and lined up the gold point to his own chest.

"Don't be a fool! That won't work. My arrow only works by my hand and my bow."

Tempted as he was, Pan knew Cupid spoke the truth. Muttering a soft, "Fuck," Pan lowered the arrow. "There's nothing I can do to change your mind?"

"If there is, I cannot imagine it."

"So, what do you suggest we do now?"

"It's time to get back on track with our plan to find your Worthy." Cupid held the bow out for Pan, who took it with great reluctance. "I can't see where I'll have occasion to use this while I'm down here without raising a lot of questions we can't answer. Will you store these for me in a safe place until we can send them back up to the Mount?"

"Fine," Pan answered. What choice did he have?

19

A CONFUSING BEAT

The next morning, the lane Cupid shared with Reed was not big enough to contain Cupid's frustration. His overzealous kicking had already propelled him onto Reed's ankles three times, this last time earning Cupid a swift kick in the face.

Reed stopped dead, mid-lap, horrified he'd broken Cupid's nose despite Cupid's assurances to the contrary. Little did either of them know something far more menacing was heading their way across the pool deck. Even with the dense concentration of pool chemicals in the air, Cupid could smell Pan's approach as soon as he walked through the locker room door and into the pool enclosure.

Reed followed Cupid's gaze to the figure of Pan, grinning wide as he strode across the pool deck in nothing but a skimpy black Speedo and a pair of flip-flops that snapped loudly against Pan's heels until they came to a stop at the edge of the pool.

Cupid mumbled an apology to Reed and waded over to meet Pan. "You're swimming?"

"Assuming I don't sink," he answered with a merry chuckle,

"but I guess we'll find out soon enough." Pan crouched down and jutted his chin toward Reed. "That's your swim teacher?"

A possessive rush took Cupid by surprise. "Yes."

"Huh. You two looked awfully cozy."

Cupid was working to sort out his emotions when his thoughts were loudly interrupted by an insistent beat coming from Pan's heart. Could Pan have been so epically stupid as to have impaled himself on Cupid's arrow? Had it actually *worked*?

"*Pan?*" Cupid asked slowly so as to keep the hysteria out of his voice. "What did you do?"

"What's the matter?" Pan's mouth twisted into a scowl as he glanced at Reed. "Worried I'll cramp your style?"

Just then, Reed swam up and grasped the coping next to Cupid, who had no choice but to introduce them. "Pan, meet Reed. Reed, Pan."

Reed lifted his goggles and took in Pan with eyes popped wide. At this angle, in that bathing suit, there wasn't much left to the imagination. "So *you're* Pan."

"And you're Reed," Pan said with a grin as he extended his hand. "My friend here told me you taught him to swim."

"My role is supervisory at best," Reed said, warming Cupid with his smile.

Pan chuckled. "He's a quick learner."

Cupid was beginning to feel like a steak being passed back and forth between two hungry lions. Well, maybe one lion and one of those tabbies that could always be found skulking around the palace halls.

"I'm more of a weight-room guy myself, but I thought I might add swimming to my routine," Pan said. "They say cross-training is healthy. What do you think, Reed?"

Reed's eyes took a slow ride down Pan from head to toe. Whereas Pan knew little about the body parts Reed was concealing underwater, Reed could see every ripple of muscle in Pan's thick thighs and abdomen. "Whatever you're doing seems to be working," he said. Not exactly an invitation to join them in the pool, Cupid noted.

"Nice of you to say," Pan said.

Cupid had heard enough. "Will you excuse me, Reed?" Cupid catapulted out of the pool and dragged Pan by the arm until they were well out of Reed's earshot.

"What is your damage, dude?" Pan asked, amused.

"You're beating!"

"I *am*?" Pan held his hand up to his heart. "I can't feel anything different. Are you sure?"

Was he sure?

"Mr. Innocent. What did you do, Pan?" Cupid grabbed Pan by his shoulders and shook hard. "Tell me you didn't fall on that arrow!"

"Whoa. Chillax, man. I didn't fall on your arrow. Come on, think about it. Why would I take that chance when I didn't even know if you'd be the next person I'd see?"

"Yeah, okay. But—"

"But nothing." Pan cupped Cupid's face between his hands. "Everything has changed. We're free to be us. To do what we want now . . . to have each other!"

He twisted out of Pan's grip. "That's not how it works."

"I would've thought by now you would have learned the rules can change at any moment. Someone is having a bad hair day up there, and *poof*, you're a constellation. It's just that easy. Maybe someone decided it was our time."

"I don't like it, Pan. It's too convenient." A harsh splash drew Cupid's attention to the water. Reed had started up his laps with a labored, aggressive rhythm completely unlike his typical, smooth strokes.

Pan met Cupid's gaze as he turned back from the pool. "Were you planning to tell me?"

It was complicated with Reed, and Cupid didn't owe Pan any explanations. "No."

"*No?*"

"We agreed not to talk about our . . . hookups."

"This is no hookup. I see how you two are looking at each other."

"You're right, Pan. Reed's special," Cupid said, "but he's not you."

"Well, here I am." Pan spread his arms wide, as if Cupid hadn't noticed him earlier. "You're beating for me, I'm beating for you, and you're *still* flat-out rejecting me."

"Can we talk about this when we both have more clothes on?"

Pan followed Cupid's gaze to his Speedo. "That would be the exact opposite of what I had in mind."

Cupid groaned. "I'm going back into that pool and working off my stress, and I suggest you do the same."

"You're exasperating!" Pan said, glaring at him.

"You came here to swim, didn't you?"

Bluff called, Pan jumped into the pool in the lane beside Cupid. His body wasn't the most aerodynamic, and his technique would not have won any style contests, but after watching Reed's breaststroke for a half a lap, Pan managed to propel himself across the pool. Seeing that Pan was not about to drown, Cupid found his opening and fell in sync behind Reed, the two of them kicking up matching whirlpools now that Pan had agitated them both. It was a great relief to all three when Pan decided he'd had enough and hoisted his body out of the pool. So much for working off stress.

Cupid climbed out of the pool after Pan, and Reed slowed to acknowledge Cupid's goodbye with a brief nod. Reed seemed less than thrilled to see Cupid leaving with Pan, but Cupid didn't have a clue what to say to him about it.

Cupid and Pan kept their distance in the locker room until they were safely clothed. They walked to the sub shop around the corner and worked their way into the awkward topic as their sandwiches were being made.

"Did you enjoy your swim?" Cupid asked.

"It was fine," Pan said, "but I'd probably enjoy the experience a whole lot more without a raging erection. Speaking of us . . ."

"Right." Cupid stared at the gray tabletop between them.

"Way to stroke my ego, buddy."

"You know it's not you."

"Sure feels like me," Pan shot back.

"I'm sorry," Cupid replied. "This is all very confusing."

"You know what's confusing? I don't feel any different when I'm with you. Shouldn't I feel something?"

"Trust me, Pan. You're lucky you don't feel it the way I do." Their lunches were delivered, but neither man so much as lifted his eyes toward the server.

Pan took a bite of his meatball sub. "What is it supposed to feel like when you beat for someone—I mean, if you're not being punished by the Goddess of Love?"

"I don't know. I guess you could ask Mia or Lieutenant Goode."

"Yeah, no thanks," Pan said. "What does it sound like to you?"

Cupid set down his pastrami sandwich and leaned across the table. He concentrated his complete attention on Pan's heart, and . . . nothing.

"I don't hear anything." Cupid would have liked to have been surprised by the sudden reversal; sadly, he was only disappointed.

"You can't describe the sound?"

"No, Pan. You're not understanding me. It's *gone*."

"What?"

"You're not beating for me anymore."

"That's it? I'm not a Worthy anymore?"

Cupid's own heart thumped strong and painfully true. "I'm still beating for you, so I think you're still a Worthy. You're just not beating for me anymore."

"So now I *can't* have you?" Pan was crestfallen.

Cupid sighed. "You never could. They were just messing with us."

"I don't get it."

"Neither do I, Pan. But we're going to find you your Worthy."

20

ECHO BEATS

The next day, the gods gave Cupid's heart a much-needed respite after the highs and lows of Pan's mysteriously appearing and disappearing echo beat, and Cupid knew exactly where he would pass the time. The pool had become his sanctuary and Reed his favorite diversion.

As he neared the pool, Cupid was more than a little surprised to find Pan swimming laps in the lane next to Reed. Irritation struck him first—how could Pan invade his sacred space?—but wasn't Cupid the one who'd convinced Pan to try swimming? How could he now begrudge Pan the relief he'd found?

Cupid released a sigh that carried through the thick air, causing Pan to lift his head out of the water and meet his gaze. Cupid considered turning around and leaving, coming back later after Pan and his irresistible scent had gone, and skipping a repeat of the awkward friction with Reed. Cupid would be with Pan soon enough; they had a meetup scheduled for lunch so Cupid could listen in when Pan met his next potential Worthy.

Before Cupid could make up his mind whether to stay or go, a powerful echo heartbeat reached his ears. Cupid forced his feet closer to the pool though each step felt like dragging a cement block. Pan was beating again, damn the gods! The on-again, off-again torture was extreme, even for Aphrodite!

But no . . . Cupid realized, close enough now to pinpoint the beat. It wasn't Cupid that Pan's heart was echoing. If Cupid hadn't let wishful thinking get the better of him yesterday, he would've noticed then that Pan wasn't beating for him. With startling clarity, Cupid finally grasped the situation: Pan was beating for Reed, and Reed was beating back.

The realization stopped Cupid dead in his tracks. He should have been happy for Pan, for Reed, too. He probably should have even been happy for his own wretched soul, having so swiftly matched the two Worthies. But Cupid didn't feel happy. The echo was perfect and final, and it filled him with a deep sense of loss.

Pan stood watching Cupid from the middle of his lap lane, a curious tilt to his head, while Reed swam on, oblivious to the forces that had just changed the course of his life. The desire to flee came over Cupid again, more powerfully this time, but even stronger was the physical compulsion to stay close to Pan and Reed. It wasn't worth fighting; Cupid knew that much.

He walked over to the bleachers, sat down heavily on the bench, and dropped his forehead to his knees.

"Hey! You okay?" Pan stood dripping on the pavement in front of him.

When Cupid didn't answer, because he didn't have a clue how, Pan knelt and placed his hand on Cupid's knee. "Q, talk to me."

There was no use prolonging the agony. "You're beating again," Cupid said, barely lifting his head from his lap.

"*What?* What the fuck?" Pan fought through his confusion the same way Cupid had—with faulty logic born of hope. "It has to be the water," Pan said. "Maybe we're meant to live out our days near the ocean or inside a giant vat of chlorine or something."

"It's not the water, and it's not the chemicals," Cupid said carefully. "And it's not me."

"Huh?"

"You're beating for Reed."

The rhythmic *swish* of Reed's crawl stroke pulsed in the distance like a steady, beating drum.

"That makes no sense," Pan said, as if Love were bound to reason. "I don't feel anything. At all. With any part of my body."

"You will." It cost Cupid dearly to say so.

"How are you so sure?"

"*Because*, Pan. He's beating back."

"What?" Finally, Pan glanced toward Reed's quiet movement through the water. "You heard it?"

"Yes. Nothing echoes like a natatorium. I can hardly hear myself think." The last part wasn't exactly true. Cupid heard plenty of his thoughts; he just didn't like any of them.

"How do you know he's not beating for *you*? Maybe we're all beating for each other. What if it's a big circle? Or a triangle?"

"No, Pan. There's a clear echo, and I'm not in it."

The undeniable truth started to sink into Pan's wet skull. Pan exhaled a bumpy sigh, then slipped onto the bench next to Cupid, the two of them with their eyes set on Reed. Pan shook his head with a huff. "This is fucked up."

"Yes." Losing Pan and Reed at the same time was going to be unimaginably miserable.

"I'm sorry, Q."

"It's not your fault."

"Like that matters."

"You know, you're supposed to be happy about this," Cupid said, trying his best to smile. "This is the best thing that will ever happen to you."

Pan rolled his eyes. "*You* would have been the best thing to happen to me."

"Not according to the Goddess of Love," Cupid said with a shrug. "Say what you want about my mother—" Pan snorted. *Yeah, better not.* "Worthies are sacred."

"But Reed has feelings for *you*."

True, and after all their talk about hope, Reed was going to be crushed at Cupid's unexplainable change of heart. "I have feelings for him, too, but he's not beating for me, Pan. He's beating for you."

"I'm pretty sure Reed hates me."

"He doesn't know you."

"He knows that you and I have a history together."

"None of that matters now."

Pan stared out at the pool for a few minutes, looked up toward the ceiling, and sighed. "He's a mortal."

"Indeed, he is," Cupid replied, remembering exactly how close Reed had come to his end.

"I'm sorry. I can't handle this right now." Jumping off the bleachers, Pan grabbed his towel and slung it around his neck. "I need to get out of here. I'll call you later, okay?"

"Okay."

Pan strode to the locker room entrance. As he pulled open the door, Pan stopped and turned to look back at the pool one last time before disappearing.

21

NOT A FIT

The longest shower Pan had ever taken offered little relief for the rapid-fire assault of his thoughts. Round and round went the voices in his head, taking his emotions on a wild roller coaster. *If* this Right Love hype were to be believed, *if* Cupid's judgment were to be trusted, *if* this weren't another elaborate trick cooked up by Ares and Aphrodite, *if* this Reed could be convinced, *if, if, if* . . .

Toweled off and no closer to answers, Pan squeezed a line of toothpaste onto his toothbrush and lifted it to his mouth. The rote mechanics had the unfortunate consequence of catching his reflection in the mirror. The bleary, dazed eyes blinking back at him seemed to belong to one of Pan's fallens, not the confident earth version of himself he had grown accustomed to seeing in the mirror. He bent over the sink to finish the job, scrubbing his gums so furiously he drew blood.

Pan followed a string of curses all the way to his bureau and snatched up the first shirt his fingers touched. He barely stopped pacing long enough to hop into his boxers and jeans.

Still muttering to himself, he jammed his feet into socks and sneakers—not because he would have been cold in flip-flops, but because autumn in the Midwest required some adjustments to fit in with the humans.

Attempting to be productive, he shoved his phone and wallet into his pockets, grabbed his keys, and climbed into his truck. As his dear old dad had not so subtly reminded him, Euphrosyne was sorely needed back home. Grateful to have a purpose, Pan fired up the Titan and headed for the South Side.

It wasn't until Pan was standing in the elevator in Euphrosyne's building, his finger hovering in front of the buttons, that he realized why he'd really shown up here. Olympus could damn well wait for the return of their Grace, Pan decided, then slapped the button for Cupid's floor.

A solid knock at Cupid's door went unanswered. Either Cupid wasn't home yet, or he was looking for his own answers in the shower. *Good luck with that.* As the legal tenant, Pan had a key, and he used it to let himself in. No shower running, no Cupid. No matter. Pan would wait.

Suddenly ravenous, he headed into the kitchen. How fortunate that Cupid had recently stocked up. Pan threw open the side-by-side refrigerator and freezer doors and surveyed every shelf for the available options. *Hmm, beer or cookie dough ice cream?* He briefly considered combining the two.

His face was so deep into the freezer, he didn't notice Cupid enter the apartment until he reached over Pan's shoulder to grab a beer. Wordlessly, as if Pan's presence in Cupid's kitchen were not unusual enough to warrant comment, Cupid twisted off the bottle cap and chugged down half the contents.

This cannot be good.

"You hate beer," Pan said, grabbing one for himself and shutting the doors.

"I don't think I'll ever get used to it," Cupid said, then took another swig. He strode across the kitchen floor, seemed to forget where he was going, turned around, tossed back more beer, and paced back to where he'd started.

"Will you slow down, please?"

"I will if you will," Cupid answered.

Pan hadn't realized he'd been pacing too. "Come sit down."

Cupid flopped into the seat right next to Pan at the small, square table, set down his beer bottle, and scrubbed his face with his hands.

"What did you say to Reed?" Pan asked.

"I told him you weren't feeling well."

Pan huffed. "That's accurate."

"I'm not feeling so well myself."

Pan leaned forward, elbows on his knees. "Do you love him?"

Cupid answered quickly, as if he'd already given the question a fair amount of thought. "Not the way I love you, but I do care about him."

"What if I don't want him, Q?"

Cupid swiveled abruptly to face him. "Don't say that, Pan."

"I can't help who I love any more than you can."

"You *will* love him. You two just need to cross the Liminal Point."

"Right, and he's gonna suddenly start looking at me the way he looks at you?"

"It might not be immediate, but it will happen. You two are matched."

"How can that be?"

"What do you mean, 'how can that be'?"

Pan sighed. *Was Cupid really going to make him spell it out?* "I was in the pool when Reed showed up this morning."

"And?"

A sharpness sliced through the single word, setting Pan on edge.

"C'mon, man. You've seen the way he moves. How do we make any sense as a couple?"

"You must make sense to Mother, or she wouldn't have made you beat for each other." Cupid's words dripped with envy.

"Or maybe this is Aphrodite's way of punishing me."

Cupid shot out of his chair. "That's a horrible thing to say! Reed is not a punishment."

"I didn't mean that *he's* a punishment. I have nothing against the guy, but he's not my type—*at all*." Had Cupid really not noticed Jagger's build or even the power-tool guy from Home Warehouse?

"I didn't realize you had a type, considering you've coupled with . . . oh, let's see . . . *everyone*." The insult slid off Pan's back, but he didn't appreciate that Cupid was trying to wound him.

"Until your arrival, *old friend*, there didn't seem to be any reason to be selective."

"Have you considered there might be some reason beyond the physical for the pairing?"

Pan craned his neck to shoot a disbelieving glare at Cupid. "Like what?"

"Are you really that shallow?"

"What if I am?" Did Pan want Cupid to convince him otherwise?

"Maybe you were—*once*," Cupid added after Pan's snort, "but I don't think that's who you are anymore."

"Maybe you're giving me too much credit."

"I'm not," Cupid answered carefully.

A nagging voice inside Pan told him Cupid was right; Pan wasn't a shallow asshole, which probably should have made him happy. Still, he couldn't quite wrap his head around the reality that Reed was *it* for him.

"Shouldn't there be fireworks or something?"

A hint of a smile started in Cupid's eyes, but it was quickly tamped down. "Have you had fireworks before?"

"Of course."

"And how many of those lovers are you still with?"

"None, obviously."

Cupid folded his arms across his chest. "Why do you think that is?"

Pan glared until Cupid blinked. It was the smallest of victories for Pan—and his last one. He slumped against the ladder-back chair. "Fine. Point taken."

Cupid sat down again and dragged his chair closer to Pan. "Don't give up on your fireworks, Pan. It wasn't like that for Mia and Patrick at first either. You two need to get to know each other."

Clearly, there was something about Reed that had captured Cupid's interest even more deeply than Pan had understood. If nothing else, Pan was curious. "Tell me about him, Q."

Cupid's gaze shifted away from Pan. He sipped at his beer while he gathered his thoughts. "He's super smart," Cupid said proudly.

Pan chuckled. "I don't think that would have been the first thing on my list, but okay."

"He's a really good man. Did he tell you what happened to his leg?"

"We didn't speak other than a quick hello," Pan said. "So, what happened to Reed's leg?"

"He was out jogging one night when he heard a woman cry out for help. With no thought for his own safety, Reed rushed in to help and got shot in the hip."

"Holy shit!"

"I know," Cupid said. "It's hard for me to comprehend how some mortals can be so selfless with the short lives they're given.

Even if Reed believed the Fates controlled the number of his days on Earth, there's still the fragility of the human body to consider."

"Most people would've called the police or just kept on jogging."

"Reed said he couldn't have lived with himself if he hadn't responded the way he did."

"Do you think that's why your mother made him a Worthy?" Pan couldn't know what choice he might have made as a mortal, but a sickening feeling came over him: he wasn't good enough for Reed.

"Could be," Cupid answered. "It's not necessarily about an act of bravery. Sometimes it's just about surviving without getting crushed by life." If Cupid was wondering, as Pan was, what qualified Pan, he kept his doubts to himself.

"What kind of work does he do?"

Cupid set down his beer with a heavy sigh. "Pan, you should be asking *Reed* all this, not me. You two need to get to know each other."

"I think I'm the last person he wants to get to know."

"It's not you. He doesn't socialize much since the shooting. Plus, he never really thought about men, you know, romantically, before he met me."

"Wait! *You're* the first man he's been with?"

"We weren't . . . I never even got to kiss him."

"I'm sorry, Q. That sucks." Pan briefly considered whether there was any way Reed and Cupid could have had their little fling first, but this situation was complicated enough without connecting the last two dots of the triangle.

"Please, Pan, when you and Reed finally . . . just promise me you won't break him in two."

Pan might've laughed out loud if Cupid didn't look so goddamn tragic about the whole thing. "Gentle isn't really my style. This is what I mean about not being a good fit."

"I'm sure you'll figure it out." Cupid rose and took his empty beer to the kitchen. "I need something to eat. Want a sandwich?"

"Sure." Pan watched Cupid as he busied his hands, stacking bread and meat and condiments on the counter. Cupid was no better at hiding his feelings than he was at outright lying. Cupid's pain was palpable, and Pan suspected it would get a whole lot worse before it got better. "I'm sorry, Q. This whole Right Love situation is a lot to take in. I'm probably not being sensitive to your needs."

Cupid snorted. "When have you ever been sensitive?"

"What can I say?"

"Nothing, Pan," Cupid said, now smiling. "Say nothing."

Pan tried, but he couldn't stay quiet when Cupid started pouring a bag of chips into a bowl. "What are you doing that for?"

"It's called *manners*. Would you get us a couple more beers, please?"

Oh boy. How would the Divine Council judge Pan if he returned Cupid to Mount Olympus with a drinking problem? Pan rose heavily and grabbed two glasses of water along with the beers. Meanwhile, Cupid had set the table with placements and napkins neatly tucked under the sandwich plates.

"Shall I pour your pilsner into a crystal flute, my good man?"

Cupid rolled his eyes at Pan's cheesy British accent. "Wouldn't hurt you to step up your game if you want to impress Reed."

"Impress him? The guy won't even talk to me."

"Cook him dinner. That's what I did."

"You cooked? I'm afraid to ask how that went."

"Euphrosyne helped me, and it went very well, thank you. And you're a great cook. Just . . . use utensils. Reed is very refined."

"Yet another thing we do not have in common." Pan threw back his beer, then let out a loud belch to make his point.

"Nothing attracts like opposites," Cupid said. "Did I mention he reads?"

"*Books?*"

"Rise to the occasion, Pan."

Pan shook his head, sputtering with laughter. "The gods are nothing if not ironic."

"That's one word for it," Cupid replied.

"Think about it, Q—a man who was injured saving a damsel in distress from the unwanted attentions of a brute. *I'm* the brute the nymphs were always running away from."

"You're different now, Pan."

"Hello. The man's name is Reed. Do you not think that's a big ol' *eff you* from the gods lest I ever try to forget where I've come from? Can you honestly tell me this whole thing isn't one big, sick joke? What is a man like Reed possibly going to see in me?"

"You're a Worthy. That means regardless of the past, you are deserving of Right Love. If simply speaking Reed's name out loud reminds you of your past mistakes and keeps you loyal to your best self, how lucky are you?"

Pan wanted to believe him, wanted to believe he had a chance to be this version of himself Cupid seemed to see.

And what the hell did Pan ever claim to know about who was right for him? His methods up to this point had yielded a whole lot of action but not a single relationship worth holding on to. What could it hurt to swipe right on Reed?

"Let's say I decide to give this thing with Reed a go."

"You *will?*" Cupid's expression lifted with so much hope, it made Pan's heart hurt to look at him.

"Yeah. I mean, what if Reed really is my Right Love ship, and I let him pass me in the night?"

"Exactly! Eternity is a long time to live with regret."

"No doubt." Now, to convince Reed. "I, uh, don't think I made the best first impression on Reed. Maybe you could be there when we meet up again?"

"I don't know if that's a good idea."

"With both of us wanting you, you mean?"

"And me wanting both of you," Cupid said gloomily.

"Just get us started. Then you can get indigestion or bubonic plague or something."

"You know I'm a terrible liar."

"Okay, fine. Then tell him he's my Right Love, and we're going to have our happily ever after, but that can't happen until you leave."

Cupid tapped his napkin along the side of his mouth. "I feel the flu coming on."

"That's my boy." Pan lifted his beer bottle and waited for Cupid to clink.

"Beer, lies, wild sex . . . you've thoroughly corrupted me. Are you happy now?"

"Yes—and no. You do realize you've been perfect this time. I can't imagine what more they could want from you. As soon as we make this work, you'll probably ascend."

"To be honest, Pan, my going home would probably be best for everyone involved."

Pan could only answer with a sullen nod.

22

BAIT AND SWITCH

Today was the day. Reed had made up his mind on the drive to the gym. Time to hobble way out of his comfort zone. *Yeah, look where that got you last time,* the bum leg reminded him, to which Reed answered, "No regrets" out loud just as Dr. Hannon had coached him.

It had been a while since Reed had needed to invoke the mantra, which, according to his therapist's parting words, was not necessarily a good thing. *Take a chance every now and then,* Dr. Hannon had said. *Remind yourself you're alive.*

Reed needed little reminder lately. He was alive and well—at least his libido was. Fantasies of the lovely young man mysteriously named Q had pretty much taken over all his conscious thoughts and a fair portion of his dreams to boot. And *oh,* those dreams! Just thinking about what the two had done to each other last night fogged up the windows of Reed's car.

He couldn't deny it was Q's outrageously good looks that had caught his initial attention, but once the door of possibility opened, Q had given him plenty of compelling reasons to step through. The man was alluring on so many levels—his exuberance for life and learning, his directness and lack of filter, the uncomplicated state of his intellect. Any holes in Q's scholastic knowledge were more than compensated for.

Reed genuinely wanted to get to know Q better, and that motivation was unusual and powerful enough to pull him out of his safe, boring existence. What, really, did he have to lose? He plotted and rehearsed until a solid plan came together: Reed would stretch and warm up, and when Q arrived, he'd invite him out for drinks. Get the whole thing out of the way so he could enjoy the simple pleasure of sharing a swim with his beautiful companion.

Conviction was well and good inside the safety of his car, but it frayed along with Reed's nerves as he plodded across the parking lot toward the gym entrance. He didn't even know if Q would be at the pool today. Not that Q was playing hard to get—he'd made his feelings known—but Reed had asked for time, and that's exactly what Q had given him. The next move was Reed's.

Stay relaxed. Kane's first rule of rehab.

Easy for you to say, Reed argued with the voice in his head, instantly acknowledging the insanity taking over his life. *I'm too old for this shit.*

Reed had talked himself into a lather by the time he exited the locker room into the pool area. His breath caught as he found Q swimming laps in "their lane." Reed's initial instinct was a flashing red light: *Retreat!*

"Take a chance," spoke with an insistence that wasn't going away. With a measured breath, Reed shook off the urge to flee.

"Focus," Reed whispered out loud. The last thing his ego needed was a face-plant into the pool deck. Reed managed one deliberate foot in front of the other though his heart was pounding as if he were perched at the end of the high dive, about to leap.

Reed had nearly reached the pool when Q swam to the end of the lane and floated up and out onto the deck as if a jet-pack were strapped to his heels. Water droplets skidded down his body and puddled at his feet, sending a tributary licking at Reed's toes.

"Morning," said Q, skimming his wet hair off his forehead.

"Hi." Q was standing far too close for Reed to sneak a gawk below the neck without getting busted. *Good Lord. I'm a boy with a crush.* "I, uh, didn't mean to interrupt your workout."

What the heck was it he'd wanted to ask? Oh yes, *a drink.*

"No, it's fine," Q replied. "I'm just finishing up."

So much for their swim. "Say, I wanted to ask—"

"There's something I—" Q started at the same time. "Sorry, go ahead."

Something in Q's expression crushed Reed's hopes. "No, you."

Q swallowed hard. "I just wanted to tell you I've really enjoyed our friendship."

"As have I," Reed said carefully, reading goodbye between the lines. He'd taken too long. Q was, no doubt, on to bigger, brighter, and *younger* pastures. Reed couldn't blame him, and he surely wouldn't stand in his way.

"Were you about to ask me something?" *God,* how he looked at Reed with those big, innocent eyes.

"Oh." Was it too pathetic for Reed to ask if they'd see each other again? *Yes, it was.* "I just wanted to ask if Pan is feeling better."

A wrinkle creased Q's forehead. "He's fine. In fact"—Q glanced toward the door—"there he is now."

Reed turned to look over his shoulder at the quickly approaching figure. He looked plenty healthy to Reed.

"I have to go," Q said abruptly, plucking up his towel from the bleachers. "Have a good swim."

"Yeah, okay." Reed felt like a spinning top set into motion by a giant, unseen hand.

Q and Pan passed each other with a subtle nod that could have meant anything from "I hate your guts" to "I'm so glad we're back together," and Reed had no way of knowing what was happening between them—only that something definitely was. Had Q used Reed to make Pan jealous? What did it matter anyway? Q was leaving, and his personal life was none of Reed's business. *Definitely too old for this.*

He shook his foolish head and inched toward the pool. There were laps to be swum, just like before Q turned his world upside down. At least Pan and Q had the decency not to flaunt their whatever-it-was in front of Reed. He didn't think he could handle watching the two of them frolic together in the pool right now.

Reed sank to the coping and propelled himself into the pool using his arms behind him. It wasn't pretty, but why should Reed care what Q's once-and-maybe-again lover thought of him? His chest felt tight as he slipped into the water—not the best way to start his workout—unlike Pan, who hopped into the next lane with a friendly, "Morning!" in Reed's direction.

"Hello," Reed answered coolly. Did he have to pretend to like the guy?

Pan took the hint and minded his own business though Reed distinctly felt Pan's eyes on him several times during their workouts. During his breaks, Reed watched him back. Pan wasn't elegant—he was more water buffalo than dolphin—but his powerful strokes got the job done and earned Reed's grudging admiration.

Reed was going through the motions on his side of the lane divider, but his spirit was broken. Q had slipped through his fingers. Swimming harder, longer, or faster wasn't going to bring him back. What was the point of pushing himself? Even before Reed reached the assist chair, he'd already justified his abbreviated workout. Kane would not have approved, nor would he have sanctioned Reed's little pity party, but Kane wasn't here. Dr. Hannon wasn't here. Q wasn't here. Just Pan.

As he was dismounting the lift, Reed twisted around for one last look. The awkward move threw off his balance enough to snag his right foot behind his left at just the wrong moment. Panic set in as Reed braced himself to hit the pavement, but the hard landing never came. His fall was broken by Pan's thick arms, which had somehow materialized between Reed's body and the deck.

Reed's heart pounded like a fist against his rib cage as he blinked at Pan in astonishment. The man's lower body was still half inside the pool. How he'd come to Reed's rescue so quickly made no sense. "How did you just . . ."

"Sorry," Pan answered, sounding embarrassed, as if he were the one to humiliate himself. "I saw you start to trip, and I swam over as fast as I could. Here, sorry . . ." Pan slipped away from Reed, setting him carefully onto the deck. "Are you okay?"

His concern was genuine; that much Reed could tell.

"Yes, thank you. That could have been really ugly."

"No problem," Pan said, dipping down to his shoulders in the water, giving Reed some space and some much-appreciated dignity to stand up by himself.

"I guess this is what I get for cutting my workout short," Reed said, huffing at himself as he checked to make sure nothing was actually broken.

"I hope that wasn't on my account," Pan said.

Yes, actually, it was. "No, not at all. Just not feeling it today, you know?"

"Sure." Pan smiled. "But if someone's trying to send you a message, don't you think it would be safer to get back in the water?" Pan waved his arm over the surface of the pool as if he owned the place. "Swim with me?"

What the hell was going on with Reed and these boys? Whatever it was, Reed didn't like feeling so very confused and out of his element.

"I should go."

"I wish you would stay," Pan said.

"Why?" *Why the hell do you care* was really what he meant.

Pan smiled up at Reed, his hands folded on the pool deck like the teacher's pet in the front row. "I know you think you've got this thing all figured out, Reed, but trust me. Whatever you're thinking, it's not the whole story."

"Look, buddy, I don't know how you can know what I'm thinking when I don't even know what I'm thinking." This, right here, was why Reed didn't do people anymore.

"How about we don't think for a while? Can we just swim? That's what you came for, right?"

In the end, what drew Reed back into the pool was a determination not to let these crazy feelings impact his routine. With a satisfied grin, Pan pushed off the wall, trailing a whirlpool to the next lane, where he began his plodding, chunky freestyle.

After a few labored laps, Reed settled into a groove, and the vigorous swim worked its usual wonders on his mood. He pushed himself for an extra lap, not surprised when Pan slogged to a stop at the same time.

Pan stood, dropped the goggles to his thick neck, and hitched his elbows over the pool's edge behind him. "Feel better?"

"I do. And you?"

Pan shrugged. "Sure, I guess. Swimming isn't really my thing."

Yes, Reed had noticed. "May I ask the obvious, then? Why are you here? You seemed to want no part of me when we first met."

Pan guffawed. "I might say the same of you."

"You would be correct," Reed admitted, "but it was nothing personal."

"Same." Okay, then. "Look, can I buy you a beer or something? I would really like to continue this conversation, but I can't breathe in here. If I don't get some fresh air into my lungs, I think I might be ill." The man did look quite pale behind all that sodden auburn facial hair, come to think of it.

"It's not even ten a.m." Even as Reed voiced the lame excuse, he wished he could take it back. He had too many questions to leave this alone.

Pan was not easily deterred. "Coffee, then? A walk? Sit in my truck with the windows open?"

Reed cracked a smile. "Can I hold the keys?"

Pan grinned back, a reservoir of warmth and good humor in his eyes—but something deeper as well, some kind of mutual understanding. "Sure, if you need to."

23

A VERY SHORT HIKE

They decided to drive separately and meet at Crawley Pond, a beautiful spot just down the road. Given Reed's history, Pan couldn't blame him for not getting into the truck with a near stranger. At least Reed was willing to hear him out.

They walked together in silence down the short path that led to the pond, Pan taking small, deliberate steps to match Reed's labored gait. It wasn't easy holding back, especially out in the woods, the crisp leaves crunching under his feet. He'd nearly blown his cover at the pool, diving to catch Reed like that, but what was Pan supposed to do—let Reed crack his head open?

Pan rounded the empty bench and sat down, stretching his legs out in front of him. "I've always enjoyed coming here, especially this time of year."

"It's a beautiful spot," Reed answered as he eased onto the opposite end of the bench and hooked his cane over the back. "I used to love running around this pond."

By the time Pan had arrived at this Tarra, Reed would already have been out of commission, or they might have passed each other running on this very path.

"And now, you could swim it if you wanted to," Pan said.

"Probably," Reed said, smirking. "I guess that makes me a biathlete."

Here's hoping, thought Pan, unable to contain a chuckle.

Reed's cheeks pinked up as it hit him what he'd said. Oh boy. Not just straight as Cupid's arrow, but tightly wound, to boot. *Thanks for the challenge, Aphrodite.*

Reed cleared his throat and changed the subject. "You seem much more comfortable outdoors."

"Definitely." The fresh air offered more than relief from the thick concentration of chlorine. Outside, Pan could sense minute changes in Reed's body chemistry—an ability that would come in handy while he was trying to woo the man. "You asked why I came to the pool today."

"Yes." Reed shifted on the bench and faced Pan with a wary gaze.

Pan would have to tread carefully so as not to scare him away. "Our friend Q is a matchmaker of sorts."

"You hired a matchmaker?"

Pan bit back a smile. "Not exactly."

"Well, I sure as hell didn't!"

"Believe me, I know you had nothing to do with this, Reed."

"I don't even know what 'this' is." Reed sighed. "Are you two a couple or not?"

"Not."

"But you *were?*"

"Very briefly." And it was glorious, but Pan couldn't dwell on that.

"And then?"

"And then," Pan answered, extending his arm along the back of the bench toward Reed, "he met you."

Reed's eyebrows narrowed in confusion. "Are you saying you and Q broke up over *me?*"

"We'd agreed to . . . take a break . . . and that's when he met you."

"And then you decided you wanted him back?" Pan had to admire the guy for trying to make sense of the whole convoluted scenario.

"No. Q got to know you a little bit and realized you and *I* would make a better couple than you and *he*."

"*You* and I?" Reed blinked. "Better than Q and I?"

"Yep," said Pan.

"And better than Q and *you?*"

Pan had to bite his lower lip to keep from laughing out loud. "Yes, Reed."

Reed took a moment to digest the idea. "Not that I'm complaining or anything, but how could I possibly be better for either of you two young men than you are for each other?"

Yeah, Pan would have liked to ask Aphrodite the same damn question. "Honestly? I'm not sure yet, but Q is. And I trust him."

"He's really that good at matchmaking?"

"He's kind of famous for it."

Shaking his head, Reed turned his gaze to the water. A quiet, thoughtful man was a welcome change of pace.

"Huh," Reed said finally. "I thought Q had genuine feelings for me."

"He did. He *does.*"

"I don't get it. He's willing to just step aside and pass me along to you like a bar of soap?" The shower visual wasn't helping Pan stay focused.

"He's very serious about . . . his beliefs."

"He's not coming back, then? Even if this thing he's so sure of between you and me turns out not to be right?"

"He's pretty sure it is."

Reed looked doubtful.

It was up to Pan to put that final nail in Reed's coffin, or

they'd never move past Q. "But no, he can't be with you now."
Or me.

"I can't decide if I'm angry or disappointed or just plain confused." Reed huffed to himself. "Do I get any say in this?"

"Of course." *Well, not really,* but to be fair, none of them had. "I wasn't planning to force myself on you, Reed."

"I didn't expect you were!" A sharp tang of panic wafted from Reed's side of the bench, making a liar out of him.

And just like that, Pan was the brute again, chasing down a water nymph who wanted nothing to do with him. Funny how easily centuries of confidence could be stripped away, leaving Pan feeling as vulnerable and rejected as his worst day as a satyr. "Hey, I'm sorry, man," Pan said. "I know I'm a distant second . . . if that."

Reed shot back. "You have to be thinking the same of me."

Pan leaned toward Reed and slipped his hand onto Reed's shoulder. "Actually, I was thinking I'd like to get to know you better."

Reed searched Pan's expression. "Yeah?"

"Yeah." It was an odd headspace, for sure, to start out a relationship with the knowledge you'd been cosmically matched by the Goddess of Love, a tidbit of inside information Pan wasn't ready to share with Reed. "What do we have to lose?"

"The opportunity cost of taking myself off the market." Reed laughed at his own joke until tears came to his eyes. "Is it fair to assume Q told you . . . about me?"

"If you're referring to the whole never-been-with-a-man situation, yes, he told me."

"That would be the situation, yes," Reed answered, a blush burnishing his cheeks.

"And yet, you're here." It was a risk, calling him out like that, but Pan could read the signs. Reed's interest was piqued, if not his desire.

Reed drew a deep breath and released it slowly. *Bingo.* In response, Pan gave Reed's shoulder a massage-style squeeze, a small reward for the man's courageous effort. A shiver vibrated through Reed's leather jacket and straight into Pan's bones.

"I can't quite figure out what you want with this old, broken codger when you could be with any guy—or gal—your own age."

"That is exactly what I'd like to find out," Pan replied.

Reed huffed.

"What?" Pan asked.

"I noticed you didn't correct my description of myself."

Pan shrugged. "Your age doesn't bother me." What bothered Pan was how he would explain *not* aging after a while, but that was a problem that didn't need an immediate solution.

Reed gave voice to one last gasp of skepticism. "Look, if this is some kind of con you boys are running, I can save you the trouble. I live a very simple life. Other than a few nice bottles of wine I'm saving for special occasions, any spare change I've got left after paying my mortgage and my taxes goes toward books."

Oh, Reed of little faith. When were you last loved?

"We're not con men, Reed. You probably can't tell from my broken-in jeans and sweatshirt, but I have everything I need. Even some very nice bottles of my own." Pan winked, one connoisseur to another.

Reed shifted, sat up a little taller. "Such as?"

Aha! A shared interest Pan and Reed could build on, something more productive than both of them having the hots for Q.

"How about I show you tomorrow night? Dinner at my place?"

Reed countered, "How about we do this at my house instead?"

Well now, *there* was a leap of faith. Not even Q had received that invitation. "You sure?"

"Mm-hmm. Fair warning, my family is a discerning group."

"Do you always invite your *family* on the first date?" A chill rolled up Pan's spine. Convincing Reed to give him a try was enough of a challenge. Now he was expected to win over the whole family at once as the first male partner Reed had ever brought home, no less?

Reed shrugged unapologetically. "If they don't like you, it's all over. Better to get it out of the way before I get attached. You game?"

"Sure, why not?" Pan said through gritted teeth, but only because "Do I have a choice?" seemed a bit confrontational. Addresses and phone numbers were exchanged.

With the pressure of arranging their date safely behind them, Reed visibly relaxed. Pan got him talking about the "good ol' days" of teaching, and time passed easily as they shared war stories back and forth from opposite sides of the lectern.

"Not exactly the teacher's pet, were you?" Reed made the observation with what Pan hoped was an appreciative grin.

Pan's booming laughter rang out over the pond. "Not even close."

Naturally, Pan's accomplice popped to mind—the winged prince of the palace, always causing trouble but never suffering the consequences. Well, Q was getting his fair share now—and then some. Poor bastard.

Reed's smooth storytelling drew Pan back to the here and now, the man who was destined to be his Right Love. Pan wouldn't have said he was smitten, but he found himself very much enjoying Reed's company. He could vividly picture Reed in all his glory at the front of a large lecture hall, his students rapt while Reed brought "the ancients" to life. During Reed's recounting of an incident that occurred during one of his classes, Pan even experienced a stirring of intellectual curiosity about the particular piece of classical literature Reed was describing.

How many ways did Pan and Reed challenge each other's idea of the perfect mate? How many more times would Pan turn this pairing over in his head?

Though Pan was eager to make those discoveries—surprisingly so—enough ground had been covered today. Reed would need time alone to marinate. He might not realize that his head was muddled while in Pan's company, but he'd figure it out once they were apart. Attraction was an important start, but anything meaningful and lasting would have to make sense to a clearheaded Reed. It was time to say goodbye for now and leave their conversation on a high note, with both men wanting more.

"I'm really sorry, Reed, but I have an appointment to get to," Pan said, secretly delighted when Reed's smile flickered.

"Oh. Of course."

Reed shifted back to cautious mode as he lifted his body from the bench in deliberate, practiced movements. Swimming was a safe zone for Reed, but otherwise, talk came easier to him than motion, and his confidence followed suit.

Again, Pan matched Reed's pace on the leaf-covered trail. The delicious anticipation of their next encounter swirled around the two men all the way to Reed's car. Pan subdued the urge to take a taste of Reed's lips or even draw him into one of his exuberant hugs. If the gods were watching, they were no doubt amused when Pan offered his hand instead.

Reed returned the handshake with a firm grip.

"I really enjoyed our talk," Pan said. "Thank you for giving me a chance."

Reed studied Pan as their clasped hands stilled but stayed connected. "It occurs to me I have no idea what you do for a living."

A smile came over Pan. A bit of mystery was good for a man like Reed. Pan flexed his elbow, drawing Reed's body closer and leaning in as if to whisper a secret though they were alone. "Something to talk about tomorrow," Pan said, then released his grip.

Neither man moved a muscle. A puff of Reed's sweet breath wafted up Pan's nostrils. Reed wasn't panicked now, nor was he pulling away.

"See you at six thirty," Pan said. Reed's heated gaze could have burned two holes into Pan's back as it followed him to his truck. Pan turned to wave before climbing inside.

Reed waved back with a shy smile at having been caught staring. A pleasant buzz carried Pan out of the parking lot and back to the main road. *Too pleasant, perhaps?*

Shit!

Pan whipped out his phone and dialed Cupid.

24

WHAT TO HOPE FOR

"You're still here," Pan said, breathing a deep sigh of relief when Cupid answered his phone.

"Yes. How'd it go with Reed?"

"We made a date for tomorrow night."

"That's good, Pan!" Cupid sounded genuinely happy, which eased Pan's conscience a bit.

"Yeah, I thought so too. Kind of amazing he's come this far. We really could not be more different."

"Maybe you're not as different as you think." *Hmm*, cryptic.

"Are you trying to tell me there's something about Reed I'm missing?"

"I'm sure there's a lot we both don't know about Reed, but that's not what I meant. I was talking about you. Love has a way of reflecting what we might not have seen before."

Cupid was starting to sound like the philosophers he and Pan had always made fun of, droning on with their grandiose ideas about love and purpose. Pan would have liked to dismiss his friend's so-called wisdom, but there was a ring of truth he couldn't deny. Something had happened on that bench, even if Pan didn't quite understand it yet.

"How are you holding up, Q?"

"I'm fine."

"You're still the worst liar I've ever met," Pan answered and was met by a long sigh.

"I was hoping Reed would be there for me once I crossed you with your Worthy and the pain came crashing down."

"Dammit, Q. I'm still going to be here for you. Lean on me."

"Something tells me Reed won't be too pleased about you cuddling with me in bed while I cry all over you for days on end."

A Pan sandwich with Cupid on one side and Reed on the other was a nice visual. Pan didn't need to see into love's mirror to know he was being an asshole.

"I hate knowing I'm the cause of your pain. Hate it."

"It's not your fault," Q replied.

"I wish you'd stop saying that. *Fuck*."

A tortured silence held the space between them until Cupid spoke again. "It's possible the heartache won't happen this time. If you're my last test, and I succeed . . ."

"Careful what you wish for."

"I know. I don't feel like earth is home, exactly, but I can't imagine going back up to Olympus, stuck inside my old body again, made to follow all of Mother's rules like some dumb kid. No more sex, no more love for me."

It sounded thoroughly hideous, but at least Cupid would be spared staying here with a whole town of lovers paired up all around him.

"You could have an honest talk with your mother and try to renegotiate your situation at home. This could be a game changer for the two of you."

"Maybe. I don't even know what to hope for anymore. I do want you to be happy, Pan."

"Thanks, man. I know that. Hey, why don't you hang out with Euphrosyne tomorrow night while I'm with Reed—in case it happens then. Who knows, maybe you can loosen her up a bit?"

"I don't see how I can cheer anyone up right now, but I'll try."

Pan forced a smile into his voice. "That's the spirit, buddy."

"So, uh, if it turns out I'm stuck here after you two cross, will you still help me . . . with my next one?"

"Of course! I still have a job to do—"

"Right. Your *job*."

"C'mon, Q. I didn't mean it that way. My feelings toward you aren't going to change. I will always love you."

"Good luck, Pan." *Click.*

25

CHEERING UP

"It's not your fault, I promise," Cupid said, but Euphrosyne still sat frowning across the table.

Pan would have arrived at Reed's by now. Pan would be trying to fall in love; Reed would be trying not to. Mercury could appear any second now to take Cupid home.

"I know it's not my fault you're down in the dumps," she said, "but I'm supposed to be able to cheer you up. How about another piece of cornbread? I added two ears of fresh corn to the batter, and I used half-and-half instead of milk."

"Hmm? Oh, it's delicious. Thank you." Cupid didn't have the heart to tell her he wouldn't be needing any more of her cooking tips. There would be no more dates to impress with his home cooking, not where Cupid was going.

"You know, you're not the first devastated soul I've had to pick up from the side of the road after love barreled through." Euphrosyne was smiling kindly, but Cupid felt the sting.

"You mean to say after *I've* devastated them."

"Oh! Never on purpose," she answered. "Your skill is beginnings. Someone has to spark the flame."

Sure, setting fires was way more fun than sticking around to make sure everything didn't burn to the ground. Consequences had never been Cupid's concern.

Reading Cupid's scowl, Euphrosyne tried a different course. "But have I mentioned how much I love teaming up with you on the joyous endings?"

Though well-intentioned, Euphrosyne's comment inspired a vivid mental image of the two of them working opposite ends of the Augean stable. While Cupid stood near the oxen heads, whispering sweet words into their ears and hand-feeding fresh, bright alfalfa into their greedy mouths, Euphrosyne toiled away in high boots and thick gloves, mucking manure as quickly as three thousand oxen could produce it—a labor not even Hercules could complete without rerouting two rivers to carry away the filth.

"Drumstick?" A perfectly fried chicken leg hovered between silver tongs over Cupid's plate.

"No, thank you," he answered. "I really can't eat another bite." Then again, maybe if he kept stuffing his face, he'd be too heavy to ascend tonight.

"Well, I hope you saved room for dessert. I made triple decadence brownies, and I'm serving them with ice cream and hot fudge." She rose to take the dinner plates to the sink.

Cupid followed, ferrying the serving platters to the counter two at a time until the table was cleared. Despite his heavy heart, Cupid smiled. "You really went all out for me."

"Pan might have warned me you would have a particularly rough time tonight." So now Cupid was just another job for Euphrosyne, too.

"Pan was correct."

And if the trend from Mia to Ruthie were any indication, Cupid's heartache was going to get much, much worse before it got better. This was only the beginning.

Pan would be breaking through Reed's resistance about now. Soon, it would be Reed addicted to Pan's touch, his kiss, the way those warm, green eyes flared with passion and made him believe he was the only one who'd ever mattered.

The loud whistle of the teakettle broke Cupid's morose train of thought.

"How about a cup of tea while the fudge heats up?" Euphrosyne didn't wait for an answer before pouring the boiled water into two waiting teacups.

A prettily tied sachet tumbled under the stream of hot water and floated to the top of Cupid's cup, and he chased the bobbing bundle with his spoon. Cupid hadn't drunk tea before or after Mia, whose green tea bags came tied to a little paper tab that Cupid would use to dunk and dunk and dunk until Mia told him it was ready.

"Would you like some sugar with that?" Euphrosyne asked.

"If I didn't know better, I'd think you were trying to fatten me up."

Euphrosyne answered with a huff. "Has your body changed at all since you've fallen?"

"Nothing that lasts more than a couple of days"—a fact of his Earth life for which Cupid had been extremely grateful. This was a body he did not wish to change.

Euphrosyne slid the sugar bowl across the counter. "So you might as well enjoy yourself, yes?"

What harm could come of indulging the Grace? So what if Cupid was caught in this seemingly infinite loop of heartache; he didn't have to snare Euphrosyne in his misery. He heaped two spoons of sugar into his tea and brought the overly sweet drink to his lips. Jonah would have loved it this way. The fond memory of Mia's oldest son made Cupid smile.

"Do you mind if I ask you a question?" he asked.

"Do you mind if I stir the chocolate while you do?" Euphrosyne had already turned toward the pot on the cooktop. It occurred to Cupid that she was unaccustomed to waiting for permission.

He'd once been the same. Shooting his Love arrows was a solitary endeavor that didn't require collaboration. *Besides, who would object?* he might have reasoned before his fall. The experience of being in love had taught Cupid that answer most dramatically—which, he supposed, was the entire point.

"Did you forget your question?" Euphrosyne was grinning over her shoulder at Cupid.

"I was wondering what would have happened to all these people if I hadn't fallen. Would Mia have met her Patrick? What would have become of Ruthie and Zach? Do you think Pan would have been chosen as a Worthy?"

"Ah." Euphrosyne stirred thoughtfully, her back to Cupid again. "I notice you didn't ask if Reed would have been chosen."

And Cupid noticed she hadn't answered his question. "Reed seems an obvious pick, though I do wonder if he might have been matched with someone other than Pan if I hadn't crash-landed here when I did."

Euphrosyne stirred the pot for a short while longer, then turned to face Cupid, bringing the pot of melted fudge with her. "Do you feel Pan is unworthy of Reed?"

"Of course not! I've known forever how amazing Pan is. He's my best friend. It just seems . . ." Cupid paused and drew a deep breath. *The gods are listening.* "Doesn't it seem a bit coincidental to *you* that after two thousand years on Earth, the Goddess of Love should deem Pan a Worthy *right now* when her son happens to be caught up in the middle of a divine judgment right here in Pan's backyard?"

"Chocolate," Euphrosyne said, dipping her finger into the pot and bringing it to her lips with a loud, satisfied hum, "remains one of my very finest inventions, if I do say so myself."

"No argument here," Cupid said. "To think there are mortals who believe they came up with this idea on their own!"

"Oh"—Euphrosyne waved her hand as if pushing away a bothersome insect—"the moderns take credit for all kinds of things—jazz, penicillin, the wheel, Labradoodles . . . Shall I go on?"

"No need," Cupid replied. The two exchanged knowing grins.

"I don't mind. It's all just part of the job. I should think we're all used to it by now." She turned away to remove the brownies from the oven. "Would you get the ice cream, please?"

"Sure." Cupid opened the freezer, chuckling when he saw the variety of flavors Euphrosyne had purchased. "What kind?"

"Whatever makes you happy, obviously!"

"Obviously." He chose his newest favorite, mint chocolate chip, and shoveled out two big scoops to match the giant brownie squares Euphrosyne had plated.

With the pot held high, Euphrosyne drizzled a generous serving of hot fudge over their desserts. "How am I doing in the joy department?" she asked hopefully as Cupid took his first bite. "Anything?"

"I'm feeling slightly less miserable than when I arrived." Cupid mustered the best smile he could. "Thank you. This is delicious."

Euphrosyne gave him an appreciative nod and concentrated on loading up her spoon. "You think this connection between Reed and Pan is somehow about you?"

Lousy liar that he was, Cupid didn't bother to deny it. "If it is, then I'm glad I fell when I did. They both deserve to be happy."

And they would be, assuming Cupid could get them past

their Liminal Point. What would it take this time? Was it possible they'd never cross, that all three would be cursed to less of a life than they deserved?

"It's worth it, then?" Euphrosyne asked.

"What's that?"

"Falling in love. I never have, you know." Euphrosyne released a ladylike snort, more of a sniff. "Well, of course *you* know!" Another veiled accusation? Cupid couldn't make out the expression hidden behind the tower of ice cream and chocolate heading toward her mouth.

Truth was, Cupid had never considered the Graces eligible for his Love-tipped arrows. Certainly, there were few deities more deserving, but Olympus could ill afford anything getting in the way of the sister-Graces fulfilling their duties. Love was messy on a good day.

"Yes, it's worth it," Cupid replied. "Falling in love is worth everything."

Euphrosyne parted her lips for the fork, closed her mouth around the dessert, and released a wistful hum as she savored both the mound of hot fudge sundae and the sweet possibility of love.

Now that Cupid had heard Euphrosyne's yearning, leaving the Graces out seemed unnecessarily cruel. No one understood how it felt to be sidelined better than Cupid. As soon as he had the chance, he would make it up to Euphrosyne and her sisters.

And if yes to the Graces, then why not the Fates?

Now, *there* was a scary proposition. A heartbroken Lachesis apportioning a too-short thread of life ("What's the point anyway?") or a starry-eyed Atropos choosing not to snip the thread at its time ("How could I, when life is so beautiful?")? Woe to the archer who mucks up the allotters of life!

Cupid certainly had a lot to reconsider once he returned to the Mount.

26

CLEMENCY

Ares did not appreciate being summoned to a special Council meeting to discuss Euphrosyne—especially at Apollo's behest. Every moment spent in this stuffy chamber was an eternity away from Aphrodite's warm body.

Themis tapped her gavel on the olivewood table, and they went straight to business. "Gods and goddesses of the Council, I thank you for making time in your busy schedules to hear this petition for clemency in the Euphrosyne case. Apollo, please?"

"Yes, thank you, Lady Chairgoddess. Before I read the statement from Euphrosyne's sister-Graces, I wish to preface their remarks with a personal plea. As I'm sure we can all attest, the atmosphere on Mount Olympus has been noticeably lacking in joy since Euphrosyne's descent fifty-eight days ago."

Athena exchanged a meaningful glance with Themis. Dike, the goddess responsible for ensuring fair judgment, sat up straighter in her chair. Generally speaking, unhappiness was not a justification for commuting a sentence. Personally, Ares couldn't have cared one way or another about Euphrosyne's fate, but it was always entertaining to watch Apollo squirm. Perhaps this meeting wouldn't be a complete snoozer after all.

The God of Light pressed on. "But it's worse than that. The goddesses of good cheer and splendor are unable to function effectively without their sister-Grace at their side. Two cannot dance in a circle meant for three. I ask you all, would you have Clotho spin the thread of life and Atropos cut the thread without Lachesis to allot its length?"

Heads shook.

"No."

"Impossible."

"Out of the question."

"Of course not!" Apollo continued, emboldened. "Three Fates act as one, as do our beloved Graces. Now far be it from me to question the Queen's authority, *especially* where Hera suffered personally due to Euphrosyne's failure to induce an acceptable level of mirth." Ares's snigger was conspicuously ignored. "Naturally, the Council stands behind Hera's verdict and sentence . . . *in spirit*."

Themis's pen halted abruptly. Here, just shy of heresy, Apollo paused, looked around the table, and gathered his strength to finish. Poor Dike had colored a bilious shade of yellow. Ares crossed his arms over his chest and reclined in his seat.

"I would simply ask my fellow Council members to consider the reality of our current situation, to balance"—Apollo gestured at the ivory scales of wisdom inlaid at the center of the olive-wood table—"the offense lodged by the complainant, Hera, with the certainty that all of Mount Olympus would be better off with Euphrosyne returned to the circle of merriment and mirth beside her two sisters."

Well played, Ares grudgingly acknowledged. Certainly, Apollo had the most to gain from the return of his beloved attendant to her place at his court, but he'd presented his case most artfully, appealing to the self-interests of the assembly while providing the altruistic justification they might later need to produce.

Apollo cleared his throat and read from the paper in front of him: "Gods and goddesses of the Divine Council, we, Thalia and Aglaia, hereby enter an official plea for leniency in administering the sentence imposed upon our sister-Grace, Euphrosyne. First, we offer our own most sincere and respectful apologies to the goddess Hera for our sister's unintended failing. Further, we ask you to consider the upcoming Puanepsia and Oskhophoria festivals. It is our duty and most fervent wish as goddesses of good cheer and splendor to secure the divine blessings for the autumn sowing of seeds and grapes, but without our sister's spirit of mirth to complete our circle, we find ourselves lacking in the requisite level of joy our beloved Apollo"—here, Apollo attempted to sound particularly official—"and Dionysus so richly deserve. Furthermore, as we two are diminished without Euphrosyne, so is she ill-equipped to produce mirth on Earth without her sisters. We beg you, therefore, to turn a gentle heart toward our sister and accept her penance with the knowledge that her efforts are the most generous offerings of a splintered soul. Most respectfully submitted, Thalia and Aglaia."

"Thank you, Apollo, for bringing this critical matter to the fore," said Themis. "Discussion?" As was her custom, Themis looked first to Athena, and the Goddess of Wisdom obliged.

"The Graces make an excellent point about the diminished ability of any one of a triad. In all fairness," Athena argued, "there is a certain built-in bias we should factor in when considering Euphrosyne's performance."

"Noted." Both Themis and Dike appeared relieved at Athena's endorsement. "Other thoughts?"

Dike offered her opinion next. "In light of the special circumstances surrounding this case, I would support a relaxed application of the law." Apollo shot her a look of gratitude, then spun toward Ares's voice entering the debate.

"And, of course, nobody wants Apollo's banquet to suck wind."

"Which goes without saying," Themis deadpanned. "Perhaps you would like to suggest a revised benchmark, Ares?"

"Something less rigorous than entertaining a roomful of people, apparently. It's clear the attempt at comedy was a bomb." And if Ares had to sit through another performance like the last one, he would not be adding water to his wine the next time.

"It's not the first time we've observed our humor doesn't translate well," Athena commented.

Turning toward the Chairgoddess again, Apollo said, "If I may?"

"*Please.*"

"What if Euphrosyne were to bring one noticeably joyous moment into the life of a single mortal?"

"Just *one* moment for *one* mortal?" Dike asked anxiously, her gaze rolling around the table. "Will that be enough to satisfy . . . the spirit of the law?"

Don't you mean, Will Hera eat me in my sleep? Ares couldn't fault the goddess for her trepidation. His mother could be quite the vindictive bitch when crossed.

Athena stood; the room quieted. Ares felt a flutter of anticipation in his belly, one tactician to another. Athena was a brilliant war strategist who understood how to apply her skills on an interpersonal level, a finesse Ares admittedly did not possess—as Aphrodite had pointed out numerous times in recent weeks. Yes, Athena could be a softy at times, even known to act irrationally over the occasional love interest—Who among them hadn't?—but she was a fierce warrior goddess who fought for what she wanted, and Ares admired that in her.

"I believe we can afford to let compassion guide us in this case," Athena said. "This is a first offense for Euphrosyne. Where the pain and suffering are automatically triplicated, I move that we adopt Apollo's revised standard and close out Euphrosyne's case as quickly as possible."

"All in favor of adopting Athena's motion?"

All four gods raised their hands. Ares could have voted against the petition out of spite, but what purpose would that have served? He would have looked small and been outvoted anyway. This way, Apollo owed him one.

"Motion passes. Thank you, Apollo. Please send word back to the Graces."

"Yes, of course," Apollo said, a healthy color filling his cheeks once again. "Thank you, all." Apollo's expression turned sheepish when his gaze finally landed on Ares, who returned a broad, toothy grin.

And now to hunt down Aphrodite for an emergency strategy session. Power really was the greatest aphrodisiac.

27

ANIMAL MAGNETISM

Reed's address was a surprise. The rural sprawl of sparsely situated homes set back from the main road by long, unpaved driveways was the exact opposite of the perfectly manicured section of town where Ruthie and Zach lived, where even the road medians were irrigated and hand-weeded. If you didn't mind being isolated, you could get a lot of land for your money out here.

Reed could have chosen any number of neighborhoods within a shorter commute of his work, but as Pan had learned yesterday, it was here at the end of a long, dirt drive that Reed had staked his claim when he moved to Tarra for the job at the university, and it was right here he'd stayed.

All things being equal, Pan might well have chosen this part of town for himself. It wasn't any great love for humanity that had lured him from the woods into the vast suburban in-between. Experience had taught him to stay close to his fallens, and with few exceptions, they'd needed to serve out their sentences where they could interact with mortals. Over time, Pan had prioritized the convenience of living closer to the more densely populated areas over the nature he loved. He'd turned into a city dweller by small increments with each successive move until he no longer sought out the more remote locations.

Pan's nerves jangled as he checked his reflection in the rearview mirror before palming the bottle of Duckhorn and exiting his truck. He couldn't remember the last time he'd been so anxious about a date that he'd bothered to run a comb through his hair. He'd also trimmed his beard as close to his face as he dared; any drastic appearance changes were dead giveaways as they, like flesh wounds, reverted within a few days to what Pan had come to think of as his "factory settings." For better or for worse, this was the body he lived in.

Pan inhaled the cool October countryside into his lungs—heady odors of fertilizer, chickens, and dogs. He had a private chuckle remembering Pookie, Ruthie's annoying little furball that wouldn't leave Pan's side.

Either Pan was first to arrive, or Reed's family members didn't require vehicles. Pan checked his watch again—right on time. He had an inkling the professor wouldn't appreciate tardiness.

He smoothed a hand down his crisp, blue button-down—tucked in, for a change, into rarely worn khaki slacks—and was wishing he hadn't been so cavalier about skipping the sport coat when the front door opened.

That pleasant buzz came back as Pan's gaze rolled down the man leaning against the door frame, more relaxed than Pan had seen him yet. Pan wouldn't have pegged Reed for the jeans type, but he filled them out nicely. All those hours flutter-kicking in the pool—and years of running before that—had resulted in thighs that gave his jeans something to hold on to, even if one leg hadn't pulled its weight in quite some time. He wore a thin, black V-neck sweater over a white polo. Nothing daring, but each piece was well suited to Reed's narrow physique.

Reed folded his arms over his chest, drawing Pan's gaze along the forearms and biceps and higher, to Reed's grinning face. *Oops.* Pan was still getting used to seeing Reed in his dark-rimmed glasses. The sexy professor vibe was working for him.

"You clean up well," said Reed.

"You've already seen me in my Speedo. Thought I'd try classing it up a bit." But not without reminding Reed of what was under those khakis. "Speaking of which . . ."

Pan presented the cabernet along his arm like a sommelier while Reed studied the label, his eyes widening with recognition.

"Very nice."

"Does that mean I can come in?" Pan asked.

"You wound me," Reed joked, hand to his heart. "Come in, come in." Reed waved him inside and through to the kitchen, where two wineglasses sat waiting on the counter.

"How many people did you say were in your family?"

Reed caught on to Pan's question. "Four, but they're not wine drinkers."

Reed opened the bottle with practiced grace and poured a taste into one glass. "Would you like to do the honors?" he asked, offering the glass to Pan.

"Be my guest." Pan hung back as Reed swished the wine around his glass, dipped his nose over the edge for a deep inhale, savored a sip, and expressed his approval with a soft hum—not that Pan was worried. Dionysus did not collect defective bottles.

"*Ahhh.* That's going to be beautiful once it opens up." Reed filled Pan's glass before topping off his own. "Here's to new friends with good taste."

"To open-minded family members!" Pan replied.

Reed chuckled, a twinkle in his hazel eyes. "They're actually waiting rather impatiently out back to meet you."

"Ah." Pan hoped he didn't sound as terrified as he felt.

"Will you be warm enough?" Reed asked.

"Yes, thanks for asking." Such a small question, but when was the last time anyone had looked after Pan's needs? Not that Pan needed looking after that way, but Reed couldn't know that.

Pan followed him to the door on the opposite end of the kitchen, taking a deep breath as he stepped outside.

"Meet my family," Reed said, then hung back as four dogs all beat a path straight for Pan.

Two large, dark-haired shepherds were edged out by a pair of exuberant, scraggly-haired pups that didn't quite reach Pan's knees in height. All four crowded in, sniffing and loving on Pan and demanding his attention. Pan offered his hand and was slathered by slobbery tongues. It was worth it for Reed's reaction, a mixture of amusement and surprise.

"Wow! They like you!"

"You seem shocked. Should I be insulted?"

"Sorry," Reed said, chuckling. "It's just that they're usually tougher on people."

"*Hmm*, must be my animal magnetism." Pan squatted to accept the wet kisses on his face. If the way to Reed's heart was through these dogs, Pan wasn't too proud to use his advantage.

"I guess so." That was most definitely awe in Reed's voice, but something else as well . . . something troubling.

"Reed? Are you disappointed your dogs didn't knock me out of the running?"

"No," Reed answered too quickly.

Pan cocked a bullshit brow. "You sure about that?"

Reed shrugged. "Maybe? I guess it would have been easier." He seemed both dumbfounded and dismayed by his own confession.

Pan straightened, ignoring the demands of the dogs to give Reed his complete attention. "Hey, don't sweat it, man."

Reed held Pan's gaze while an unspoken understanding passed between them. This ordeal was scary. Reed was a man who lived inside a carefully constructed comfort zone, and Pan challenged every boundary. Hell, even with the inside knowledge of goddess-ordained Right Love, Pan was scared shitless too.

"I hope you know it's nothing personal," Reed said.

"How could it be? You don't even know me."

"*Yet*," Reed added, pointing a finger at Pan. A hint of a smile played at Reed's lips. Pan took that as a good sign.

"You know," Pan said, "I could have spared you the suspense."

"How so?"

"Dogs and cats are always drawn to me." Pan failed to add he was that guy in the room who wanted nothing to do with them.

"I see." Reed suppressed a smirk. "You don't have a fur baby of your own?"

"Fur baby? Uh, that'd be a no." From Reed's expression, Pan might just have told him he'd eaten a kitten for lunch. "I move around a lot. And I keep inconsistent hours at my job."

"Well, you're a natural," Reed said.

And there was Reed again, too close to the truth for comfort. "Mind if I ask how you ended up with so many?" Pan asked.

One of the bigger dogs Pan was ignoring nudged Reed's hand with his nose. Without looking down or even appearing to be aware, Reed easily located the dog's happy spot and lavished such loving strokes that Pan nearly swooned at the thought of being on the receiving end of the man's touch.

"This pretty girl is a Beauceron. A friend of mine is a breeder. He convinced me the dogs make great running partners . . . and he was right." Reed smiled at the memory, but the pain behind it tugged at Pan's heart. "Before I met Margaux here, I had a beautiful Beauce named Socrates."

Pan cracked a smile. "Socrates was your dog's name? Seriously?" *Wait till I tell Q about that one.*

"I can't tell you how many miles Socks and I logged together in these woods." Reed glanced longingly into the opening between the trees. "When I couldn't run anymore, poor Socrates wasn't himself, so we added Margaux to the family." He ran his hand over Margaux's back. "And when Socks passed, Margaux needed a new companion. She and Andre have been fast friends ever since."

"And what about these two?" Pan rolled the two grayish-white pups around, laughing as they tumbled over each other, scurried onto their paws, and raced back to him for more.

"Pyrenean Shepherds, bred to protect—sheep, specifically, but humans will do in a pinch. The puppies need a lot of exercise and supervision, especially around young children. Bo Peep, here"—Reed pointed to the smaller of the two—"was given up for adoption after about a week with a family that didn't understand the breed. Sad, but it happens a lot. And Moses showed up a few weeks after I took in Bo."

Pan grinned. "Just happened to wander by, huh?"

Reed shrugged. "The shelter knows I'm a sucker for a pretty face."

"Lucky me," Pan said, flashing Reed a goofy smile.

An alarmed expression crossed Reed's face as he struggled to respond.

Pan rolled his eyes and gave Reed a little *thwap*. "That was me being funny."

Reed was visibly relieved. "Anyway, I know I shouldn't keep taking them in since I can't work them properly, but they have one another and three acres. I think they're happy."

"They're definitely loved." Pan couldn't stop watching Reed's hands move over the dogs. They couldn't get enough of him.

"I have yet to meet an animal I didn't like better than most humans. No offense intended."

"And none taken." Well, at least one aspect of this pairing made sense now. What better "human" for Reed than one who was part animal? "Any other family members I should know about?"

"I have a chicken coop around the side yard." Yes, Pan smelled them. Not his favorite creatures, but he'd deal. "I used to keep goats," Reed added.

Pan swallowed hard. "Used to? What happened to them?"

Reed laughed and shook his head. "The goats were a steep learning curve. I have to admit I went into the enterprise grossly underprepared."

"That doesn't sound like you."

"I led with my heart," Reed said, an adorable blush rushing to his cheeks. "Big mistake. The females are loud, and they need to be bred once a year to produce milk. The males have to be neutered."

Pan fought an instinct to cover his crotch. "That seems a bit harsh."

"Heh. Not as harsh as what happens if you don't. It's godawful—they pee on themselves, on their food, everywhere. I shouldn't trouble you with the gory details when we're about to eat dinner."

"Couldn't you just let the goats roam free?" Pan asked.

"Not out here with the cats and bears. They wouldn't be safe. And don't get me started on the pen. They're like four-footed magicians. If they can get their head through a hole in the fence, that's it! They're as good as free."

"What about that fence?" Pan asked, pointing to a pretty wood lattice wall along the garden. "That looks like it would hold them."

"See those roses?" Reed said.

"Yes."

"You wouldn't if I still kept goats back here."

"Flowers are overrated." Pan was unable to keep the sour note out of his voice.

"My last girlfriend didn't think so."

"You chose the girl and the roses and kicked out the goats?"

Reed shot him a quizzical look. "Don't you think you're taking this kind of hard?"

Whoops.

"I don't see any girls here now." Pan looked around, just to make sure.

"True. I thought about that too," Reed confessed with a grin, "but it wouldn't be fair. Goats need a lot of interaction. They love to play. I feel bad enough about not being able to run the dogs anymore."

"I love a good run through the woods."

Pan was pleased to note that Reed took his comment for exactly what it was—an offer. Reed had been crystal clear that Pan would be out if the dogs didn't like him, but would he risk letting the dogs become attached?

Pan sipped at his wine and practiced being patient. Reed was a challenge.

"You know," Reed said after a bit, "I think they would like that very much."

"Thank you, Reed. That means a lot to me." Pan raised his glass, and Reed clinked it with his.

"Mind if we sit down?"

"Of course," Pan said, following him to the table and chairs.

"Must be all this talk of running," Reed joked. He sat down with a sigh. "I miss it sometimes, you know? I don't want to give the impression I feel sorry for myself. That's not who I am. Swimming saved me, and I'm grateful for everything I can do, and I honestly don't dwell on the 'poor me.' Once in a while, though, I just miss feeling the ground under my feet and that sense of flying when you really get going. And now, meeting you?" Reed stared into Pan's eyes as if testing the waters in earnest for the first time. "How great would it be to take a run together?"

Reed, Pan, and the dogs. *It would be glorious.* Pan held Reed tightly in his gaze.

"But this body just can't," Reed said.

Pan nodded once. "I get it. My body used to get in the way of what I really wanted."

"*You?*" Reed allowed his eyes to wander down Pan's chest. "What could possibly be wrong with your body?"

"Nothing—now." Pan was quick to reassure him. "Let's just say I spent my formative years getting rejected."

"Ouch."

"It's okay," Pan said with a wink. "I've more than made up for it."

Reed's gaze skittered away, his unspoken question buzzing in the air between them.

"Ask me," Pan said.

Reed twirled his glass on the table while he summoned the boldness to meet Pan's eyes again. "Okay. Are you, uh, only interested in men?"

"No," Pan answered easily. "But at the moment, I'm only interested in you."

At Pan's declaration, Reed's mood shifted noticeably—*shit just got real*—but there was more to it than desire. Pan sensed Reed's apprehension—not enough to arouse the dogs' interest but more than enough to put Pan on high alert. He had a decent understanding of the conflict Reed was working through right now.

Reed raised his glass to his lips, buying himself some time to sort out his feelings.

While Pan was confident he could lead Reed through the nitty-gritty of man-on-man, there was the long run to consider, and that took Pan way out of his wheelhouse. The blind was now officially leading the blind.

But Reed needed something from Pan right now, and Pan wasn't about to let him down.

"If it helps any, having, *ahem*, extensive experience in this area, I can promise you it's not all that different from being with a woman. Aside from the obvious."

Reed huffed. "To be perfectly frank, it's 'the obvious' that freaks me out. I just wanted you to know in case that was a deal-breaker."

"It's not," Pan assured him. Freaked out or not, Reed's body had been responding all along to Pan. He wasn't worried.

"You don't mind if we don't"—Reed's gaze flickered away—"get physical?"

"Oh, I mind plenty, but I'm in no rush." Pan finished off his wine, wishing he'd had the foresight to bring the bottle outside.

"Ah, the conceit of youth. I remember it well," Reed said. "You think you're invincible, you'll live forever. You know what they say about death and taxes."

"Yes, I've heard."

"Sorry." Reed shook his head, eyes downcast, frustrated with himself. "I'm afraid I sound like a bitter, old man."

Pan reached across the table and covered Reed's hand with his own. Reed's head popped up to meet Pan's gaze. "No, Reed. You sound like a man who met up with a harsh circumstance, but you haven't let that define you. You've kept an open mind, invited a perfect stranger into your home—"

"Don't remind me," Reed said with a sly grin.

"You've given me a chance to win you over. Given *love* a chance. That's no small thing, my friend." Pan chanced a squeeze of Reed's hand and felt the man's pulse quicken.

Reed cleared his throat. "You were very convincing."

"I've seen the evidence. Q's success rate is nothing to sneeze at."

"Just out of curiosity, did you two know you weren't 'meant to be' or whatever when you started dating?"

"We did," Pan answered. "Not every successful coupling ends in wedding bells and vows, if you know what I mean."

"Okay, true, but somehow I get the feeling there's way more between the two of you than you're letting on."

Pan nodded. Reed was a smart guy. "I'll cop to a bit of wishful thinking—"

"Aha!"

"—but we both knew we were just killing time."

"I see." He didn't, but he was sure as shit trying to. Pan could respect that.

Pan heard a car turn off the main road and start down Reed's driveway. It occurred to him there might be some human family members stopping by to check him out. "Were you expecting someone else?" Pan asked.

Reed checked his watch, genuinely puzzled. "Huh?"

"I thought I heard a car in the driveway."

Reed pushed himself out of the chair. "I'll go check."

"Would you be offended if I wash my hands before we head out for dinner?"

Reed boomed out a laugh. "I'd be slightly horrified if you didn't."

28

THE TRUTH

Reed opened the front door, answering Cupid's immediate question—where had his heart signal led him this time?—but it seemed Reed was equally confused as his gaze bounced from Cupid to Euphrosyne and back. "What the—wait! Don't tell me!"

Cupid blinked back at him. "Don't tell you what?"

"You've brought me another last-minute substitution?" Cupid was wrong. That wasn't confusion on Reed's face. It was irritation, bordering on anger.

Cupid was in no shape to sort out Reed's puzzling reaction after the painful drive over. "Is Pan here?"

Reed folded his arms over his chest, effectively blocking the doorway. "Why? Have you changed your mind about letting him go? Think you'll pull another switcheroo just when we've started to get to know each other?"

"No, Reed. Nothing like that." Cupid knew he should be happy that Reed was so fiercely protecting his time with Pan, but he hated that his new friend was feeling so betrayed.

"Then what are you doing here?" A perfectly fair question Cupid had no reasonable answer for.

Just then, Pan came up behind Reed, placed a hand on his shoulder, and poked his head around. "Q. Euph."

Reed rounded on Pan. "Why are you not surprised to see him?"

The truthful answer would have been, "Because I smelled him from the opposite end of the house," but Pan opted for, "He has a habit of turning up," which was also valid. "So, friends, to what do we owe this pleasure?"

"I'm not really sure," Cupid answered carefully.

A glint of recognition flared in Pan's eyes. At least he knew where to place the blame for the intrusion.

"You're not about to . . .?" He jerked his chin toward the sky.

Reed was looking awfully territorial toward Pan, who was looking awfully touchy-feely with Reed. Had they crossed? Didn't feel like it.

"I'm sorry to bother you both. Euphrosyne and I were just finishing dinner when I felt like I needed to . . . go somewhere."

"I understand," Pan said, turning to Euphrosyne. "Everything all right with you?"

"I had to leave half of my brownie fudge sundae uneaten, but other than that, I'm fine."

"You better come in," Pan said.

Reed cleared his throat, not moving an inch to clear a path. "Actually, we were just leaving for dinner."

"I know we were," Pan replied, appealing gently to Reed, "but this is part of his process."

"Invading our date?" Pan couldn't help but grin, which only flustered Reed anew. "You know what I mean!"

Pan leaned in and murmured in Reed's ear. "Maybe it's already working."

Reed rolled his eyes, then turned back to his unwanted guests. "Won't you both come in?"

Reed led them through the kitchen to a patio outside where four dogs went berserk, jumping on Cupid and barking at Euphrosyne, who had ducked behind him. Pan moved to Reed's side, purposely drawing the dogs toward them using soothing tones, much to Cupid's astonishment. He had certainly never welcomed Pookie's attention like that.

"They won't hurt you," Pan explained. "They just think they need to protect us."

Pan and Reed were already an "us." This was happening. Then why had the gods driven Cupid here if everything was going fine? Maybe Pan could shed some light.

"Reed, would you mind if Pan and I spoke privately for a minute?"

Reed's anxious gaze traveled from Cupid to Pan. "I don't suppose I have a choice."

Offering a reassuring smile, Pan squeezed Reed's arm. "Let me take care of this. I'll be right back. Euphrosyne will entertain you in the meantime. Just don't tell him any of those horrible jokes of yours," Pan said, wagging his finger at the Grace.

"Hey, that's not fair. I have some new material," Euphrosyne said. "Have you heard the one about the three priests who go to the strip club?"

With an exaggerated eye roll, Pan yanked Cupid by the elbow and dragged him inside past Reed and into a cozy, book-lined room. "Okay, they've revved your heart and sent you here. The only question is, to help or to delay this union?"

"Delay?" Cupid moaned. "I can't sit around like this for much longer, waiting for something to happen between you."

"How long does this part usually take?"

"There's no 'usually.' It's different every time. There has to be something that signals you're meant for each other."

"I can tell he's interested."

"Have you kissed yet?"

"No. He's not ready for that."

"When do you think he'll be ready?"

Pan glared at him. "We were getting somewhere before you two barged in."

"Not my choice."

"I know," Pan said, scratching his head. "What do you want me to do, go out there and kiss him?"

"No. What good's a stolen kiss? If you attack him, he'll just think you're a jerk, and you'll set the whole thing back."

"Let me think," Pan said, pacing back and forth. "He's definitely anxious about the whole guy-on-guy thing."

"Yes, he was just warming to the idea of trying with me, even if he was a bit confused about why. And then I had to break it off." That horrible conversation at the pool yesterday. If Reed had only known how painful it had been for Cupid to walk away.

"Poor guy doesn't know what's hit him."

"Maybe that's the problem," said Cupid.

"I don't follow."

"How do you expect him to love the real you if he doesn't know who you are?"

"You're suggesting I tell Reed my true identity?"

Cupid shrugged.

"What makes you think he would even believe me?"

"I really don't know, Pan, but Reed is a man of integrity and honesty, and you are keeping a rather large secret from him."

"Do I need to remind you why we keep these secrets?"

"No, you do not." Cupid's heart knocked against his chest, lest they forget why they were all here.

Pan sighed. "You and I would have been so easy together."

"I get that it's not easy, Pan. It wasn't easy for Mia to trust another man. It wasn't easy for Ruthie and Zach to admit they were losing each other."

"This 'Worthy' thing is for the birds."

"If it were me, Pan . . ." Cupid spoke slowly and clearly to make sure Pan heard him this time. "If *either of you* were meant for me, I can't think of anything I wouldn't do."

Pan hung his head. "Okay, I get it, I get it. Look, I'd gotten Reed to the point where he's accepted you're a matchmaker, and he was willing to give this a try. You're telling me now I've got to tell him everything?"

Cupid shrugged. "I don't know. He did invite you into his home. There's a certain level of trust in that."

"He told me I was meeting his family."

"Well, there you go."

Pan barked out a booming laugh. "Right. I'll just take Reed home to meet my family."

Reed stepped through the door just then, trailing dogs and Euphrosyne behind him. "Hey, I get it," he said sadly.

"What? What do you get?" Pan asked.

"Why you would be embarrassed to introduce me to your family."

Pan snorted. "Mortified is more like it."

"I'm sure I'm nothing like the other men you've brought home."

Pan turned to face Reed, taking both hands into his. "Reed, I've never brought anyone home. It's not you. It's them. You have to trust me when I tell you the term 'dysfunctional' doesn't begin to cover my family tree." Pan let out a frustrated groan. "It's crazy we're talking about this right now. We barely know each other."

Cupid seized his chance to speak up. "Exactly my point."

Reed slumped into one of his overstuffed reading chairs, and the other three followed suit. "May I ask what you get out of this? Pan told me he didn't ask you to do this, and I know I didn't. So why? Just answer me that, please."

Pan answered. "It's just who he is. He can't help it."

"That's *partly* true," Cupid added, tired of the half-truths.

Reed replied. "I'm listening."

Cupid looked to Pan. They both had much to lose, and Cupid wouldn't go ahead without Pan's consent. Pan lifted his eyes toward the gods and sighed loudly, then tipped his hand in invitation. Cupid didn't give him a chance to change his mind.

"I'm being punished."

"By whom?" Reed looked at Pan and Euphrosyne, who were staring unflinchingly at Cupid.

"My mother, mostly." It still hurt to admit it, but there was little question Aphrodite was making it more challenging for Cupid to get home.

"Aren't you a little old for that?"

Pan guffawed, then made a lame attempt to cover his mouth with the back of his hand. Cupid shot him a potent glare.

"Be that as it may," Cupid continued with all the pride he could manage, "I don't have a choice in the matter. I'm here until I serve out my sentence to the satisfaction of the Divine Council."

"Here in Indiana?"

"Here on Earth."

Reed's eyes popped wide open.

Pan muttered, "Heeeere we go," under his breath.

"Divine Council? I've never heard of them. Is that some sort of religious group?"

Euphrosyne stood. "Reed, can I pour you a drink? Do you have any brandy? Grain alcohol?" She left the table to search his cabinets.

Cupid answered Reed as best he could. "I don't think it's what you call religion down here." He looked to Pan for help.

He'd tried with Mia, and she'd decided the gods were products of the poets. Clearly, Cupid didn't know how to describe their world to mortals.

Pan jumped in. "The Divine Council is basically the judicial branch. They represent the pantheon—"

"*The* pantheon?" Reed asked. "As in, the gods of ancient mythology?"

"'Mythology' isn't the word we use, but yes," Pan explained. "It got to be too clunky for all the gods and goddesses to weigh in on every punishment meted out, so they elected a subgroup to manage the fallens."

"Are you saying you three are fallen gods?"

"*We* are," Cupid said, indicating himself and Euphrosyne. "Pan's not really a fallen anymore if you take into account—"

"Whoa." Reed pressed his fingers to his temples. "Is the room spinning, or is it just me?"

Pan leaned in and placed his arm around Reed's shoulders. "I realize this is a lot to take in. It wasn't really my choice to lay all this on you at once. I've never told another mortal who I really am. I must apologize for my friend here. He's on somewhat of a schedule."

"On account of the punishment by his mother, the goddess."

"Yes," Cupid answered, "and Ares, of course."

"Of course," repeated Reed. "And your mother would be . . .?"

"Aphrodite."

Pan moaned, but Reed stuck with it. "Aphrodite, Goddess of Love, mother of Eros."

Cupid smiled broadly. "Yes, but I prefer Cupid."

"Q, short for Cupid!" Reed's voice grew louder as he put the pieces together—or lost his mind. "The matchmaker! That makes sense."

Cupid nodded. "Yes." What a relief to have it all out in the open now.

Reed turned to Pan. "You're shitting me."

Pan shrugged. "I told you he was good at his job."

"Isn't he supposed to have wings?"

"This is my Earth form," Cupid answered, drawing Reed's attention again.

"I see," Reed said thoughtfully. "Well, I'd have to say it's working for you."

"Thank you," Cupid replied as Pan shot him a murderous glare.

Reed pressed on with his questions. "What about your bow and arrow?"

"They're at Pan's house for safekeeping."

"But don't you need them to—" With a sharp gasp, Reed brought both hands to his chest and began tapping around. "*Wait!* Did you—?"

"No." Pan squeezed in closer and tightened his grip around Reed's shoulders. "No, Reed. He didn't."

Reed's frantic search slowed. He glanced up to meet Pan's reassuring gaze. "No?"

"Q would never take a chance like that," Pan said. "We have no idea what might happen if Cupid were to shoot anyone while he is down here." Pan failed to mention he had begged Cupid to shoot him with that arrow just five days ago. "You're completely safe, Reed."

"Completely safe"—Reed's hand fell away from his chest as he slipped out of Pan's grasp—"says Pan, the satyr."

Pan's expression fell. All the shame and rejection and despair of his long, miserable existence as a satyr filled Pan's green eyes to the brim. A lump formed in Cupid's throat.

Reed shook his head in amazement. "My dogs figured it out before I did."

"I'm not a satyr anymore, Reed." Cupid could hear the effort it took Pan to push the sentence out.

"No, I can see that," Reed said. "But what are you, exactly?"

"I'm just what you see. I'm a man," Pan answered.

"Actually, he's a demigod," Cupid added, earning a scowl from Pan.

"No need to split hairs," Pan said.

But there was, Cupid knew, because the smallest of lies could drive a wedge between two people—even two Right Loves just trying to protect each other from pain.

"Gods and demigods walking around town like the rest of us . . ." Reed followed the thread of logic, shaking his head and mumbling to himself. "It's a wonder I haven't bumped into Poseidon at the pool. Or have I?"

"You haven't. Poseidon is not in trouble right now," Euphrosyne added helpfully. She pressed a dark drink into Reed's hands. "Here. This might help."

"Bless your heart." Reed looked hard at her. "Would you be Euphrosyne of the three Charites?"

"Actually, my sisters and I adopted the Roman 'Graces' during the Syncretism."

"You mean a *literal* syncretism of the Greek and Roman systems?" Poor Reed. Just when he'd begun to make some sense of them all.

Euphrosyne shot a puzzled look at Pan, who answered, "Why don't you tell the story since you were there?"

Pulling out the chair to sit beside Reed, Euphrosyne began to explain. "After the Greeks suffered defeat at the Battle of Corinth, morale sank to an all-time low on Mount Olympus. The Romans overwrote our stories and damaged all credibility with the mortals. For six centuries, the gods languished while worship and offerings all but died out."

"Sounds rough," Reed observed. "How did you all manage to eat up there for 600 years without animal sacrifices?"

Poor Reed. He wanted to believe them, but to do so would unravel a lifetime of logic and intellectual pursuits. Cupid and Pan exchanged anxious glances, but Euphrosyne kept talking.

"When Romulus Augustus became emperor at the age of fourteen, that was the last straw. After ousting Romulus, Zeus put in place a—"

"Whoa, whoa, whoa!" Reed's hands flailed. "You're trying to tell me it was Zeus, not Odoacer, who deposed the emperor?"

All three divines cringed. Zeus did not appreciate others, especially mortals, receiving credit for His victories.

"That's right," replied Euphrosyne. "The forces at work are rarely visible to mortals. As a species, your understanding of history is quite skewed."

Reed pulled his drink to his lips and silently gulped down half the contents of the glass. "Is that so?"

Euphrosyne gave him a gentle smile. "Zeus decided the best way to regain the awe and respect of the mortals was to merge all the stories floating around about us. Where there were conflicting details, our names being the most obvious, the gods were empowered to choose what made it into the canon."

"The gods?" Reed guffawed. "What about the poets who *invented* the gods? Hesiod's *Theogony*?"

Euphrosyne blinked hard at Reed. "Surely you know it was the gods who created the poets"—Reed's eyebrows shot up at the same time his mouth dropped open, transforming his face into one, long question mark—"and the Muses who put the words into their heads."

"Says the Grace who fell from grace!"

Laughter bubbled up and out of Reed like a fountain getting its first uneven blast of water. He smacked his drink down on the table as the laughter shook his shoulders and sent tears rolling down his cheeks.

"I made someone laugh!" Euphrosyne exclaimed, her face lit with joy for the first time since her fall.

Mercury zipped into Reed's study, stole Euphrosyne into his arms, and disappeared.

Reed stopped laughing long enough to ask, "Where did she go?"

"Home," Pan said, sharing a private moment of victory with Cupid.

Cupid pointed up, and Reed followed his finger to the ceiling. "Mount Olympus."

Reed downed the remainder of his drink and tipped his head back against his chair. "I have a few more questions," he said.

Pan let out a bark of laughter. "I'd be horrified if you didn't."

29

Q & A

"Are you sure I can't get you something to eat with your whiskey? There must be some crackers in here somewhere," said Pan—the former satyr, if these creatures were to be believed—as he opened and closed every cabinet in sight.

"Thanks anyway, but I think that ship has sailed." Still, it was nice to see the virile young man scavenging about his kitchen and attempting to fill Reed's belly with carbs. "Go ahead and help yourself to whatever you like, though. Something tells me we're not going to make it to the restaurant tonight."

Pan craned his neck to check on Cupid, who was anxiously perched on Reed's living room sofa. "I'm sorry, Reed. I just can't leave him alone right now."

"No, I get it." Reed had seen Euphrosyne vanish right before his eyes, and Pan had explained that Cupid was likely to be taken from them in the same manner, possibly never to be heard from again.

These last two weeks since meeting Cupid had given Reed the dizzying sensation of sliding down a rabbit hole, so he wasn't actually as surprised as he probably should have been to find himself living inside the stories he'd studied and taught for so many years. Truth be told, Pan's explanations made more sense than any other scenario Reed had come up with to justify the insertion of these two strangers into his life.

Reed's whiskey-muddled brain couldn't remember any Eros-Pan myths that would explain the unlikely pairing of the archer and the satyr, but a person would have to be devoid of emotional intelligence to miss the close bond between the two. Reed's house vibrated with their energy. And yet, they'd both insisted it was Reed who was the "right love" for Pan, whatever the hell that meant.

"You know," Reed said, "if our being together is going to make you lose your friend forever, maybe we should reconsider making this happen."

Pan had found the bread and the almond butter, and he was busy slapping the two together. His kitchen technique matched the way he swam—ugly but effective. "We don't have a choice. Cupid's failure is not an option. Every cycle he's gone through has become increasingly more painful. Nobody wants to see what the next one might look like."

The poor sonofabitch. Reed knew of the gods' ruthless punishments, often over the most minuscule infractions and petty jealousies. As myth, the stories of the gods offered entertainment in much the same vein as fairy tales: dark stories of betrayal and jilted lovers, familial relationships at their worst, anthropomorphisms to solve nature's mysteries where science had not yet advanced a logical explanation, a rudimentary system of divine hierarchy to keep the ancients on their best behavior. Reed understood these fundamentals well; they were, in fact, the backbone of classical studies. He couldn't have imagined reading the stories as nonfiction, much less living in such a random world order, even with immortality as the ultimate reward.

Immortality. That was a concept Reed had yet to wrap his head around. From time to time, Reed might have conceptualized an eternal being as central to his personal theology, might even have glimpsed the Creator's form for a brilliant, fleeting moment in a rainbow, a perfect wave, a spectacular supermoon. Never in his wildest dreams would Reed's God have looked anything like the red-headed hulk standing across his kitchen washing down almond butter sandwiches with soy milk.

Then again, now that Reed knew the truth, it wasn't at all difficult to reframe both Pan and Cupid as gods. Or maybe that was the whiskey talking. Either way, was it any wonder he was attracted to them both?

"Honestly, Reed"—Pan paused to wipe his mouth with the back of his hand—"the sooner we do this, the better for all of us."

Whatever the "this" was, doing it with a Greek god definitely intrigued Reed. "I guess we better get serious, then."

Pan set his green eyes to "smolder" as if lowering a dimmer switch; Reed squirmed in his seat. "An hour ago, you wanted your dogs to chase me off. Now you want to lock it in?"

"Hey, who am I to argue with Cupid?"

Pan huffed. "Trust me, it's not worth it."

Oddly, instead of diminishing the thrill, their mutual declarations had the opposite effect on Reed. Gamesmanship being rendered unnecessary, the certainty honed Reed's anticipation to a point.

Pan scooped up a sandwich from the counter and tore a paper towel off the roll. "I need to feed my friend out there. Hold that thought you're having right now?" A grin spread from one edge of Pan's beard to the other.

Jesus, can he read my mind? As if to answer, Pan winked.

Desire buzzed through Reed's system. He shook his head to clear the haze, but if anything, the disorientation worsened when Pan clapped his hands loudly to announce his return.

"So . . . where were we? Right! You wanted to get serious."

Reed felt the blush reach the tips of his ears. "I think you skipped the part where you were going to answer all my questions."

If Pan was discouraged by Reed hitting the brakes, he didn't let on. "How about I refill your drink first and maybe pour myself a little something?"

"Sounds like a grand idea," Reed answered.

It felt weirdly natural for this stranger to be making himself at home in Reed's kitchen. Reed liked watching Pan move; he was purposeful without seeming rushed. Pan possessed a confidence Reed had ascribed to youth and good looks, but it was exactly the opposite, he realized now. Because Pan had lived many lifetimes over, he was wise beyond the years of his physical embodiment.

There was so much about Pan that Reed wanted to know. Where did this man's reality intersect the literature Reed had made his life's work, and where did they diverge? If the gods really were alive and well overhead right now, what did they think of humans? What was it like to live forever?

Pan set two highball glasses with fresh ice on the kitchen table, poured three fingers of Bushmills into each one, and plunked down in the chair next to Reed. He'd rolled his sleeves just past the elbows, and as Pan slid one of the glasses toward Reed, his bare forearm captured Reed's attention. He could barely resist the urge to run his fingertips along the tufted bronze hairs.

Pan glanced up, his gaze locking on to Reed's. As Reed held his breath, frozen in place, Pan's eyes creased at the edges, and his lips curled into a smile.

"Can you read my mind?" Reed asked.

"No more than you can read mine." Pan released Reed's drink and picked up his own. "To us?" He cocked a mischievous brow and waited for Reed to tap his glass against Pan's.

Reed would need a better answer to his question, but first, he drank to Pan's toast.

Pan tipped his head back, eyes closed, and enjoyed his first taste. "*Mmm*, you do have exquisite taste."

"I'm not sure I can take credit for . . . everything." Reed's blush supplied the part he couldn't say: *for choosing you.*

Pan chuckled. "Touché." With a sigh, he glanced into the room where Cupid was sitting. "To be honest, I'm not sure he can either."

"What do you mean?" Reed asked. "I thought he was the matchmaker."

"Yes, but there are other forces at work here."

"Meaning?"

Pan took another sip of his drink before filling in the finer points for Reed about Cupid's punishment, how the gods had been manipulating his heart to pull him toward love only to tear it away. How Pan was the latest in Cupid's string of lovers, about their brief affair—which Pan emphatically insisted was over—and the real reason Cupid was unable to leave Reed's house.

"Normally, he's not the guy I'd want hanging around when I'm trying to impress a date," Pan admitted. "It's a bit like Jimmy Olsen inviting Superman along as a chaperone. Know what I mean?"

Reed laughed. "This is a very odd first date." He was starting to feel differently now, but he certainly understood where Pan was coming from. "So, how long do you think he'll be . . . with us?"

"Just until we reach our liminal point."

"Some kind of point of no return?" Reed asked.

"That makes it sound dark," Pan replied. "From what we have gathered, there's a moment of recognition, when both people believe in their love. At that point, the gods release Cupid's heart from his love connection—in this case, that would be with me—which is when his real heartbreak begins. Trust me, Reed, a brokenhearted God of Love is one of the saddest sights you will ever see."

Reed's most recent heartbreak happened three years ago, a nice enough girl he'd been dating about six months when Reed somehow went from sexy nerd to intellectual bore though he could never pinpoint a single thing he'd done differently.

"Poor bastard. I can't imagine what he could've done to deserve that."

Pan leaned forward and lowered his voice to a whisper. "Apparently there was some kind of family gathering at the highest levels. Might've been one of the gods' famous festivals, I really couldn't say. Anyway, Hades brought Cerberus as his plus-one from the Underworld, and Cupid waited until Cerberus was standing in front of Hera, then shot the hound in the ass with one of his arrows."

Hera was every evil queen in every fairy tale and arguably the most vindictive of the gods. "Oh dear. What a poor choice for a practical joke."

Pan snorted. "Exactly. It's fair to say Hera's not a dog lover like yourself. Multiply that by three snarling, slobbering heads, and you can see how Cupid ended up here."

"I'm not even sure *I* could find love for Cerberus," Reed admitted, "but then, he is three-quarters snake."

"True," Pan added. They both had a little chuckle over the genetics of mythical creatures, leaving Reed pondering Pan's heritage, but that was a topic to explore when they had more time.

"If the merciful act is to send Cupid home quickly, how do we get past our liminal point?"

"I don't know," Pan said, relaxing into the back of his chair. "It's been different every time."

"But we're definitely not there yet?"

"No. He would've told me. Or just shrieked in pain." A grimace flickered across Pan's mouth.

"How awful."

"It's hideous. Look, Q felt I should be as honest as possible with you, so that's why we told you everything. I realize this is a lot to take in—"

"That is the understatement of the century." Reed guffawed.

"I'm doing my best here to be truthful with you even though it's terrifying. I've never shared this much with *any* mortal in the two thousand years I've been down here—"

"You're two thousand. Years. Old."

"Actually, I'm well over three thousand."

As in a thousand years before the coming of Christ. *Welp.* "You look quite good for your age."

"Probiotics," Pan said with a wink.

"Well, it might have escaped your notice, but I am edging ever so slowly toward old age and death."

"I'm digging the gray highlights."

Reed rolled his eyes. "You're immortal."

"As far as I know."

"And you're not going to age?"

"Nope."

"So, while I get shriveled and senile, you will stay exactly like this?"

"Within a very narrow range of variation."

"I think I need a minute to process."

"Just a minute?" Pan said, cocking his head, to which Reed

replied with a huff. "Would you care to apply more alcohol to the situation?" Pan gave him a silly grin and wiggled the bottle over Reed's glass.

"No, thanks. I better not." It didn't seem wise to remind Pan yet again of his human frailty, and Reed really didn't want to end this life-changing night with his head in the toilet.

"Take your time, Reed. I'm not going anywhere." Pan topped off his glass and took a leisurely sip while the newest batch of data banged around inside Reed's brain.

He'd consumed just enough whiskey to vacillate between believing every word and writing off the whole story as one huge crock of shit. Gods and satyrs and immortality? *Really?* And why Reed?

Ahh, at last. There it was, the one puzzle piece Reed couldn't fit into the perfect picture. Not the completely outlandish idea that the figure sitting next to him—*Pan, the hot-bodied demigod*—was who he said he was, or even that Cupid—*hello, the God of Erotic Love*—was not only real but sitting in the next room—*Cupid was sitting in Reed's living room*—waiting for this love connection to kick in.

No, the real snag holding Reed back from buying this whole scenario was the fact that Aphrodite had chosen *him* to be Pan's partner. Or at least, his partner-for-now.

Concern furrowed Pan's brow. "You have a tortured look on your face," Pan said.

"It doesn't seem fair for you to be stuck with me."

"That's your thought?" Pan shook his head, clearly amused. "You're sitting there worrying about how this all works out for *me? Pshh* . . . Wow." More headshaking but also, Reed decided, something deeper than dismissal. Maybe Pan was having his own troubles piecing the puzzle together.

"I was under the impression that's how people who care about each other behave."

For once, Pan didn't have a snappy comeback. His jaw dropped open, and he studied Reed as if he'd never seen any-one like him before. Unlikely, Reed thought, considering how long Pan had been alive. He must have seen everything by now.

Pan leaned forward, wrapped both hands around his drink on the table in front of him, and frowned. "You've probably figured this out already, but I have no idea how I'm supposed to behave."

Pan had offered up his shortcoming on a silver platter, and it might have been the most attractive side of him Reed had seen yet. He never could resist an Achilles heel. *Holy shit! Pan knew Achilles! Be still, my intellectually curious heart.*

"I'd venture to guess this situation is unprecedented." What Reed wished to say was *Let me teach you,* but he'd already been around long enough to understand Pan would navigate this—whatever this was—his own way, much as he chopped through his laps at the pool. And let's face it, Reed was no relationship expert himself.

"Fair guess," Pan replied, chuckling softly to himself. "But I'd hardly call it being 'stuck with you.'"

"Look, Pan"—would he ever get used to saying that name?—"I know there are couples with big age differences who make it work, but I have to say, I've always felt the younger part-ner was getting the short end of that stick. And I'm talking about ten, twenty years, maybe . . . not a gap that starts at twenty-five and grows bigger every day."

"Well, I've seen you in wet swim trunks—yep, I was looking—and I'm not too worried about either end of your stick." Pan had clearly reverted to his comfort zone, and Reed was back to feeling hot and bothered. "And if we're being real here, let's acknowledge that *I* am the ancient one here—and my stick hap-pens to be in fine working order, thank you very much."

Good lord. Reed had looked, too, and he was pretty sure Pan knew it.

"Whatever," Reed muttered, already chiding himself for sounding like one of his petulant students.

"Respect, whippersnapper," Pan said with mock sternness, his grin widening.

Reed huffed, but he was smiling too. Pan had his own charming way about him. Unconventional, to say the least, but disarming, nonetheless.

"Okay, I get it," Reed said. "The age difference is not a problem for you."

"One thing you'll learn about me is I appreciate a broad range of sexual experiences."

"Are you saying you're attracted to me because you're not picky?"

"No, Reed. I'm attracted to you for a dozen reasons I'd be happy to rattle off right now—starting with those very sexy, cut shoulders and curvy thighs of yours and the way you rake your eyes down my body when you think I'm not watching." Reed's cheeks felt like they were on fire. "Want me to keep going?" Pan asked.

"No, thank you," Reed replied. "That was meant to be rhetorical."

"Was it?" Pan asked, raising his brows in a gentle challenge.

Reed eased against the back of his chair and let out a sigh. "I honestly don't know."

Pushing his drink aside, Pan leaned forward on folded arms. "Look, I get it. But I really do like you—a lot—and if it makes you feel better, remember I've already lived twenty mortal lifetimes on earth, time enough to have experienced every kind of sex as a human, and I don't really think we need to get into my life on Mount O."

"Thank you for small favors," Reed replied, earning a snort from Pan.

"Whatever." Pan echoed Reed's words, adding a wink.

"You mean to say you've gotten sex out of your system?"

"*Hell* no," Pan said so quickly, they both burst out laughing. "I'm a physical guy. My voracious sexual appetite is always going to be a big part of who I am." Reed was both intrigued and terrified. "But I'm not an animal. I can hit the pause button if I need to."

"Of course, just a pause. You'll be here long after I'm gone." The words came out easily; the concept might never sink in.

Pan's lifeline appeared to Reed in a shimmering blur, stretched behind Pan to an unfathomable beginning (the specifics of which would require a reread of his dusty tomes) and in front of Pan toward an unknowable infinity. Three thousand years he'd already lived, and in that time, Pan had watched a whole world come to life: the separation of sky and water, the evolution of man, the invention of fire, epic battles of Good and Evil. The present—Reed's lifetime included—was a mere blip in time, a slow-motion snippet of a cosmic continuum Reed had never felt a part of as much as he did in this moment.

"Eternity *is* a long time," said Pan, giving away nothing about his feelings on the subject.

"I wouldn't want you plotting my demise or anything."

A little grin poked through Pan's reply. "I can think of far more pleasant ways to address the dilemma than murder."

"Glad to hear that," Reed answered.

"You know, Reed, we don't have to solve all our future problems while we're still trying to get to know each other."

"Agreed." Reed certainly wasn't ready for a conversation on polyamory or whatever other "solution" was going through Pan's mind right now. "Do you really think this can work?"

"I know Aphrodite doesn't mess around when she makes up her mind."

Whatever Reed believed or didn't believe, Pan was all in with his story.

"I guess that explains why you're not fighting this," Reed said.

Pan's swagger fell away long enough for a serious response to Reed's question. "There's a lot I don't understand about my existence and even more I can't control. I've learned to enjoy the extraordinary gifts that come my way without fretting about when they'll be taken away."

Pan might have lifted the message right out of one of Kane's rehab sessions, but the humility felt every bit as genuine. Reed was filled with a profound sense of gratitude.

Pan smiled at him, unspoken understanding in his immortal eyes.

Reed slowly released a breath he might have been holding since he'd let Pan through the front door. "I'm starting to appreciate why someone might think you'd be good for me."

"Careful, Reed. You're gonna turn my head with all that pretty talk." Pan slid his hand along the table and extended the tip of his pinkie up and down the length of Reed's thumb, raising goose bumps all over the surface of Reed's body.

Reed was working out if and how to respond when Pan started toward a noise in the living room.

"Q? Fuck!" Pan jumped up and darted into the other room. "Q? Are you here?"

A toilet flushed. A door opened. Q, sheepish, reappeared. "Sorry."

30

HOMECOMING PLANS

Aphrodite wasn't one to loll in bed after the deed, not even with the glorious God of War lying naked beside her. "We should get dressed," she whispered as she rolled away from his side.

Hephaestus's workshop was too close to the bed chambers for comfort though he toiled at his forge later and later into each passing night and rose earlier each morning to start again. Aphrodite wasn't sure he slept at all anymore.

"Stay." Ares stretched his arm across the bed but not in time to trap her.

"Oh, wouldn't you love for Hephaestus to discover us together in his bed?"

Dark laughter rumbled out of Ares. "Maybe I just enjoy seeing my lover's exquisite skin kissed by these luxurious satin sheets."

Aphrodite answered with a huff as she pulled on her robe. "Maybe you enjoy winning."

"*Ahh*, there is that," he admitted. She didn't need to look back at Ares to know he was grinning.

Her pulse quickened as she plucked the gaiascope from its stand. She'd have to endure Ares's teasing for spying on Cupid again, but the situation on Earth had reached a critical point. Cupid would be returning to his life on Olympus any day now, and Aphrodite barely recognized this man her son had become.

"If I didn't know better, I might be jealous of the time you spend with your nose in that glass." Ares slipped his arm around Aphrodite as he crowded in next to her and peered through her window to Earth.

"And how *are* the lovers today?" boomed a voice from the other side of the chamber.

Aphrodite snapped her head up. There stood Hephaestus in his leather blacksmith's apron, arms crossed over his chest, glaring at them across the crumpled bedcovers. Thankfully, Ares had tied his robes.

"Getting closer every day," Ares said, tightening his grip on Aphrodite's waist.

"I was referring to the couple you're watching," said Hephaestus. There was no emotion in his voice. As many years as they'd been married, Aphrodite couldn't read his mood.

"You're home," she said cautiously.

Cheating on her husband in his own bed was beyond cruel, and yet she'd let Ares convince her that relocating their strategy session to her palace would offer a fresh perspective on the Cupid problem. When he suggested they move the conversation to her bedchamber, she really should have protested. But here they were.

"Yes. I was summoned for a meeting, but I didn't realize the meeting was to take place under our bedcovers." Hephaestus cocked his eyebrows at Ares, then shifted his gaze to Aphrodite. Aphrodite held as still as a statue. It was important she and Ares present a united front. She'd play along with the ruse now and deal with Ares later.

"You found us," said Ares, who was looking extremely proud of himself.

Hephaestus screwed up his face in obvious distaste. "I followed your scent."

"Well, we are all here now," Aphrodite said as cheerfully as possible under the circumstances.

"So we are." Hephaestus untied the strings at his back and kicked off his sandals while discarding the leather apron.

"What are you doing?" asked a horrified Aphrodite.

"I'm undressing so we can resume the meeting," said Hephaestus as he began to throw off his chiton.

"Stop that!" Aphrodite's outburst drew raucous laughter from Ares and feigned confusion from Hephaestus.

"You do not wish to continue?" Hephaestus asked.

Gods! The two of them were driving her mad with their games!

"Yes, I do," Aphrodite answered calmly. "Can we please discuss the topic at hand with our clothes on?"

"There's a refreshing idea," Hephaestus replied with a huff.

Ignoring her husband's theatrics, Aphrodite updated him on Cupid's situation. "Pan and Reed are close to reaching their Liminal Point—no thanks to that stunt you pulled with the arrow." She was still cross with Hephaestus for interfering though a part of her admired his gumption.

"We should have reported you to the Council," grumbled Ares.

Aphrodite turned to give Ares a pointed glare. "We don't need to air our dirty laundry in the public square." Three pairs of eyes shifted to the crumpled sheets. Ares let out a grunt.

"Oh, Aph," Hephaestus said with a sad sigh. "You know I was just trying to do the right thing."

"Well, you nearly spoiled everything!" she said. "Cupid and Pan would have been a royal mess together."

Hephaestus shrugged. "They looked like the perfect couple to me . . . but *clearly*, I don't know the first thing about what makes a relationship work."

"Which is *why*," Ares was quick to reply, "we leave matters of the heart to the Goddess of Love." Lavishing Aphrodite with pure reverence, Ares tucked a strand of hair behind her ear. She shivered at his touch.

"I do have to give you credit there, love," Hephaestus said. "Pan and the professor are one of your more brilliant pairings."

"You think so?" She did love flattery, and Hephaestus wasn't one to dole it out without justification.

"I do. Tell me, how did you come up with the idea?"

The tiny hairs on the back of Aphrodite's neck stood at attention. Before she could answer, Ares jumped in. "She's brilliant, obviously."

Hephaestus continued to stare at Aphrodite, quirking his bushy brows in anticipation of her answer as if he had not heard Ares at all.

"Honestly, Heph, I just let Cupid do his job."

"You're too modest, Goddess." Despite the menacing glare Aphrodite shot him, Ares kept talking. "We all know Cupid didn't find Reed for Pan. Cupid was going to take Reed for himself until this clever one"—Ares wagged his thumb at Aphrodite—"saw the possibilities."

"To shatter Cupid's heart?" said Hephaestus.

Ares jumped in to defend her. "Collateral damage is to be expected."

Hephaestus glared at Aphrodite as if *she'd* offered the cavalier response. "Have you thought about what you'll do with our son once Pan and Reed cross?"

She let Hephaestus's claim on Cupid pass unremarked this time. "Of course. We've been strategizing daily."

"Multiple times, some days," added Ares with a flash of teeth.

"You don't say," said Hephaestus.

"We have to make sure we consider all possible angles." The god truly had no shame.

Hephaestus rounded on him with a massive eye roll. "Congratulations, Ares. You're screwing my wife. As soon as I return to my shop, I'll make you the biggest cock-shaped trophy ever crafted. Now, can we return to discussing Cupid's future?"

Ares's jaw fell open like a door with a broken hinge. If Aphrodite hadn't known how torn up her husband was over the affair, she might've guessed he was just plain bored. In any event, she was relieved to bring the conversation back to Cupid.

"Assuming nothing unforeseen happens before the couple crosses their Liminal Point—"

Hephaestus huffed so hard, Aphrodite could feel the breeze on her cheeks. "You two aren't planning to interfere again, are you?"

Ares's back stiffened. "You wound me."

"Collateral damage," Hephaestus replied with a shrug.

"No, Heph," Aphrodite answered quietly. "We won't stand in the way of Pan and Reed."

Hephaestus nodded. "Good. And you'll make a positive recommendation to the Council on Cupid's behalf?"

"We haven't decided," said Ares.

"Actually, um . . . I have Mercury standing by," Aphrodite said. "You *do*?"

"Oh, did I forget to mention that?" she asked Ares. "I was sure I'd mentioned that."

"No, we definitely did not discuss that," Ares replied sternly.

Aphrodite pressed on, shaky but determined. "It's time for Cupid to return to the palace. I've planned a lavish banquet upon his return."

Hephaestus harrumphed. "That's a bold move."

Aphrodite swiveled her head toward her husband. "What's that supposed to mean?"

"I'm just a little surprised you think he's going to feel like celebrating."

"Why wouldn't he?" Aphrodite demanded.

"Look at him, Aph! Look what you did to him. He's all twisted up inside!" Her husband's voice broke with emotion. "You think a troupe of acrobats and a bunch of old men reciting poetry are going to make your son forgive you?"

"Forgive *me*?" Aphrodite's hand flew to her heart. "I'm not the one who set the hound of Hades on your mother—"

"*Goddess.*" Ares wrapped his hand around her elbow and squeezed hard.

"No, you didn't shoot the arrow, but you—" Hephaestus cut himself off abruptly, waving his hands in front of his face where the ugly words almost went. He didn't need to say them out loud. She knew what Hephaestus thought, what *everyone* thought, of her parenting skills. "Look, Aph," he started in gently, "try to imagine what it will be like for him if you bring him up to Olympus right now, tearing him away from Pan again, in the throes of the worst heartbreak of his life."

"But he'll be home again where he belongs, with his family."

"Oh! You mean *this* little family right here?" Hephaestus swirled a chubby finger in a circle, indicating all three of them.

She wouldn't rise to the bait. "He'll have to be a little more careful with his arrows going forward, but he's proven himself now. He can go back to the life he loved."

"The life of pairing up everyone else and never participating in love himself? Tell me, Goddess, how is that any different from his punishment?"

"I have to agree with Hephaestus," Ares said.

Well, that would be a first, though Ares had his own selfish reasons for stalling Cupid's return.

Hephaestus strode across the room and took Aphrodite's delicate wrist inside his massive hand, and Ares squeezed tighter, two dogs gripping opposite ends of the same bone. "Aph, I'm afraid if you pull him out now, Cupid is going to resent you for a very long time." Hephaestus glanced into the gaiascope. She couldn't bear to follow his gaze.

Tears welled in her eyes.

Hephaestus softened. "May I offer a suggestion?"

Much as it pained her to admit, Hephaestus had always understood Cupid better than she did. "I'm listening," she said.

"Why not release Cupid from his sentence, but let him stay on Earth—"

"Let him *stay?* I can't lose him, Heph."

"Not forever, love. Just give him some time to heal. You've opened up his world and shown him how it feels to love. Hasn't he earned the right to experience that for himself, just once?"

"Why can't he do that here?" A dozen reasons tumbled through her mind even as the plea rolled off her tongue. Which of the deities who had known Cupid as the perma-pubescent rascal of the palace would ever take him as a lover?

Hephaestus answered simply with a kind smile.

Ares was smart enough to keep his mouth shut.

"Fine," Aphrodite finally agreed, "but we all know he won't appreciate love if it falls easily into his lap."

Seeing he'd convinced her, Hephaestus chuckled, filling the chamber with the warm roll of laughter that had so often shaken their marital bed. "Then give our boy a challenge."

31

RESEARCH

Settled in for the evening in his favorite silk pajamas and fleece-lined slippers, a generous pour of whiskey in hand, and four dogs snoozing nearby, Reed kicked back in his recliner. He sipped at the drink, closed his eyes, and smiled. The memory of Pan's touch was still fresh enough in his mind three hours later to bring goose bumps to Reed's skin.

This can't be happening, argued the logical side of his brain.

If he hadn't stood next to the two gods, hadn't swum with and spoken to them both, Reed might have written this whole experience off as the musings of a mad professor who spent far too much time isolated in the boondocks with his dogs and his ancient stories. Even still, Reed might have called on his oldest, wisest friend in the Classical Studies Department for a reality check if not for the secretive nature of the situation. The whole thing was surreal, but at the same time, as real as reality could be.

This *was* happening. The only thing preventing Pan from being here with Reed right this second was Reed's reticence.

Pan had been understanding enough as Reed shooed him away but left Reed's house only after making it clear he was ready and willing whenever Reed was. A heated flush washed over Reed as he remembered Pan's sexy wink on the way out.

Goose bumps, blushing over boys, and gods throwing themselves at his feet! *How is this my life?*

With a happy shrug, Reed traded his drink for the book at the top of his carefully curated stack waiting on the side table. Reed wasn't one to watch porn. Staged sex scenes for the sole purpose of titillation had always left him cold. Words were his aphrodisiac—the bigger the better, and poetic, if you please. Sure, he'd purchased *Penthouse* in his day, but more likely than not, it was the letters section Reed turned to first. Not that they were any great literary masterpieces, but Reed much preferred the visuals in his own mind to a photo that left nothing to the imagination.

But of course, no scholar of the classical period could claim a firm grasp of his material without developing an appreciation for the renderings of the gods and mythical beings that populated the literature. Music, statuary, and paintings were all instructive elements of the landscape, each reflective in its own way of the creator's bias toward the source material and each worthy of study. So yes, Reed could well have started his "literature review" by rereading the poems, hymns, and legends written about Pan, but he felt perfectly, academically justified starting with the visual arts.

Yes, that must have been intellectual anticipation that buzzed through Reed as the heavy textbook met his lap. Prior to meeting Pan, Reed would have characterized his own sexual appetite as healthy enough: always happy to indulge with a committed partner or to relieve the tension himself when the need arose. He'd never been overly preoccupied with sex, and he'd always been fine with that. It didn't take long for Reed-the-scholar to acknowledge the only real difference between himself and every other creepy stalker checking out nude photos of some guy he liked was that Reed had twenty-five hundred years of material to crawl through—an embarrassment of riches.

Tonight wasn't Reed's first walk through the volumes of imagery of the Greek god Pan, not by a long shot, though it was his first time viewing the provocative images through the eyes of a potential lover. Last week, he might have labeled his interest in Q as "bi-curious." Having now met Pan as well, Reed readily admitted there was more than curiosity at work.

He turned to the first flagged page—Reed had gotten straight to work bookmarking every image in his extensive library after Cupid and Pan's exit—one of the earliest works, a red-figure bell krater from the fifth century BCE, depicting a goat-headed Pan chasing after a young shepherd boy. The artist left no room for misinterpretation as to what was on Pan's mind, with his exaggerated erection in plain view as he ran on goat-hooves after the boy with his arms outstretched and greedy. Judging by the shepherd's anxious gaze at said erection, Pan's ardor was presumably the reason for the boy's determined retreat. Reed didn't have to stretch for empathy for the awed but frightened shepherd boy.

The next Post-it brought Reed to the sculpture *Pan and Daphnis*, discovered in the sixteenth century, attributed to the sculptor Heliodorus from the second century BCE. A white marble Pan leaned against a low wall, gripping the upper body of the young, nude figure of the shepherd boy, Daphnis, beside him. Supposedly teaching the boy to play the flute Daphnis held against his chest, Pan's expression had always read as slightly wicked to Reed. Now there was no mistaking Pan's intentions or the massive endowment between his splayed legs.

Reed stared hard at the photo, trying to reconcile the human version of Pan he'd started to get to know with this mostly goat form. How much of this beast lurked inside the man? Reed wondered with a shiver. Pan had certainly made no bones about his sexual appetite.

He flipped to a sculpture of Aphrodite, Eros, and Pan, dating back to 100 BCE. "Oh my god!" Reed's sudden outburst startled Bo Peep from her sleep. "Sorry, girl. It's okay."

But it really wasn't okay. Knowing what Reed now knew, he'd never regard the sculpture the same way again. Pan was making a lascivious play for a nude Aphrodite, attempting to tug her hand away from covering her genitals, while she prepared to whack him with a sandal in her other hand. While this drama was playing out between Pan and Aphrodite, Cupid flew between them, grabbing at Pan's horns to distract the beast—his best friend—from raping his mother.

Yeah, that's highly disturbing. Could twenty-one hundred years possibly be enough time for Cupid to burn that image from his memory?

How many times in how many different permutations had the two best friends bumped up against each other during their long and storied past? Wrapping his head around the vastness of the life span his new friends had already experienced was damn near impossible, never mind attempting to grasp the infinite future. Maybe Reed would get used to the idea by the time he was seventy and Pan was still thirty-three-ish.

Of one fact, he was certain: life would never, ever be boring again.

Reed paused for a slow sip of whiskey while he contemplated the big picture. Everything Reed thought he'd understood of gods, poets, artists, and philosophers, all the layers shifted like sliding mirrors in his mind's eye. He was Clara, watching his beloved nutcracker come to life.

The gods of the ancient world lived; they lived still! The Greeks had their names for them, as did the Romans. There were stories and statues and hymns and frescoes, but Reed would find nothing recent in his tomes. Modern man had traded Pan and Cupid and Zeus and Aphrodite for new theologies, but that didn't mean they had all just faded away. Their existence never depended on mortals believing in them.

Reed turned to the next flagged page. A smile spread across his face as he studied *Nymphs and Satyr,* the famous Bouguereau painting exhibited in Paris at the 1873 Salon and hailed by one critic at the time as "the greatest painting of our generation." In the painting, Pan was surrounded by four beautiful, naked nymphs who were gleefully pushing and pulling at him, attempting to drag him forward toward the stream. Reed had always loved this painting for revealing a different side of Pan. His body language clearly reflected an uncharacteristic resistance to their attentions: his whole body tensed backward, hooves firmly planted on the ridge, straining to hold his position, a look of sheer terror on his face. His reluctance only made sense in the context of the quotation from Latin poet Publius Statius, which was posted alongside the painting at its debut: "Conscious of his shaggy hide, and from childhood untaught to swim, he dares not trust himself to the deep waters."

Poor Pan. Reed chuckled to himself. He hadn't been joking when he'd casually tossed out that he might sink, which only made his appearances at the pool that much more impressive.

Reed flipped idly through the volume in his lap, page after page, nude after nude. Holy shit! Was there a single image of Pan where he wasn't displayed in the buff? Kraters and sculptures and paintings . . . the character of Pan was certainly a darling of the artists of the day, appearing in every variation of goat parts from head to hoof but almost without exception, naked and aroused.

Walk back the snub nose, pointy ears, and horns, and there was some version of the childlike face of the Pan that Reed was beginning to know. The goat hindquarters were easy enough to replace with the thick, tree-trunk legs the human version walked around on. Of course, it helped that Reed had seen pretty much every part of Pan that first day at the gym when Pan had pranced across the pool deck in nothing but a tiny Speedo. At that point, Reed was still getting used to the idea of being attracted to Cupid; nonetheless, the image of Pan remained burned into his memory. The Greek god of the wild personified as a human male in his early thirties was not a sight even the straightest of men easily forgot. And speaking of sights—

"Holy shit!" The *Barberini Faun.*

Reed lurched forward in his recliner, snapping the footrest closed and nearly catapulting himself across the room. Bo let out a thick *ruff!* Moses growled. The Beaucerons lifted their heads and waited for Reed's word before settling down again.

"Sorry, gang. Nothing to see here but a horny old man."

Reed lifted the book, bringing the figure of the half-reclining marble satyr toward him for a closer look. My god, he was a spectacular specimen of the Hellenistic Baroque style, a sharp departure from the reserve of the Classical period and its obsession with the heroic form.

Reed had always appreciated the blatant eroticism of the piece: fresh from a Bacchanalia, Pan's legs were wide open as he reclined from utter exhaustion, the drunken drowsiness in the slack cheeks and sensuous, slightly opened mouth, the tension evident in the raised right leg, the plush leopard skin shielding the figure from the harsh rock beneath him, the right arm, thrown luxuriously behind his head, setting off the stunning musculature of the abdomen, chest, and neck.

What didn't happen to Reed the last time he'd viewed the sculpture was the erection now tenting his pajamas.

Replacing the bookmark, Reed gently closed the book and replaced it on top of the stack. All of this was Reed's for the taking. He finished his drink and headed to bed. He'd start on the words tomorrow.

32

KEEPING AN EYE ON Q

"Don't let the speed bag get past your hands. Here, watch me again."

Cupid stepped back and watched while Pan tapped the bag slowly at first, every muscle in his back engaged with each punch thrown. His whole body worked as one powerful, efficient machine, legs pistoning, shoulders and arms strong and tight, his breathing perfectly synchronized to the task before him, a ball of energy barely contained by his earthly body and skintight gym shorts. And Cupid wasn't the only one staring.

"Your turn," Pan said, slowing the bag with the backs of his hands.

"I feel like everyone is looking at us." Not just looking, Cupid realized, but *wanting.* He recognized several familiar faces from their visits to Versailles.

"Because they are," Pan replied without taking his eyes off Cupid. Since leaving Reed's, Pan had insisted on keeping his eye on Cupid. As Cupid was keeping both eyes on Pan. "Let's go, man. Left, left, right, right, that's it." Pan shadowboxed next to

Cupid until he'd mastered the sequences. It wasn't long before he had the bag moving like a seasoned boxer.

Yoga and swimming offered a great release, but Cupid could definitely see the appeal of the speed bag. There was something satisfying in the *pop* of his fist meeting the leather and sending the bag hopping around on its hook. He remembered that sickening sense that Ruthie's husband was contemplating punching him in the face and how defenseless he'd felt at the time.

"I think I could hold my own in a fight now," Cupid announced without slowing his fists.

Pan snorted. "This would be the wrong place to test that theory."

Cupid took a break from his punches to glance around the muscle gym: guys bench-pressing what had to be twice Cupid's body weight, the rhythmic *clank* of weights and *jhoozh* of cables as machines and humans pushed and resisted each other, the telltale grunts of exertion all around the room, all those muscles bulging out of stretchy clothing. There was a definite pecking order to the room, and Cupid had no doubt Pan was at the very top.

"I bet *you* could take down anyone in here, couldn't you?"

"You're unbelievable." Pan huffed, shaking his head with a hint of a smile playing at his lips. "I bring you to the best hookup spot in town, and all you can think about is beating someone up?"

No, that was not all Cupid had been thinking about since their arrival at The Back Door. He'd been wondering which of these men Pan had already had sex with. As the atmosphere had thickened with sweat and pheromones, Cupid couldn't help adding colors and flavors and textures to those wonderings.

"You've got me punching things!" Cupid said. "How am I not supposed to think about punching people?"

"Think of this as a dance." Pan stepped in front of the bag again. He scissored his feet on the mat, lighter on his toes and more elegant than Cupid had ever seen him, then gradually brought his arms and hands into it. Maybe this little expedition to the gym wasn't such a great idea after all. "Rhythm, timing, awareness of your partner . . . it's all here. You wouldn't punch your dance partner, would you?"

Lust gathered into a fire in Cupid's groin as Pan performed for him. In his mind's eye, Cupid peeled off Pan's tight clothes, pictured his body hard and tight, moving over him as it had when they were alone and naked together.

"Q?"

Oops. "Hmm?"

"And we're done here," Pan said with a chuckle. "Speed bag isn't for the wandering mind. To the mats with you!"

Cupid followed Pan's gaze to the row of sweaty bodies in various stages of sit-ups, push-ups, and stretches, laid out along the floor like chocolates in a box. *Deep, cleansing breath,* Cupid told himself, tugging his T-shirt as low as it would go but unable to conceal his arousal. This place was almost worse than Versailles, but the worst temptation was the man who plopped down onto the mat next to his. Cupid's heart knew Pan belonged to Reed now, but that didn't stop Cupid from wanting him in the worst way.

"You want to hold my feet first?" Pan asked as he stretched out on his back, clasped his hands beneath his neck, and raised his knees.

"I don't want to hold your feet at all."

Pan rolled his head to the side, his bearded cheeks pressed into a lopsided grin against the mat. "You doin' okay over there?"

Inhale . . . exhale. "I'll be fine. Just don't ask me to touch you, please." Cupid settled onto his back and set his focus on the ceiling. "Or look at you."

"Fair enough," Pan replied.

As if Cupid wouldn't smell him or hear him grunt with each sit-up or feel the roll and flex of muscle by his side. As if any of that lessened when Pan rolled onto his belly and began a series of Olympic-worthy push-ups designed purely to capture the attention of every eye in his vicinity—and it was working. A bucket of ice would have been helpful, but in its absence, Cupid opted for the next best spoiler.

"So, what's happening with Reed?"

Flexed halfway into his one-armed push-up, Pan turned his head just enough to send his upper body crashing to the mat. "Seriously?"

"Sorry," Cupid mumbled back.

Pan let out an exasperated sigh and flopped onto his back. "*Nothing* is happening with Reed."

Cupid tipped onto his side, propping his head up with his hand. "Nothing?" It had been two full days since the scene at Reed's, two days of Cupid holding his breath, waiting for Mercury to appear and take him away.

"Reed said he needed some time to review his materials." All the confidence of gym-rat Pan dissolved before Cupid's eyes.

"He's rereading the old stories about you."

"Yep. His 'mythology' texts," Pan said through clenched teeth.

"That's slightly terrifying."

Pan huffed. "Ya *think?*" Pan pulled his knees into his chest. Despite his perfect *Apanasana* pose, tension was rolling off him in dangerous waves.

"Hey, give Reed a chance, Pan. He'll figure it out."

"Or he'll go running for the hills . . . so to speak." He grimaced at his own awful joke, then crossed his right leg over his left thigh and rolled his lower body to the left while turning his head and arms toward Cupid. "And all I can do is sit here and wait for him to come back and give me a chance to show him the real me."

"Sometimes waiting is all you can do."

"Have you ever known me to be patient?" He reversed his legs and flipped to the other side, turning his gaze away from Cupid, who peered over Pan's body to answer.

"You've been extremely patient with me." Ignoring Pan's eye roll, Cupid went on. "And Euphrosyne. And probably every other fallen who's tried your patience down here."

"*Humph.*" A tiny smirk appeared as Pan stretched his arms above his head and extended his legs straight out along the mat, revealing a swath of skin and a trail of copper-colored fluff dividing his belly in half. "Nobody's tried it quite like you, my friend."

Friend. The word hardly began to describe their complicated relationship. It definitely didn't describe Cupid's feelings right now toward the span of sinew and flesh on display beside him. Their eyes caught. Cupid looked away before Pan could give him another of his pity-filled stares.

"This is one hell of a catch-22," Pan said.

"What's that?"

"Sorry," he said, "sometimes I forget you just got here. I meant, there's a part of me that wants this part to drag on for-fucking-ever so you don't ever have to leave, you know?"

Cupid nodded. He suspected Pan also quite enjoyed being so completely desired by him, but Cupid didn't have the heart to hold it against him.

"But then there's this part of me that wants to get going with Reed already. I mean, if he's supposed to be my Right Love and all that happy shit, bring it on! Am I right?"

"Sure," Cupid answered, though it broke him to say it.

"And there's always the chance you'll still be here after we cross." Pan scrambled into a sitting position and stretched one arm over the opposite shoulder. "I mean, you must've fucked up *something* somewhere along the way, don't you think?" he added hopefully.

"Probably." If Cupid had messed up this time, he sure couldn't imagine doing any better the next time. Maybe he'd never get home.

Pan switched arms. "Not that I wish you another round of this crapola. I wouldn't wish that on my worst enemy, but you know what I mean."

"Of course I do."

"So, you gonna do some work over there or just watch me?"

"I think I've had enough for today," Cupid said, rising to his feet. "I'm just gonna get my bag and head out."

"Whoa! Hang on!" Pan jumped up and grabbed him by the shoulder. "The whole reason we came here is waiting for you inside the locker room. Hookup Central, a.k.a. the steam room." He finished with an unsavory wink that clogged Cupid's head with visions of a steam room tryst with Pan.

"Okay, fine. I'll have a steam."

"That's more like it," said Pan, following him.

Cupid rounded on him at the entrance to the locker room. "What are you doing?"

"Supervising," Pan answered, pushing open the locker room door and urging Cupid to pass under his stinky armpit.

"I don't think that's a good idea."

Pan rolled his eyes, hard. "I realize I'm not the matchmaker you are, but I've, uh, sampled most of the goods. I can definitely save you some time."

"No offense, Pan, but I think I can manage on my own." There were at least a dozen men to choose from, and Cupid wasn't feeling all that picky.

Pan gave Cupid a careful stare, then clapped him on the back. "Okay, man. I can take a hint." It was more sledgehammer than hint, but at least Pan was finally backing off.

"Thank you. And let me know if you hear from Reed?"

"You'll be the third to know," he said with a grin, then pointed toward the sky and whispered, "Not counting them."

They, who were always watching.

What would they think of Cupid picking up some random man at the gym? Would this be the strike against Cupid that would keep him here for another round of *Follow Your Heart 'til It Hurts?* Part of him wondered if that was exactly why he intended to go through with it.

"Before I cut you loose," Pan said, "let me at least leave you with two pro tips."

Cupid sighed. "Okay. What?"

"One, nobody *wears* a towel. Sit on it, dry yourself off after your shower, whatever you need to do, but don't walk around with it knotted at your hip."

A quick scan of the locker room supported Pan's advice. Modesty was definitely not an issue. "Got it. Number two?"

"If you get caught doing something nasty in the steam room, you do not know me."

33

A KNOCK AT THE DOOR

Celibacy was a new and different challenge for Pan. His sex drive from his former nymph- and shepherd-chasing days hadn't diminished with time or evolution. Happily, though, Pan-the-man didn't spend a lot of time running around naked, sporting a jumbo erection for all to see. Also happily, Pan had somewhat civilized his physical urges. As long as Pan could unclog his pipes when needed, abstinence was bearable.

As a general rule, the gods didn't seem to object, hence the boatload of quality time he spent shining his flagpole—every night, most mornings, and the occasional afternoon. In recent weeks, he'd found himself relying more and more on that mid-day tug to get him through the day. Lately, a visual of Cupid was the quickest route to release, specifically the sweaty, swole, horny version Pan had just left at the gym. But Reed was an intriguing option, and Pan didn't mind investing the extra few minutes it took him to reach his destination, forging a new path through uncharted territory. In fact, Pan found he was quite enjoying the challenge.

Can you read my mind? Reed had asked. Technically, Pan's response was truthful, but he hadn't exactly been forthcoming about the fact that a demigod could glean an awful lot from his five senses. Pan could smell Reed's desire and his fear as surely as those dogs had sniffed out Pan's wild nature. He could see all the obvious and not-so-obvious signals Reed telegraphed: dilated pupils, the subconscious lean-in, the way his mouth hung open just enough to reveal a hint of tongue. He could hear Reed's heartbeat when it quickened for him; whether that was affection or excitement was Pan's to interpret. He could see the bump pushing against the zipper of Reed's jeans, loved it even more when it was a proper pair of trousers straining but unable to hold the professor's secrets. He could feel the rush of goose bumps along Reed's skin whenever Pan touched him. He could taste the sweet desire on Reed's breath, and Pan wanted more of that. So much more.

A roughly spliced film played for Pan now in the shower—a vivid picture of naked Cupid, a fantasized first kiss with Reed, Cupid getting blown in the steam room—but it was the image of Reed in his dark, round glasses, tweed jacket, and bow tie, sinking to his knees, that made Pan shoot his thick stream across the shower. The stirring image remained lodged in Pan's head while he scrubbed a towel over his wet hair, pulled on his sweatpants, clicked the TV to some recap of some football game, and went to answer the knock at his front door.

Lo and behold, it was the professor himself!

There stood Reed, not wearing the tweed and bow tie from Pan's latest fantasy but looking youthful in a pair of slim jeans and a very snappy olive-green Henley beneath his jacket. Both looked suspiciously pristine, unlike the well-worn wooden cane Reed held near his right hip.

Reed swallowed hard when he saw Pan standing there

without his shirt on, which was pretty darn amusing since he'd seen Pan wearing a whole lot less than sweatpants at the pool. The poor guy couldn't seem to make his mouth work to say hello or anything else. Pan helped him out by breaking the ice.

"Reed. You look hot."

"Not bad for an old goat . . ." He blushed beet red. "Oh my god, I'm so sorry, I . . ."

Pan grinned and waited for Reed to pull his loafer out of his mouth.

"I apologize for showing up here without calling first. I don't know where my manners have gone today." *That*, Pan suspected, was his poor influence rubbing off on Reed.

"Not a problem. What brings you to my abode this fine afternoon?" If it was just to stand there and gawp, that was a step in the right direction, though Pan hoped it would be more.

"I'm pretty sure I know how to get us across the finish line."

This announcement made Pan downright giddy. Even if Reed's idea didn't work, the fact that he was trying was huge. "This sounds promising," Pan said, leaning into the open door. "Would you like to come in?"

"Thank you."

"Step into my lair." Pan resisted the urge to wrap his arms around the very adorable professor as he passed through the doorway. Knowing Reed had spent the last three days immersed in Pan's sordid history, the last thing Pan needed to do was prove himself the aggressor.

Reed glanced down at his own hand, seeming surprised to find a book. "Oh. This is for you." Reed passed the thin paperback to Pan. There was a picture of a dog on the front and the title: *Le Berger de Beauce*. "I thought you might be interested in the history of my Beaucerons." The beautiful dog on the cover resembled two of Reed's "children."

"Thank you for this," Pan said, humbly turning the book over in his hands. Nobody had ever gifted him with a book before. "I'm embarrassed to admit I haven't learned French."

Waving his hand through the space between them, Reed added, "Please forgive the pretentious gesture. It's the only version that's bound and published. I wrote my own translation in the back for you. It's really a beautiful story, and I had a feeling you'd appreciate the folklore."

If anyone had told Pan the way to his heart would be through his intellect, he surely would have scoffed. And yet, here was Reed, appealing directly to his mind. And yeah, it was sexy.

Pan was a little surprised to note that his hand had moved to cover his heart—Cupid rubbing off on Pan, perhaps? "Thank you, Reed. This is a beautiful gift."

Reed strode to the middle of the great room and spun in a slow circle with his cane at the center as he took in the furnishings. "Nice place you've got here."

"Thanks." Pan clicked off the TV. "Can I offer you something to drink? A beer, maybe?"

"Do you have iced tea?"

"I have lemonade."

"That'd be lovely." Was Pan going to have to start drinking tea and saying words like "lovely" now?

Reed shrugged out of his jacket and followed Pan to the kitchen, barely making a sound with his genteel leather shoes and rubber-tipped cane. Pan grabbed himself a beer and poured Reed's lemonade into a tall glass with ice.

"You caught me just out of the shower. I can go grab a shirt . . ." Pan trailed off. If Reed wanted him to cover up, he was going to have to say so.

Reed's hand shook as Pan handed him the drink across the island. "Please, don't go to any trouble on my account,"

Reed said, licking his lips before gulping down his drink. *Atta-boy, Reed.*

"You seem a bit nervous." The man was shooting off phero-mones like bottle rockets.

"You could say that. I've been brushing up on my mythology."

"I see," Pan replied cautiously.

"I thought maybe reviewing the stories could help me get inside the heads of the gods . . . and I could help solve the puzzle of how to cross."

"Way to go, Professor." Pan wanted to kiss the hell out of him right now.

"So, I reread the stories about you." Reed's gaze met Pan's, then bounced away as if he'd touched hot coals. *Fuck.*

"Reed, we talked about this. You think puberty was awk-ward for you? Try it with hooves and horns. Seriously, not my finest thirteen hundred years."

Reed reached across the counter for Pan, set a hand on his arm, and squeezed. "You don't have to go there, Pan. I get it."

Despite the ice-cold touch, Pan was warmed from the inside out by Reed's gesture. Of all the humans on earth, Reed alone knew Pan's truth. Reed, arguably one of the most well-versed scholars of Pan's life as a satyr.

"You get it?" Was this love's power, then? The ability to understand and transcend all of that?

Reed smiled. "Every relationship has that sweet getting-to-know-you phase. I expect, with you, there may be more to learn and discover than your favorite color and what sign you were born under."

"Hey, if you want to talk astrology, we could be here all day with the backstories," Pan said. "You see stars. I see jealousy, passion, revenge . . ."

"It was meant as an expression," said the professor, all serious.

"And as for my favorite color . . ." Reed leaned in, eyes wide, as if Pan were about to unlock the innermost vault of his private thoughts. Pan met his gaze. "What color are they, hazel?"

A pungent exhale left Reed. "My eyes?"

"Mmm, my new favorite color. Hazel."

Cheesy, but effective. Reed's cheeks pinked up. It took all of Pan's self-control not to ghost his fingertips over that blush. Reed eased back and sipped his lemonade.

Don't pressure him, idiot.

The cold drink snapped Reed back to his train of thought, which seemed to be leading somewhere Pan very much wanted to go. "So, I got to thinking," Reed said, "all those stories, and you're always the one doing the chasing. It doesn't really seem fair. I mean, if it's true love, shouldn't it be fifty-fifty?"

Well, that was unexpected. *Where are you going with this, Professor?*

"It occurred to me that maybe the gods were waiting for someone—for *me*—to want you enough to chase *you*."

"I see." Oh yes, Pan liked his theory very, very much.

"So here I am." *Fuck yeah, you are.*

"Indeed." Pan was cranked up inside like a roller coaster that had *tick-tick-ticked* to the top of the highest peak, front wheels teetering over the crest.

He glugged down the rest of his beer, if only to occupy his lips with something other than Reed's mouth.

"And I thought maybe," Reed said, gaining courage as he laid out his plan, "since we'd already tried talking and logic and dogs and friends and other people's heartbeats"—god*damn*, Pan wanted to jump the man—"maybe we could just try being alone together for a little bit?"

"Just being alone?"

"Together," Reed added.

Please let sex be involved.

Pan leaned over the counter, inches from Reed's lips. "I have to say I really like the way you think."

Reed picked up Pan's phone from the end of the counter and waggled it in the air between them. "*Alone*, alone. Put each other first. Do you think you can do that, Pan?"

The professor had some balls on him. Reed knew about Cupid's tenuous situation, understood the enormity of what he was asking of Pan. They stared each other down until Pan gave in to his ultimatum.

"Sure." Pan took his phone, switched it off, and showed the dark screen to Reed. "I'm all yours." A shiver shuddered through Pan. He was ready for this—electrified, even.

Emboldened, Reed rounded the counter so he was standing in front of Pan, all business—then nothing.

"The thing is," Reed started, "I've never actually seduced a man before."

Pan stifled the urge to smile. After all that buildup, the professor didn't have an actual plan? "Could've fooled me."

"Yeah?"

Pan stepped closer, arms locked by his sides, his gaze lowered slightly to meet Reed's. "Mm-hmm. Consider me seduced."

Relief crossed Reed's face but was immediately replaced with tension. "So, I should probably . . ."

"Kiss me?" Pan suggested.

Reed blinked up at him. His Adam's apple bounced hard. "Do you think?"

Holy hell, how Reed tempted him. But he'd made a good point about the chasing. "That's usually a good start." Pan's tongue felt sluggish, like he'd just downed a milkshake in one go. Pretty soon, he wouldn't be able to form words.

Reed met Pan's gaze, and Pan saw real fear in the man's eyes.

"The answer is yes," Pan said. "Whatever you want, Reed. The answer is yes."

"Okay," he whispered, his breaths coming shallow and quick. *So fucking sexy.*

"So . . . what *do* you want, Reed?"

Reed raised his hand to Pan's beard and rubbed his fingertips up and down over the sideburns while Pan stood motionless except for the choppy rise and fall of his chest. "I'm trying to process the idea of kissing a person who has a beard." Reed traced his thumb across Pan's mouth, leaving his first hint of flavor on Pan's lips. Pan couldn't resist trailing his tongue after. *Clean laundry, dog fur, the pages of a book.*

"And how's that working for you?"

A twinkle lit Reed's eyes. "I think I need to just go for it."

"Sounds like a plan," Pan replied, doing his best statue imitation lest the gods interpret any movement as taking the initiative.

Reed's mouth opened slightly as he leaned in and touched his lips to Pan's for the first time. A shy tap, a mere tease, and he fell away.

Pan groaned; he couldn't help it. The man was trying his patience.

"I'm sorry," Reed said. "I know this all must seem really silly to you, considering how many times you've done this, but I feel like a teenager having my first kiss." The years fell away, and Pan saw Reed as that young man he once was, awkward and tentative, eager and scared.

"It's not silly at all. I think it's exciting."

Reed's gaze snapped to Pan's. "Are you making fun of me?"

"No," Pan said, his words so ineffective compared with what a kiss could have conveyed. "I'm dead serious"—Pan laughed as the realization caught him off guard—"which is actually highly unusual for me."

Surprise lifted Reed's eyebrows. "You mean that, don't you?"

"I'm barely holding it together over here." Reed visibly relaxed at Pan's confession. "So how about kissing me for real this time? Because once you get this party started, I am done holding back."

A nervous chuckle escaped Reed. "Thanks for the warning."

"It wasn't a warning," Pan said with a wink. "It was a promise."

Reed licked his lips, nodded once, and—credit where credit was due—dove right in for Pan's lips, this time like his life depended on it. Maybe it did. Maybe Pan's did, too, and for sure, Cupid's.

As far as kisses went, it certainly wasn't the best Pan had ever had, at least not at first. Reed was all over the place, trying too hard and thinking too hard and kissing too hard. He slashed his mouth this way and that. Pan did his best to stay with him, but it felt more like boxing than kissing.

Pan brought his hand to Reed's face, gently cupping his cheek. "Relax," Pan whispered, taking the lead, slowing their frantic kisses.

The tension leaked out of Reed with a low moan that vibrated on Pan's lips and sent shock waves through his body. Pan slipped his tongue gently along Reed's lower lip. The swift answer of Reed's tongue pressed against Pan's made him dizzy with want.

They found their rhythm together inside a kiss that could only belong to the two of them. Pleasure buzzed in Pan's head. Tiny explosions of light and color *pop-pop-popping*.

Holy shit! Fireworks.

Pan pulled away, stunned at his epiphany.

Reed's lips, glistening, curved into a shy grin. Pan could feel his own smile stretch wide across his face, changing the landscape of his facial hair enough to trip up Reed's fingers. The two of them laughed softly together.

"Well? What's your conclusion, Professor?" Pan asked, a light note of teasing in his voice. "How was it after all, kissing a person with a beard?"

Reed scrubbed his fingers through Pan's beard one last time before letting his hands fall away. "Different from what I'd imagined."

"How so?"

"It was . . . tender-er," Reed said, chuckling at himself and melting Pan's insides with his goofy sincerity.

Yes, Pan had been especially gentle with him. He had plans for Reed, plans requiring stamina and an open mind. He slid one hand to Reed's and twined their fingers together.

"Do you trust me?" Pan asked.

Reed pondered the question. "Yeah," he answered, seemingly surprised by his own response, "I guess I do."

"Good." Pan brought their joined hands to his bare chest, flattened Reed's palm against his skin, and slowly drew Reed's hand over the hard mounds of his pecs. Reed stilled, watching his own hand crawl across Pan's body as if it belonged to someone else.

"Hey," Pan whispered.

Reed's steady gaze shifted to Pan's face. "Hmm?"

Pan shot him a wink. "Don't forget to breathe, okay?"

Reed smiled shyly, then drew in a choppy breath through his plump, ripe lips. Pan couldn't resist leaning in for another taste. Reed found his stride quickly, seeking out Pan's tongue and taking control of their kiss.

Turned out the professor was excellent at multitasking—or maybe the more distractions, the freer his body was from the burdens of his overactive mind. As Pan dragged Reed's thumb over his nipple, Reed pinched the sensitive knot, causing Pan to groan into Reed's mouth.

They broke apart, gasping for air.

Reed shook his head. "Wow."

"You know you're making me completely crazy, right?"

A blush bloomed on Reed's cheeks. He didn't need to say it back; Pan knew damn well he was having the same effect on Reed.

"I don't want to rush you," Pan said, "but I'd really like to bring you to my bed right now."

Reed answered with a shuddering sigh and a clipped nod. Pure joy surged through Pan.

He slipped his arm around Reed's waist and coaxed him toward the bedroom. If Pan had needed a reminder to go easy on Reed, his uneven gait down the hallway would have done the trick.

At the foot of Pan's bed, they stood facing each other. Reed let his cane drop to the floor. Without speaking, Pan tugged Reed's shirt free of the jeans and slid it up over his head. Reed's skin pebbled with goose bumps as his arms dropped to his sides. Pan ran his hands up the length of Reed's arms and across his shoulders, lean but strong from years of swimming. Reed swiped his tongue across his lips; they wouldn't stay moist for long.

Pan trailed his fingertips downward. The bands of muscles tensed and rolled under his hands as if Pan's touch held the power to breathe life directly into Reed's belly. Pan's knuckles knocked against Reed's belt and the soft fuzz behind it. Reed's Adam's apple bobbed hard.

Pan worked open the buckle, and the belt fell open. He reached for the zipper.

Reed thrust out his hand and gripped Pan's wrist with a firm grasp that stopped him dead in his tracks.

Pan's gaze snapped to Reed's face. "Sorry. Too fast?"

"I, uh . . ."

If he'd wanted Pan to stop, Reed could have pushed his hand away instead of trapping it there. Pan wasn't sure what that meant, other than he was going to have to wait and see. Patience wasn't exactly his strong suit. It seemed he was going to have to work on that for Reed.

"Sorry," Reed said. "I just wanted to tell you, to *warn* you . . . it's, uh, a bit rough under there. Scarring." Reed closed his mouth and swallowed hard, waiting and watching for Pan's reaction through pleading eyes.

The tiniest misstep on Pan's part—a twitch, a grimace, a squint—could do real damage to Reed, and to Pan's chances of a future with Reed. He wanted to reassure him that a little scar tissue was not going to repulse a man who recently had a tail stub growing out of his ass, but that didn't seem like a productive direction to take the conversation.

"If you can kiss a person with a beard, I'm pretty sure I can handle whatever you've got going on down there."

Reed huffed, a small smile overriding his anxious pout.

"Look, Reed, this is something we're going to have to get past. If we don't do it now, it's going to become larger than life."

Reed nodded as a sigh escaped him.

"Hey, I get it," Pan said. "This isn't your first time down this path."

"No." Reed dropped his gaze, no doubt recalling every humiliation in his past.

"*Well*," Pan said, drawing out the word until he was sure he had Reed's full attention, "if we're both really lucky, it *could* be your last."

The impact of Pan's words caused Reed's head to jerk up. *Yes, Reed. Let that sink in: I might be the last person you ever have sex with.*

On second thought, maybe Pan shouldn't have let those words fly. If Reed were to stop him now, he was basically rejecting the whole idea of Right Love—and Pan along with it.

The hand on Pan's wrist fell away.

"You asked me if I trusted you." Reed's voice sounded as shaky as a note blown through Pan's flute. "I've known you all of . . . what, a week? First, the God of Love just happens to seek out a retired professor of classical studies for *swim lessons,* of all things! Now, it's pretty obvious the man is, *ahem,* physically gifted, but that kind of thing never affected me any more than, say, viewing a particularly compelling painting or sculpture— *shoot,* that's an unfortunate example . . ."

Had Pan pushed Reed too far too soon? The poor man seemed to be coming unhinged.

"Anyway, I find myself completely consumed by this baffling attraction—I mean, not that it's baffling why anyone would be attracted to the embodiment of the perfect man—"

Pan cleared his throat so hard, he could have coughed up a family of four. It wasn't that he disagreed with Reed about Cupid's perfection, but there was only so much a guy could bear. Reed shot him a sheepish look.

"What I meant was, if I liked men *that way,* wouldn't I have already figured that out by now? I've been alive for . . . a good, long while now. But okay, I'm an old dog. That doesn't mean I'm afraid to learn a new trick. It just takes my mind a few days to open to the invitation my body has already accepted. And wouldn't you know it? On the very day I've worked up the guts to give this man-on-man thing a try, out walks Q and in walks his big, kind of scary-looking friend Pan . . ."

Ouch.

". . . and lo and behold, he casts his spell on me, too."

Pan didn't know whether he should throw Reed down on the bed and rip his clothes off or prepare himself for the worst breakup of his life.

"Ah, but don't worry, folks. This all makes perfect sense because Q and his friend Pan are—yes, you guessed it! Greek gods!"

"Demi," Pan cut in, immediately wishing he hadn't. "Sorry. Continue, please."

"Right. Yes. Make that *one* god and one demigod-satyr who's not a satyr now." Reed broke off the tirade to his imaginary audience and set his focus on Pan. "On top of all that, I'm informed my heart is beating for you and yours for me, which makes us each other's destiny—or at least, I'm *one* of your destinies because of the whole immortality situation—" Reed stopped and shook his head. "You do get that this is insane, right?"

Agreeing seemed like a terrible idea, and Pan couldn't figure out how to disagree without agitating Reed further. He shrugged.

"The point is . . . if you really think about it, there's absolutely no reason I *should* trust you."

Pan's heart plummeted. Was that it, then? "Dammit, Reed, at least give me a—" Reed's hand closed over Pan's mouth.

"But I *do* trust you." Reed's whole face surrendered to a warm smile while the words drilled through Pan's thick skull. Reed dropped his hand from Pan's mouth.

"You do?"

"Yes." Tears welled behind Reed's glasses. "Please don't hurt me, Pan."

"Reed—" Pan lifted his hands to Reed's glasses and gently lifted them off his head. He placed a soft kiss over each of Reed's eyes, then pulled back to meet his shimmering gaze. "Wait, can you see me?"

Laughter bubbled out of Reed. "I can see you well enough, but if you break my glasses, I won't be able to drive home."

"Huh. Is that right?" Pan grinned and pretended to snap Reed's glasses in two.

"*Ever!*" Reed added, fake-scowling at him.

"Okay, okay." Pan slipped Reed's glasses onto his face,

teasing his fingers through Reed's hair. "Luckily, you look ridiculously hot in glasses."

Reed rolled his eyes as he straightened the frames. "Whatever," he said, working hard to stifle a grin.

This lighter moment felt good. There were plenty of serious conversations ahead of them, assurances to be made. The truth was, Reed's body would always require special consideration, and he deserved to know if Pan could handle it.

Inside that flare of clarity, Pan committed his full heart to rising to the occasion. In fact, he couldn't wait to be that man. His conviction stole the breath from his lungs.

For the first time since Cupid's heart set on Pan, he felt like he might deserve to be a Worthy after all.

"Look, Reed. I know I can be a real jackass sometimes, but I swear to you, I will do everything in my power not to hurt you."

"I believe you," said Reed.

"Good. *Now* can I get in your pants?" Pan batted his eyelashes, and Reed snorted and threw his arms wide to the sides.

"I believed you about the jackass part, too," Reed said, "but thanks for the demonstration."

"Any time."

Reed's skinny jeans didn't need nearly as much coaxing as the man wearing them. Pan peeled off the pants and boxers in the same smooth motion, heading off any further debate. As he followed the clothes down Reed's legs, Pan sank into a crouch. He steadied Reed while he stepped out of his jeans and loafers, then lifted his gaze to the sight of his lover's naked body.

If not for their conversation, Pan would have tactfully ignored the scar, at least until he'd paid appropriate homage to his Right Love's genitalia—now staring him directly in the face. Of all the moments in his life to step up, Pan had to go and choose the one that required him to delay the gratification of his carnal desires with arguably the most important partner of his existence.

If the gods weren't testing Pan, they were certainly enjoying a hearty chuckle at his expense.

In the bright afternoon light, there was no missing the lumpy, pink starburst of scar tissue at Reed's hip. It reminded Pan of the time he'd accidentally smashed one of Dionysus's kraters and tried to repair it using boiled birch tar.

Here was the bullseye of Reed's most noble act and his most intimate secret revealed to Pan. A lump of gratitude rose in Pan's throat.

Reed gasped at Pan's first touch. With each circuit of Pan's fingertips around the edges of the bullet wound, Reed's tension seeped out. Pan feathered a soft kiss on the ravaged skin, drawing a low moan from Reed. His libido stirred to life. Whatever Reed had needed to ease his mind, Pan had provided.

Now, it was time to convince Reed he would never want for another lover.

Grinning up at Reed's dazed expression, Pan gave Reed's stiffening length its first loving caress. Reed answered with a whimper that straightened Pan's dick faster than the filthiest porn.

Oh, Reed. There's so much more where that came from.

Pan kiss-walked Reed backward to the bed, then gave him a playful shove onto the mattress. Reed lifted his head to watch Pan push his sweatpants to the floor. There was nothing underneath.

"Oh my god," Reed said, wide-eyed at the erection headed his way.

Be gentle. Be gentle.

Pan lifted one knee onto the bed—*be gentle*—followed by the other—*be gentle*—and crawled toward Reed.

A loud crash coming from the garage caught Pan's attention, but the last thing he was about to do was leave Reed and go deal with some idiotic burglar. *Fuck it.* Let him steal the truck; Pan would buy another one tomorrow.

A door slammed. "Pan! I know you're here!"

Reed jolted upright. "Is that Cupid?"

Motherfucker.

34

DESPERATION

"Don't even think of going anywhere," Pan warned Reed with as much gravity as possible. "I'll get rid of him."

Pan extracted his crumpled sweats from the pile, tugged them up his legs as quickly as he could, and folded his erection inside. Reed chuckled, clasping his arms beneath his head to watch the show.

"This better be good," Pan muttered, adding a few choice curse words having to do with the state of his aching balls.

More crashing—drawers and cabinets—this time from inside the house. "*Pan! Get out here!*" The God of Love was in a foul mood.

"I'm coming! Don't get your toga in a twist!" With one last, ardent glance at the naked man stretched out on top of his bed, Pan closed the bedroom door behind himself.

Whatever he'd been doing, Cupid stopped to glare at Pan, arms crossed and eyebrows knit into an angry line. "You didn't answer your phone," he said evenly.

Crap! His phone! "Sorry, man. This *really* isn't the best time . . ."

"*Obviously*," Cupid answered. Yes, of course he'd smelled Reed and arousal all over him. Well, that sucked, but that was just the way it was.

"Q, *buddy*, are you having an emergency? Because I'm trying to consummate over here, and your little visit—"

"You already did."

"Uh, no. We definitely did not." The proof was straining against his sweatpants.

"You and Reed crossed your Liminal Point."

"Wait, *what*? We did?"

"Oh, you definitely did."

Pan had seen that anguished expression twice before. Yep, they'd launched Cupid into his heartbreak phase.

They'd crossed! Pan was well and truly mated with his Right Love.

Under other circumstances, the news might have kicked off a super-obnoxious victory dance, but Pan tempered his excitement so as not to be a complete asshole. This was something to celebrate with Reed when they were alone again.

"When did this happen?" Pan asked.

"The worst thirty-three minutes of my life ago."

Thirty-three minutes. Reed's kiss.

"But you're still here," Pan said, realizing at once how cold that sounded. "Sorry."

Cupid's hand had migrated to his chest, and he was squeezing hard. If the poor bastard could've reached inside his own rib cage to choke off the last heartbeat, he surely would have.

"Here, come sit down." Pan took him by the shoulders and drew Cupid to the couch. "I can't understand why they didn't take you this time."

"I couldn't say," Cupid mumbled. He was agitated, edgy, eyes darting all around the room. Neither of them sat down.

"How are you holding up? You want a drink?" Pan started for the kitchen.

"Where's my arrow?"

"What?"

"I know you still have it here somewhere." The desperation in Cupid's eyes made Pan's blood run cold. So that's what he'd been looking for.

"What the fuck, man?"

"I need to end this, Pan."

"You cannot kill yourself."

A dark chuckle left Cupid. "You don't actually know that."

"I know I won't let you, so yeah, I know."

Cupid's chin jutted out. "Maybe you can't stop me now."

"Seriously? One day at the speed bag and now you're stronger than me? Think again, chump!"

A long stare-down followed. Cupid looked away first. Pan breathed a sigh of relief until he realized Cupid was spinning slowly while scanning the room, still searching for the arrow. Cupid's gaze fell on the closet and froze. By the time Pan figured out that Cupid had been reading his responses like a treasure map, it was too late.

Cupid bolted for the closet. Pan lunged. Pan was stronger, but Cupid was quick. He easily beat Pan to the door, yanked it open, and snatched his bow and arrow from the floor.

Pan grabbed him by the arm. "Stop, okay?"

"Let go of me."

Pan relaxed his grip. Might was not going to win this battle. "C'mon, Q. What are you hoping to accomplish here?"

"I am hoping I can figure out a way to shoot myself in the heart and set the next Worthy into motion so I don't have to keep feeling like this for another second."

"But what about all that stuff you said to me when I begged you to put that arrow in my heart? What if you nail the wrong person? What if they get angry you chose for yourself? What if you *die?*"

"I don't care," Cupid said, and Pan could see he meant it. "Literally *anything* would be better than this. I know what I'm talking about. The two times before were nowhere near this bad. If I don't end this soon, I'll—"

"Don't do it, Q." Pan and Cupid spun around, and there was Reed, striding toward them, barefoot, his shirt hanging out over his jeans. His face was ashen.

"Reed," Pan said, stepping in front of Reed and grasping him by the arms, "it's not what you think."

"I think you're wrong," he said, then slipped past Pan.

This was about to get dicey. Pan's mind raced, but he could not figure out how to regain control of the situation.

"Q—" Reed stopped, then began again, "*Cupid.* You look like what I used to see in the mirror. A more handsome version, obviously . . ." Reed smiled at Cupid but did not get a response. "Come sit down." Reed looped his arm around Cupid's shoulders and glanced at Pan. "Can you get us some hot tea?"

"I have lemonade."

"Lemonade's fine," Reed said gently.

Pan glanced from Reed to Cupid, shrugged, and retreated to the kitchen. It wasn't as if he had a better idea. He worked quickly, scooping ice into glasses while keeping ears and eyes peeled on the pair in the next room. He could always leap the counter if need be.

Reed sat Cupid down where the couch turned a corner and settled in next to him, knee to knee. Pan had almost forgotten how close Reed and Cupid had become, but it was hard to miss, seeing the two of them together like that.

Cupid lowered the bow and arrow to the floor. At least he was listening.

"Pan explained to me how your, uh, predicament takes its toll on your heart. Your pain is palpable, and I feel for you. I really do."

A ragged sigh left Cupid. His shoulders drooped like a shirt slipped off a hanger.

"I also understand," Reed continued, "there is much that is beyond your control"—Cupid huffed—"but there are choices you *can* make. Do you remember our conversation about fate?"

Pan returned with the lemonades. "Don't worry, it's decaf." Pan's humor fell flat as Reed and Cupid took the glasses.

"Thank you," Reed said, his gaze catching on Pan's bare chest. "How about putting on a shirt?" The way Reed was looking at him, Pan knew it wasn't a question. What Pan couldn't tell was whether it was for Q's benefit or Reed's.

"Sure." Pan squeezed Cupid's shoulder as he walked past. "Be right back."

The voices carried into Pan's bedroom. He monitored the cadence and the gist of the conversation as he covered up his tempting flesh with a loose-fitting T-shirt. He returned to find Cupid and Reed inclined toward each other, their foreheads nearly touching.

"I think I know somebody who can help you," Reed was saying. "You do?"

"Yes. A therapist who helped me through my trauma."

Cupid looked to Pan, who sputtered at Reed. "A *shrink?*"

Reed nodded.

"Whoa!" Pan's hands shot up in the air. "Slow down. Nobody's sending the God of Love to therapy!" Reed's eyes opened wide, and Pan rushed to cover his tracks. "Not that there's anything wrong with therapy . . . for *mortals*."

Pan stopped to take a breath. Hysteria wouldn't help anything. He hadn't even told Reed their good news yet, and here he was insulting the man. *What a shit show.*

"Look, Reed," Pan started again, "you are literally the only mortal alive who knows our true identities, and we need to keep it that way. I can't let Q go talk to some expert extractor. Did you not notice he has zero filter? We'll be outed before the guy can say, 'Time's up. That'll be three hundred dollars.'"

Reed waited for Pan's outburst to wind down, then answered using that calm, teachable-moment tone Pan was already starting to find endearing. "He'll keep all your secrets, Pan. In fact, he's legally and ethically bound to do exactly that."

"But he'll *know* them," Pan replied.

"True, but I believe the trade-off is well worth it. Dr. Hannon was the only person who could get through to me after I was shot."

"*Doctor?*" Cupid looked to Pan again for answers he didn't have.

Of course Pan knew what a doctor was; he'd even slept with a few. He just had no frame of reference for the experience of being a patient.

The Olympian healers, Apollo and his many descendants, had always applied their healing techniques to the humans who worshipped them. Immortal, self-healing bodies did not require medical care. A decent *mental* health practitioner, though . . . *that* person could find a steady stream of business on the Mount, now that Pan thought of it. Up to this point, Pan had never entertained the notion of seeking treatment for a fallen's emotional distress. Wasn't the mental anguish part of the punishment?

"He's a psychologist," Reed replied.

"What's that?" Cupid asked.

"A psychologist is someone who studies the mind and human behavior. It comes from your Greek root *psyche*, which means soul—" Reed cut off with an embarrassed chuckle. "Oh, but look who I'm lecturing to about psyche!"

Cupid stared blankly at Reed. "Me?"

"Well, obviously, you would know better than anyone why our modern study of the human soul would be named for her."

"Her *who?*" Pan asked.

"Psyche!" Reed said.

"Who's Psyche?" Pan asked, turning to Cupid, in case he'd missed this important development in Cupid's life while they were apart.

Cupid shrugged. "I'm not aware of anyone named Psyche."

Reed bolted off the couch. "Psyche? The voluptuous youngest of the three daughters of the mortal king and queen? Cupid—uh, *you*—were sent by Venus to set ruinous love on the girl, and instead, the two fell in love . . . and this isn't ringing *any* bells?" Reed's smile died when he realized nobody else was in on the joke. "Are you two serious right now?"

Pan shrugged at Cupid, who mirrored his confusion right back at him. "Reed, what are you talking about?"

"The myth of Cupid and Psyche?"

"*Ohhh,*" Cupid said, standing to join the others. "A myth. No wonder." He and Pan exchanged nods.

"I don't understand," said Reed, his expression twisted with confusion. "I thought you said those stories were your history."

"Just the ones that are true." Pan clapped both hands onto Reed's shoulders. "Don't believe everything you read, Professor. For every ten stories told about us, only three are true, and often, those are so wildly embellished, they barely resemble what really happened."

But oh, the retellings of the exaggerations provided for endless entertainment on Mount Olympus! In fact, Pan had often wondered whether the poets had stolen some of the more fantastical myths from the dinner-table lore spouted by the gods themselves. How else were immortal beings meant to amuse themselves century after century?

Cupid chimed in, nudging Pan with his elbow. "Hey, how about that old story that Hephaestus split open Zeus's head with an ax to free Athena?"

"Right! Nothing like an ax to the head to relieve a head-ache!" Pan huffed. "As if Zeus would have let old Hephaestus keep both testicles after a move like that!"

"I guess the true story wasn't interesting enough," Cupid said.

"The true story being . . .?" Reed asked.

"That Athena sprang from Zeus's forehead in full body armor," said Pan, grinning, "after Zeus swallowed her mother!"

"Oh, and don't forget I'm my own mother's father!" Cupid said with a giggle that brought Pan right back to the childhood friend he'd abandoned so long ago.

"Yeah, remind me how that's supposed to work again?"

Cupid and Pan tossed stories back and forth while Reed watched like a man trying to memorize the answer key to his whole life. Pan was just happy to take Cupid's mind off his pain for a little while. The two had a good hoot until Reed cleared his throat, effectively halting the frenetic ping-pong of tall and taller tales flying around the room.

"So, what is your true, uh, origin story, Q . . . if you don't mind my asking?" *Damn*, if Reed's delicate way with words didn't make Pan want to tackle the man right where he stood.

"Oh," Cupid answered without the slightest hesitation, "I'm the illegitimate offspring of Mother's sordid affair with Ares."

"Huh." Reed nodded slowly, studying Cupid as if looking for evidence of the unholy union that had produced him. "And everyone knows this?" he asked cautiously.

"Yes," Cupid answered. "Personally, I've always believed that my stepfather—"

"Hephaestus, yes?" Reed asked. Pan had to give the guy credit for keeping up.

"That's right. I think he had to have sensed Mother was preg-nant before he threw his chain-link net over her bed, trapping Mother and Ares underneath it—"

"*Naked*," Pan added, earning a thanks-for-reminding-me glare from Cupid.

Cupid sighed. "But there was nothing to be done about it at that point."

Pan added, "Other than humiliate all three of them."

And now, according to Mercury, Ares and Aphrodite were at it again. Poor old Hephaestus, always paying for his "fortu-nate marriage" to Aphrodite one way or another. Would he even try to stand in their way this time?

"Well, that's dark," Reed said, shaking his head.

A knot tightened in Pan's belly. Is this what Reed feared when he'd spoken of Pan being trapped in a relationship with him? Surely, Pan and Reed's Right Love union was superior to the marital arrangement ordered by Zeus in order to keep peace among the gods.

With all his affection flowing to Reed, Pan squeezed his shoulders. "I know it's a lot to take in."

"Actually, this makes perfect sense."

Pan burst out in a loud guffaw that pulled him away from Reed. "I was not expecting that."

"No, really," Reed said. "I've never been able to reconcile all the different origin stories. It's hard to accept some stories as true when some are so outlandish. A mathematician would never accept the logic of a solution to a problem if he couldn't prove the foundational theorems. You understand what I'm saying?"

"Sure," Pan answered. *I have the answers you seek, my curi-ous lover.*

"And the art . . ." Reed stared off past Pan. "So many different interpretations of the physical form throughout the centuries."

Here, Cupid interjected. "I find the pudgy, diapered versions particularly upsetting."

Pan chuckled again. "What's more disturbing than the idea that the Goddess of Love would hand a bow and a quiver filled with love-tipped arrows to a flying baby?"

"Seriously! I couldn't even hold the bow until my tenth birthday."

"Yes, exactly *this*!" Reed's face lit up with a new fire Pan had not yet witnessed. Oh, he was glorious, each new discovery buffing away layers of confusion, revealing a glow burning inside Reed as bright as the source of all light.

"And you, Pan?"

Startled, Pan met Reed's questioning gaze. "Hmm?"

"All those changing representations of you through the ages, were they actual sightings or artistic imaginings or what?"

Pan cleared his throat. "All of the above, I guess."

Reed nodded. "And the stories?"

Cupid snorted out a laugh. Pan glowered at him. They both knew where this was heading—the last place Pan wanted to go.

Fixing his expression for Reed, Pan replied, "Which stories are you referring to . . . *specifically?*"

"You and Syrinx?"

"Mm, afraid so," Pan replied.

"Pitys?"

"Okay, yes, that's true too."

"And Selene?"

"Ah, my sweet moon goddess. That was a beautiful affair—until Selene set her heart on that lazy shepherd boy, Endymion."

"Yes, of course. Endymion," said Reed, nodding, "Selene's great love."

Pan half snorted. "Right. She loved him so much, she made a deal with Zeus to cast him into an eternal sleep because she couldn't bear the thought of losing her mortal lover."

Reed's eyes went wide as he connected the dots. He opened his mouth as if to ask the question of Pan—*Would you ever do that to me?*—then thought better of it. "And what about Echo?" he asked instead.

"Guilty," Pan admitted.

". . . *guilty . . . guilty . . . guilty . . .*" added Cupid, earning him an eye roll from Pan though he was grateful for the comic relief.

"In my defense," Pan said, "those were the adventures of a wild beast. I won't deny my past, but all of those escapades from my life as a satyr don't represent who I am now."

"Understood," said Reed. "Aphrodite must have had good reason to choose you for love."

A blush rose up Pan's neck, making it awkward to meet Reed's gaze. Adoration was going to take some getting used to.

A gentle nudge at his elbow caused Pan to glance down as Reed slipped his arm through Pan's. "Does this mean you can play the flute?"

Pan's blush burned hotter.

Cupid answered for him, ignoring Pan's stink eye. "Yes, he still plays beautifully."

"I'd love to hear you play sometime," Reed said, "if you feel comfortable."

"Of course I'll play for you, Reed." Pan's voice caught on his lover's name. Reed heard it too, his gaze melting into two warm pools of grayish-green.

A low groan from Cupid drew them out of their googly-eyed moment. Poor guy was in agony. Pan shot him a sheepish shrug.

"Right," Reed said. "Where were we?"

Cupid was quick to answer. "Something about someone who might be able to do something to help me not feel like I'm walking through the pit of Tartarus?"

"Yes, yes, and you were saying you'd never heard of Psyche."

Pan shook his head. "Definitely sounds like a fabrication of some human's overactive imagination."

"Huh. Is it possible it happened so long ago you simply don't remember?" Reed looked back and forth between Cupid and Pan; both returned blank stares.

"Hmm." Pan rubbed his chin, summoning wisdom in the manner of generations of great thinkers. "In this myth of yours, does Cupid lose his virginity?"

"Uh . . ." Reed's gaze slipped over to Cupid and darted back to Pan as quickly as it could. "Many times over."

"That *definitely* did not happen!" Cupid said. "There is no length of time that could ever make me forget that."

"Okay. Well, not to get hung up on the etymology, but do you think you might give therapy a try?"

Cupid turned desperate, yearning eyes on him. "*Pan?*"

Back in the day, Pan would have relished the power rush of being looked at just the way Cupid was looking at him this very moment. There was no satisfaction in it now that Pan was, as Reed had put it, legally and ethically responsible for his best friend's welfare. *Just when I thought this job was getting easier.*

Pan lifted his eyes toward Olympus. This was a Big Decision. He needed to get it right.

On the one hand, Pan had just barely been able to drag Cupid's heartsick ass through the first two breakups by sticking to Cupid like Velcro until the gods had released his heart to inflict the next torture. Even if Pan devoted himself to Cupid twenty-four seven, there was little chance he could provide much comfort, being the one who'd smashed Q's heart to smithereens this time.

On the other hand, it made Pan physically ill to imagine Cupid stretched out along some random doc's couch while the contents of his existence were dragged out of him like the entrails of a deer carcass left to rot at the side of the road. The mortals had as much chance making sense of Cupid as the scientists who dissected E.T., and the results would be no less disastrous.

Best-case scenario, they'd take Cupid's stories as the rantings of a madman and lock him away to languish in some hospital for the mentally ill. Worst-case, they'd believe him.

Meanwhile, Cupid was looking at him like a kid who'd just asked his dad for a pony. Pan let out a moan. There was nothing he disliked more than being the grown-up.

"I'm sorry, Q. I have to be honest with you. I think this is a terrible idea." Beside him, Reed tensed. *Fuck. Way to stick your hoof in your mouth.* Pan whirled around. "No offense, Reed."

Reed lifted his hands in surrender and gave his head a sad shake. "I shouldn't have stuck my nose in where it doesn't belong," Reed said as he started toward the bedroom.

Pan bolted toward Reed and grasped him by the elbow. Reed whipped his head around; their gazes caught and held.

"No," Pan said, "it's not that at all. I *want* you to stick your nose in, and you definitely belong."

Reed huffed, shrugging off Pan's hand. Pan could practically see the hurt eking out of every pore.

Be gentle. It wasn't just Reed's body that required care.

"He's right, Reed," said Cupid quietly. There was so much pain behind Cupid's eyes, it seemed impossible he had room to worry about anyone else's feelings. "*I'm* the one who doesn't belong here."

Dammit, Q! Pan felt like a wishbone being tugged in opposite directions, and he was dangerously close to snapping.

"You better tell him, Pan."

"He better tell me what?" Reed demanded.

"*Now?*" Pan mouthed to Cupid, whose eyes closed as he nodded.

"*Pan?*" Reed's broken plea tore at Pan's heart.

Cautiously, Pan took Reed's hands, lacing their fingers together. "So, it turns out your bold little move worked."

"My move? Oh! You mean pursuing you?"

"Kissing me," Pan replied, oozing pride for his brave mortal. "You did it, Reed. You crossed us."

Understanding lit Reed's expression like a spark catching on a pile of tinder. "Huh! Well, what do you know!"

Completely overcome with emotion, Pan drew Reed into an urgent kiss, a bright burst of bliss that mellowed into a solemn commitment. They were bound together now.

A soft click pulled Pan from their kiss. Cupid was gone, his bow and arrow leaned against the closet door.

35

DOMESTIC BLISS

Reed's head weighed pleasantly on Pan's outstretched arm as they half dozed under crisp, white sheets. Morning sun streamed into Reed's bedroom.

"Someone forgot to close the blinds last night," Pan said with a smirk. As if either of them would have given a thought to window treatments in the throes of their all-consuming passion.

"Maybe we should just leave the blinds closed all the time," Reed said, snuggling closer. "Who cares what's happening out there?"

"That's you, Reed. Always thinking."

It was a nice dream, staying right here in this little bubble with Reed, just the two of them learning each other's bodies and minds as they'd been doing nonstop for a week now. Pan studied the man lying beside him, looking much the same as he did just after one of his vigorous swims—hair tousled, muscles spent, a healthy flush in his cheeks. Yeah, that was Pan's doing, and the knowledge left a contented hum in his chest.

Reed's eyes drifted closed, his drowsy smile curling along Pan's bicep. "That was nice last night."

"It was." Pan rolled closer and stroked his fingers through Reed's hair, watching to see if sleep would take him again. Pan was hungry, but he could wait out one more catnap.

Reed's eyelids flickered open. "Was it really okay for you?"

Seriously? "I haven't figured out how to fake an orgasm yet, so you can be pretty sure that was me enjoying myself."

A blush rose to Reed's cheeks. "But we didn't . . ." He didn't complete the sentence, nor did he need to.

Pan ran the backs of his fingers over Reed's warm cheek. "No, we did not, and yet . . ." Pan popped his eyebrows, hoping for a smile, but Reed's forehead remained creased, a dead give-away to the turmoil inside.

Oh, Professor.

"What's up, Reed?"

"I wouldn't ever want you to feel as though you're compromising who you are to be with me."

It hurt that Reed still worried about not being enough—young enough, fit enough, fun enough, *gay* enough—and Pan had tried to be reassuring in those moments he could feel Reed hesitating.

"*Still good?*" Pan would ask carefully so as not to break the mood.

"Yes," Reed would assure him, "*feels good, keep going, don't stop . . .*"

"*You'd tell me if—*"

"*Shush, Pan. I trust you.*"

And that trust was everything. That was Reed checking his professor glasses on the nightstand and leaving the teaching to Pan.

"As long as you'll promise me the same," Pan replied, staring into the eyes of the scholar who knew more than Pan could accumulate in fifty of Reed's lifetimes. Over the span of the last week, Pan had read more, debated more, listened and learned more than in all his formal schooling combined, and still, he couldn't get enough of his hot professor. "I would never want you to dumb yourself down for me."

"Deal!" Reed agreed. "Just let me know if I'm boring you to tears."

"Oh, you'll know!"

"Haven't figured out how to fake that either?" Reed chuckled at his own joke.

"Well, if I *had*"—Pan climbed on top of Reed and stretched out over the length of his body as if to do push-ups using Reed for a mat—"I wouldn't have gotten myself into nearly so much *mischief* at the academy." Pan flexed his hips at "mischief," and he felt the man below him stir.

Reed pulled his fingers through Pan's chest hairs like Apollo plucking the strings of his lyre. "*May*-be," Reed said, coy as can be, "you just didn't have the right teacher to inspire your curiosity."

"Hmm, I guess we'll find out, Professor," Pan said, dipping his head to give Reed a slow, steamy kiss.

A faint gallop of dog paws striking wood floors snowballed into a full-blown stampede on the other side of the bedroom door. Reed turned from Pan's kiss and peered over his shoulder toward the exuberant barks and scratching at the door.

"You closed the bedroom door?" Reed asked.

"Yeah, I did. Moses almost took out my left nut yesterday when he jumped on us."

Reed shrugged, unimpressed. "I thought you said your regeneration period is three days."

"Oh yeah?" Pan reached down and cupped Reed's balls, applying a not-entirely-loving pressure. "Tell me, which one of *your* balls would you like to do without for three days?"

"Fair point," Reed answered, wriggling free of Pan's hand as he rolled out of bed. "We'll keep the door closed from now on."

Pan liked the permanent ring to that.

In fact, Pan grinned all through his morning leak, kept grinning around his toothbrush, and was still grinning when he came upon the happy scene in the kitchen. All four dogs stood in a neat line at their bowls, heads down, working away at their breakfast while their tails wagged their asses so hard, it was a wonder they didn't fall like dominoes. And there was Reed in his furry slippers and flannel pajamas, filling the coffee maker with enough water and coffee grounds for two.

"You know, I think you might need a few more creatures to take care of," Pan joked, drawing Reed's attention to his entrance.

Leaning back against the counter, Reed stared at Pan's naked form with great amusement. "Aren't you cold?"

"I don't actually get cold. I only wear clothes so as not to arouse suspicion."

Reed burst out laughing. "If you plan to walk around the house buck naked all day, you're going to arouse a lot more than suspicion!"

"Works for me," Pan replied with a wink.

"I guess modesty is not a concern."

It was Pan's turn to laugh out loud. At the sound, Margaux lifted her head from her bowl and trotted over to greet him. "Hey there, girl." He bent to give her ears a scratch, careful to protect his dangling bits from errant teeth and a sloppy tongue. With her fierce loyalty to Reed, Margaux had been slower to warm to Pan than the others, but once she'd decided he was okay, she was all in. She'd quickly become Pan's favorite, and he was pretty sure she knew it. The others gave him no more than a quick sniff before clamoring to go out.

"Tough crowd this morning," Pan said with a chuckle as he strode to the door.

"We did make them hold their bladders longer than usual this morning," Reed said, a sly smirk playing on his lips.

"Worth it." Pan stepped out of the way of traffic as he pushed open the door.

"Better make sure my mailman's not outside. Flashing a postal employee is a federal offense."

"Now how would you have come by that little nugget of information, Reed?"

A sense of well-being swept through Pan as he took the proffered coffee mug and dropped a kiss on Reed's cheek. The phrase "domestic bliss" entered Pan's head.

He was reminded of his visit to Mia's, how those three boys had wrapped themselves around Cupid like monkeys hugging a tree, how the little one in diapers had rolled his dump truck up and down Pan's legs, and how Pan had dashed all their hopes of becoming a happy family that day. And how Ruthie had invited Cupid into her home but was never his to have or hold.

And here was Pan, strutting around Reed's kitchen, letting it all hang out and growing more attached to Reed each day, while poor Cupid was drowning his sorrows in gym rats, booze, and random women. According to the text Cheri had sent Pan last night, she'd cut Cupid off after his third Kamikaze, and he'd left the Stagecoach soon after with two girls on each arm.

"Hey, what just happened?" Reed's ability to read Pan was scary sometimes.

Pan shook his head. "Sorry. What should I make us for breakfast today?" He tugged open the refrigerator door and hid his face among the shelves. "Ooh, how about an omelet? Oh, whoops, we're out of eggs. Hmm, how about a smoothie with . . . oh, nope. No yogurt. Shit, sorry, I guess I've been eating you out of house and home. I was thinking of grabbing a few things from home today anyway. I'll stop at the store on my way back. Or we can take a ride together if you—"

"Pan."

Pan shut the refrigerator with a sigh. *Busted.*

Reed sat nursing his coffee and watching Pan with way too much worry in his eyes. "What's got you so rattled? Are you not happy with me?"

"*What?* Of course I'm happy. I'm deliriously happy! That's the whole problem!"

The puppies were whining to be let in. Pan started toward the door.

"Leave the dogs for a minute," Reed said tightly. "Please, just sit down and talk to me."

Pan sank into the chair beside Reed. "I'm sorry. I didn't mean to pee on our parade."

"You haven't peed on anything. C'mon, Pan." Reed slid his hand palm-up on the table between them. "We're a couple now. We're supposed to work together. If something's bothering you, maybe I can help. At least get whatever it is off your chest."

Moved by Reed's empathy, Pan set his hand atop Reed's and curled his fingers into the spaces. "It's Q. I'm worried sick about him, and every second I'm here with you and feeling happy, it makes me feel lousier."

Judging by Reed's nod, he wasn't surprised to learn what had been plaguing Pan. "Whatever happens, we're in this together now. All three of us."

Unease seeped into Pan's bones. Reed was right. Whatever the Divine Council held in store next for Cupid, somehow Reed was now situated smack in the middle of it. Pan's protective instinct surged so swiftly and so violently, it nearly threw him from his chair.

So this is how it feels to love.

Reed tipped his head forward and gazed over the rims of his glasses at Pan. "You know you don't have to worry about me, right? I'm a big boy."

"Of course I'm worried about you. I'm worried about all of us. Cupid's in for the ass-whooping of his eternal life, I'm completely useless, and now, thanks to me, you're tangled up with the most powerful mayhem machines in the cosmos."

Reed offered a gentle smile. "Did you ever consider maybe that's why I'm here?"

"For *Q*?" Pan was surprised by the pang of jealousy that snuck up on him.

"For *you*, Pan. To help you . . . if you will allow me."

Help? For two thousand years, Pan had been a solo act. Could he make room for Reed? Hell, Pan had just admitted he had no idea what to do for Cupid. Might be nice to have a whip-smart, levelheaded partner with vast knowledge of the inhabitants of Mount O to help Pan think things through.

But what about Reed's safety? Clearly, the man had a bad habit of throwing himself in harm's way. That didn't mean Pan had to encourage him.

"Listen, Reed, I would love to have your help, believe me, but I don't think you appreciate exactly how dicey things can get." *Impotence, priapism, tails . . .* "There's no reason for you to put yourself in danger. Q and I don't have a choice, but you do."

"Exactly, and I made my choice when I showed up at your front door." A triumphant grin spread across Reed's cheeks. "Besides, somebody up there likes me, or there wouldn't be a naked god sitting at my kitchen table right now."

The gods giveth . . .

"Those same gods can be cruel and random." And hopefully, they all had more pressing things to do than listen in on this conversation. "Look, Reed, I know you see me as some all-powerful being, but I need you to understand I cannot protect you from everything."

"Noted," said Reed, still gazing at Pan with wide-eyed invincibility. He wasn't taking this seriously enough.

Pan hated to burst Reed's bubble, but the man's very life depended on it. "You could die, okay?" Speaking the bleak truth out loud gutted Pan.

"Oh, I'm definitely going to die," Reed said as casually as if he'd just told Pan he was heading to the corner store to pick up a gallon of milk. "That's the contract we all sign at birth." Reed bent forward and left a coffee-flavored kiss on Pan's scowl. "Point is, I've never felt more alive in my whole life."

Taking in Reed's serene expression, Pan could only shake his head in surrender. "Okay, fine. I give up. You want in on this insanity? I will not stand in your way."

Eyes gleaming with victory, Reed planted a hand on Pan's shoulder and squeezed. "There you go. That wasn't so hard, was it?"

Pan snorted. Why did he have the feeling this was the first of many battles he was going to lose to his sly lover? "Lemme guess—you already have a plan," Pan said.

"Matter of fact, I do. We are going to bring the mountain to Muhammad."

"Okay, I have no idea what that means."

"It means trust me," Reed said, "the way I trust you."

Trust a man he'd met just two weeks ago—a *mortal man!*—with not only his own cosmic fate but Cupid's too?

"Pan?"

"Hmm?"

"*Do you* trust me?"

Their eyes caught and held, and for the briefest sliver of time, Pan was able to grasp the exquisite perfection of their Right Love . . . but it was like trying to hold infinity in his hands. Before he had a chance to turn it over in his mind, the glorious insight slipped out of reach.

In the still of Reed's kitchen, Pan listened with all his might. The only sounds that reached his ears were four panting dogs, Reed's slow, measured breaths, and the wild pounding of his own heart. "If I can't hear the echo beats now . . ."

Reed's face fell. "Oh."

"No! *Shit!*" Pan cupped Reed's head between his hands. "Yes, Reed. I trust you. I just meant, if I can't hear it now, I never will."

Reed's mouth widened into a broad smile. "Are you trying to say you love me, Pan?"

Heat rushed to Pan's cheeks. He wasn't a man of words, but Reed was. And that was what mattered.

"Yes, Reed. That's exactly what I'm saying."

36

PIZZA FOR ONE

Cupid flipped over with a groan, tugging the pillow over his head to drown out the noise coming from the hallway outside his apartment. More sleep, that's what he needed. It seemed the longer he was down here sucking up Earth's air, the heavier his limbs, the droopier his eyelids, the less urgent the drive to leave his bed each morning . . . or was it afternoon already? Since Reed and Pan had crossed a week ago, Cupid had been lost in a lonely fog.

For three days straight, he'd pounded the punching bag at the muscle gym—but what was the point? His body didn't need it, and all those brawny jocks strutting around just made Cupid long for Pan. He'd shifted from workouts to steam room hookups, and when that failed to quench his thirst, he'd returned to the boys at Versailles.

Looking for a change of pace—someone soft and sweet and as un-Panly as possible—Cupid had hit the jackpot last night at the Stagecoach. He would've had a hard time choosing just one of his dance partners to bring home; luckily, he didn't have to. Had he brought three or four girls home? It was all a dizzying blur.

If only he could switch off all of his memories so easily and slip back into blessed oblivion . . . but who could sleep with all that racket out in the hallway? The hateful brass knocker *tap-tap-tapped* against his skull. And now, a *ding-dong, ding-dong, DING-DONG,* and a shout at his door: "Anyone home?"

Cupid gathered his voice and shouted back. "Wrong apartment!"

"Pizza delivery for 6D!" came the answer, and a quick sniff into the air confirmed what was waiting just on the other side of Cupid's door—pepperoni and sausage, to be precise.

No matter whose pizza had mistakenly arrived at his door, Cupid's innards twisted and growled out loud in anticipation of that first bite.

"Be right there!" He hopped out of bed, plucked his jeans from the same spot of floor where one of his visitors had peeled them off him last night, and bounded toward the door before the pizza's rightful owner beat him to it. "How much do I—"

Reed.

In his hungover, pizza-crazed haze, Cupid struggled to process the image of the professor of classical studies standing at his door with a cane in one hand and a pizza box in the other.

"You deliver pizza now?"

"You could say that," answered Reed, warm smile firmly in place. "May I come in?"

Cupid ducked his head out into the hallway. "Are you alone?" He could not survive seeing Pan right now.

"Just me and the pizza," said Reed.

"Sure, come on in."

As he passed through the doorway, Reed offered up the pizza box and Cupid took it, a makeshift hug with a cardboard box in the middle. A subtle whiff of Reed's neck told the story of a recent swim and shower at the gym but not a hint of Pan.

"Please tell me you haven't stayed away from Pan on my account."

"No," Reed answered, his expression going mushy. "I ordered extra garlic on the pizza in case the chlorine and two showers didn't work."

Of course Reed would have been considerate that way. "Thank you."

"No problem."

Cupid's gaze chased Reed's over the wreckage of the past week: dirty clothes strewn across the floor, dishes piled on the counter, curtains drawn against the light of day. Even Reed's mortal nose would've picked up evidence of last night's coupling. *Groupling.*

Their eyes met; both looked away.

"Will you join me for lunch?" Cupid cleared a spot for the box on the small dining table.

"I can't stay."

More disappointed than he would have cared to admit, Cupid met Reed's eyes. "You really just came here to drop off a pizza?"

Reed's gentle smile settled in once again. "I came to ask you to answer Pan's call."

Pan had been calling multiple times a day to check on him—Reed less frequently but no less earnestly. Together and separately, they'd tried to coax Cupid over for a visit or to share a meal out or join them at the pool. Lately, though, even the phone calls had become too painful to endure, and Cupid had whittled down all communication to emojis.

"You didn't have to make the trip all the way over here just for that."

"Didn't I?"

Cupid shrugged. "I don't have anything to say to Pan right now." *And just hearing his voice feels like drowning.*

"You two need to talk. It's important. I'll let Pan know you're available now." He crossed the room at an impressive clip for a guy with a bad limp. "We'll talk again soon."

"But Reed—"

"I'll let myself out. Goodbye, Q."

And just like that, Cupid was alone with his free pizza that wasn't so free after all.

He threw back the lid and lifted the nearest slice to his mouth. *Divine.* How else could the crust rise just so, sculpting warm pockets of soft, airy dough inside *and* a satisfying crunch around the edges? And who but the gods could have engineered the playful stretch of melted cheese, making a sport of every bite?

Cupid sank his teeth into a pepperoni round and bit straight through the hot cheese. The blistering tomato sauce met the roof of his mouth like a lick of the chimera's tongue. Within seconds, his scalded mouth was fully healed. The sting, a faint memory.

Not so for the ruthless torment of his love for Pan.

Three times Cupid had been tested with increasingly sadistic punishments. And yet, the gods had granted him one small mercy—each new compulsion had brought relief from the previous heartache. Cupid's only chance of surviving his current agony was for his heart to be set swiftly and profoundly upon his next Worthy.

Be careful what you wish for, Pan would have warned him.

But Pan wasn't here to intervene, and Cupid couldn't go on like this. Anything was better than this gaping hole in his heart, even a new love he had no hope of attaining. Besides, he'd surely endured the worst of his tortures now. Not even the all-powerful gods could invent an ordeal more savage than loving and losing Pan.

"Bring it on," Cupid whispered to himself.

The words made him bold, a welcome change from the desperation that had been his constant companion. "Bring it on," he said again, louder this time, then tipped his chin toward Mount Olympus and repeated his brazen dare a third time. Only the stutter step of his ravaged heart betrayed his bravado.

Alone in his stale, still apartment, Cupid waited and waited for a response—a new heart signal to obey, another outlandish decree from his mother and Ares, feathers sprouting from his spine, *anything*—but he was met instead with a cold, conspicuous silence.

Cupid's buoyed spirits turned to worry. No news was rarely good news. The gods would not be baited. They would impose their tortures in their own sweet time.

He peeled off another slice of pizza and took a cautious bite. This time, the pizza did not burn his mouth. He closed his eyes to savor the complex blend of flavors, but his momentary pleasure was interrupted by a most unwelcome intrusion—Pan's ringtone. If Pan's call was the gods' reply to Cupid's provocation, he strongly preferred their silence.

Cupid reached for his phone to send "Wild Thing" straight to voicemail, then remembered the sneaky bargain Reed had struck. Cupid's days of dodging Pan and shirking his divine duty were over.

Swallowing the bite of pizza that had soured in his mouth, Cupid answered his phone.

CAST OF DIVINE CHARACTERS

AUTHOR'S NOTE: The primary name (all uppercase) for each divine is consistent with the narrative of the "Great Syncretism," an invented departure from Greco-Roman mythology. The character snippets offered here are based on canon; where multiple stories exist within the classical sources, I have chosen my favorite version.

ADONIS: Aphrodite's young, beautiful lover.

AGLAIA: One of the three Graces (sister-nymphs), Aglaia is the goddess of splendor.

AION: God of Time.

APHRODITE (Venus): Goddess of love, beauty, and fertility. Married to Hephaestus, bore four children to Ares, including Cupid.

APOLLO: God of light, music, prophecy, and medicine.

ARES (Mars): God of war. Son of Zeus, brother of Hephaestus, father of Cupid.

ARTEMIS (Diana): Goddess of the hunt, protector of new brides. Twin sister of Apollo.

ATHENA (Minerva): Goddess of wisdom and war arts. Sprang from Zeus's head fully formed.

ATROPOS: One of the three Fates ("allotters") responsible for spinning men's fate. Clotho spins the thread of life, Lachesis determines its length, and Atropos cuts the thread with her shears.

CERBERUS: The vicious three-headed hound of Hades who guards the gates of the Underworld to prevent the dead from leaving.

CLOTHO: One of the three Fates, Clotho spins the thread of life.

CUPID (Eros): God of erotic love. Illegitimate son of Aphrodite and Ares. The winged archer of Mount Olympus.

DAEDALUS: Inventor, architect, and sculptor famous for building the Labyrinth for King Minos of Crete to imprison the Minotaur. Father of ICARUS, who plummeted to his tragic death after flying too close to the sun with wax wings designed by Daedalus.

DIKE: Goddess of justice and the spirit of moral order and fair judgment.

DIONYSUS (Bacchus): God of wine and ecstasy. Son of Zeus.

ECHO: Mountain nymph deprived of speech by HERA, except for the ability to repeat the last words of another.

ENDYMION: Handsome shepherd loved by the moon goddess Selene, who entreated Zeus to grant Endymion eternal sleep so he would never leave her.

EUPHROSYNE: One of the three Graces, Euphrosyne is the goddess of good cheer, joy, and mirth.

GAIA: Goddess of earth. One of the primordial elemental deities born at the dawn of creation.

HADES (Pluto): Ruler of the Underworld. Brother of Zeus and Poseidon.

HELIOS: God of the sun.

HEPHAESTUS (Vulcan): God of fire and forge, blacksmith and divine craftsman. Son of Zeus, married to Aphrodite, stepfather to Cupid.

HERA (Juno): Queen of the Gods, sister and wife of Zeus. Famous for her ill temper.

HYPNOS: God of sleep. Father of MORPHEUS.

ICARUS: Plummeted to his tragic death after flying too close to the sun with wax wings designed by his father, DAEDALUS.

IRIS: Goddess of the rainbow.

LACHESIS: One of the three Fates, Lachesis determines the length of the thread of life.

LYSSA: The personification of mad rage and insanity.

MERCURY (Hermes): Messenger of the gods, father of Pan.

MORPHEUS: God responsible for sending human shapes to mortals' dreams. Son of HYPNOS.

PAN (Faunus): Demi-god of the wild, protector of the herd. Satyr (half man, half goat). One of the only gods thought to have died. Son of Mercury.

POSEIDON (Neptune): Ruler of the seas. Brother of Zeus and Hades.

SYRINX: Nymph who begged the river nymphs to turn her into a marsh reed to escape Pan's unwanted advances.

THALIA: One of the three Graces, Thalia is the goddess of youth and beauty.

THEMIS: Goddess of divine law and order, a prophetic goddess who presides over the most ancient oracles.

ZEUS (Jupiter): Ruler of the gods. Father of many, *by many*—divines and mortals alike.

To get your free, full-color, downloadable guide to the mythology of the Cupid's Fall series, visit www.bethcgreenberg.com/mythology-guide

ACKNOWLEDGMENTS

Thank you to the readers who hung off the cliff at the end of book two and shouted for book three. I'm thrilled how you've taken Pan into your hearts, and I sincerely hope you are excited about how his story unfolded.

To my pre-readers of *Quite the Pair*–Shelley, Maggie, L.J., Tammy, Betti, and Larry–thank you for your enthusiasm for this part of Cupid's journey and your help in making Pan's story shine. To Karen and CeCe, thank you for helping me find new readers far and wide. To Stacey, thank you so much for sharing your expertise in metalworking and teaching me about the odd, fascinating chemistry of gold. Hephaestus has nothing on you, lady! To Di (a.k.a. Nixie), thank you for all kinds of wisdom but mostly for bringing the Beauceron legend to life and helping me match Reed and Pan with the perfect breeds.

To the uber-gifted Betti Gefecht, thank you for the (third) cover of my dreams! Of all the series covers, this one brought us the most laughs, and for that I will always be grateful. Thank you for creating the perfect cartoon incarnation of Pan—carefree, joyous, and bigger than life. Thank you for enduring my nearly endless pestering about eyebrows and splash angles and Qs fashioned into something different each time. Thank you for finding the ideal title that not only fit the cover design but captured the exact essence of this story.

My sincere appreciation for the professionalism and patience of the talented Domini Dragoone, who continues to put all my words in their proper places and beautify everything between the covers, including the lovely "falling" graphics accompanying the title page and each chapter heading.

To my partners in grammar and style, Susan Atlas and Lisa Hollett, I'm so grateful for your wisdom on issues both broad and detailed. To quote Aphrodite, "We don't need to air our dirty laundry in the public square." Thank you both for spoiling me with your great counsel.

To family and friends who continue to support my publishing journey, your enthusiasm means the world to me. To the book groups who have hosted me, thank you so much. I have truly loved seeing your reactions to the characters and their stories. To my friends at Wellesley Books, thank you for being a great partner. To my daughter Lindsay, thank you for helping me with the big, scary world of social media and trying to teach this old dog some new tricks.

To Larry, who loved Pan first, thank you for encouraging me always—and thanks for never complaining about leftovers.

ABOUT THE AUTHOR

BETH C. GREENBERG is a former CPA who stepped through the portal of flash (1000-word) fiction into the magical world of creative writing and never looked back. She lives outside of Boston, where she and her husband are occasionally visited by their daughter and grand-dog Slim. *Quite the Pair* is book three of the Cupid's Fall series.

To sign up for Beth's email list and get sneak peeks, special deals, and exclusive content, visit www.bethcgreenberg.com/ newsletter

If you enjoyed *Quite the Pair*, please consider leaving a review wherever you go to find your next read. Just a line or two really means a lot, especially to an indie author.

COME SEE WHAT'S HAPPENING:
Website: www.bethcgreenberg.com
Facebook: facebook.com/bethcgreenberg

Made in United States
North Haven, CT
07 October 2021

10208536R00173